Praise for Andrew M. Greeley

"A fascinating novelist . . . with a rare, possibly unmatched point of view."

—Los Angeles Times

The Bishop and the Beggar Girl of St. Germain
"Full of unexpected turns and twists."

—Publishers Weekly

The Bishop and the Missing L Train
"The lighthearted Bishop Blackie returns with this thoroughly beguiling entry in Greeley's series detailing the misadventures of venerable Bishop John Blackwood Ryan."

—Publishers Weekly

"The inimitable Bishop Blackie Ryan resurfaces in fine form to solve another new mystery set on the streets and in the parishes of Greeley's native Chicago. . . . As usual, the author interweaves the central plot with a couple of tangential romances cleverly designed to culminate with the resolution of the mystery. Vintage Greeley fare."

—Booklist

The Bishop at Sea
"Blackie goes overboard . . . enabling the literate and erudite Father Greeley to include ancient mythology in his Bishop's latest adventure."

—Publishers Weekly

THE BISHOP
AND THE
BEGGAR GIRL
OF ST.
GERMAIN

THE BISHOP
AND THE
BEGGAR GIRL
OF ST.
GERMAIN

A BLACKIE RYAN STORY

ANDREW M. GREELEY

FORGE®

A TOM DOHERTY ASSOCIATES BOOK
NEW YORK

This is a work of fiction. All the characters and events portrayed in this book are either products of the author's imagination or are used fictitiously.

THE BISHOP AND THE BEGGAR GIRL OF ST. GERMAIN

Copyright © 2001 by Andrew M. Greeley Enterprises, Ltd.

A Forge Book
Published by Tom Doherty Associates, LLC
175 Fifth Avenue
New York, NY 10010

www.tor.com

Forge® is a registered trademark of Tom Doherty Associates, LLC.

ISBN: 0-812-57597-0
Library of Congress Catalog Card Number: 2001023203

First edition: July 2001
First mass market edition: June 2002

Printed in the United States of America

0 9 8 7 6 5 4 3 2 1

For Nan and Peter

All the characters in this story are products of my imagination, including the Parisian priests of whatever rank. I do not intend to suggest that the Paris Curia or the Paris Dominicans are at all like those in the story. However, the characters do represent clerical tendencies that exist everywhere.

Paris, however, is not fictional.

1

"Blackwood, I need a favor."

Sean Cronin, Cardinal Priest of the Holy Roman Church and by the Grace of God and heroic patience of the Apostolic See, Archbishop of Chicago, leaned casually against my doorjamb.

I was instantly wary. Cardinals don't need to ask for favors. Something was afoot, something more serious than Sherlock Holmes's "the game."

"I cannot recall that there is a marker on the table," I said cautiously.

I was appealing to the Chicago School of economics, not that made famous by all the Nobel folk over at The University but by Chicago politicians: its premise was that you can ask for a favor from someone who owes you one for a previous favor (a "marker"). I owed Milord Cronin no favors, not that it mattered.

"I want you to go to Paris," he said, ignoring my appeal to proper procedure.

"Paris, Illinois?" I asked, blinking my eyes in feigned surprise.

"Paris, France!" he said impatiently as he strode to the cabinet where I stored various liquid refreshments. "You've been there, of course."

He poured for himself a more than adequate amount of John Jameson's Twelve Year Special Reserve (now at least a quarter century old). In the reform of life imposed on him by his twice-widowed sister-in-law, Nora Cronin, he was permitted one of those a day and two cups of coffee. It was early in the afternoon for him to fill his quota.

"As you know, we Ryans travel only in cases of utmost necessity. The journey to Grand Beach, Michigan, represents the outer limit of our travels, save for an occasional venture to the Golden Dome to cheer in vain for the fighting Black Baptists."

This was surely the case. We risked going beyond that limit only for reasons of business or love, new or renewed. Neither of these issues impacted on my life.

We never, of course, drove to Milwaukee.

"You have to visit Paris, the City of Light."

"The city where they kill cardinals and bishops in front of your good friend Victor Hugo's cathedral."

"That was a long time ago," he noted, removing a stack of computer output from my easy chair and sinking wearily into it.

If he wanted me to go to Paris, then I would go to Paris. However, it was necessary that we act out the scenario.

"Nonetheless, the French do it periodically."

"I owe a lot to Nora," he said.

"Patently your health, arguably your life."

"So, I want to take her to Paris for her birthday."

"A virtuous intent."

"And I want you along to add an air of legitimacy to the trip."

Aha! So that was the nature of the game!

"My abilities as a chaperone are even more modest than my other abilities."

"All you have to do is to be around."

"Patently, I am quite unnecessary. While arguably your virtue might appear under suspicion to some among the uninformed, the virtue of your admirable sister-in-law is beyond question."

Foster sister and sister-in-law to be precise since Nora had been adopted by the Cronins as a child and later in life married her late foster brother Paul Cronin.[1]

"If an auxiliary bishop is in tow, no one will be suspicious."

An auxiliary bishop plays a role not unlike that of Harvey Keitel in the film *Pulp Fiction*: he sweeps up messes. This was a somewhat new extension of that role.

"The uninformed trust me less than you."

"Nora deserves this trip."

He was actually pleading with me, indirectly and circumspectly as befitted his role.

"This is a busy time in the parish."

All times in the parish are busy.

"One of your young guys can take care of it for a week."

In fact, any one of them could take care of it better than I could.

"Perhaps."

"Besides, Blackwood, the Cardinal Archbishop of Paris has an interesting little problem. He hasn't asked for your help, because he doesn't know about you, but he needs your help just the same."

"Ah?"

This was the bait, the double chocolate malted milk on the table.

"It would seem that one of his most talented young priests has disappeared from the face of the earth."

"Indeed!"

---

[1] See *Thy Brother's Wife*.

"Into thin air, so to speak." He swilled the whiskey around in its Waterford goblet. "Do you want a drink? It's your whiskey, after all."

"What sort of thin air?"

"Third-century Gallo-Roman thin air!"

"Remarkable!"

"Yeah, a famous TV priest, young, good-looking, great preacher, a little too right-wing maybe for your tastes, name of Jean-Claude Chrétien."

"The Church in France seriously needs right-wing TV preachers if it is to succeed in its efforts to bring back the Bourbon monarchy. Whether such a preacher will speak to the needs of the twenty-five percent of young people in that country who are unemployed is perhaps an open question."

Milord Cronin peered at me over the rim of his drink.

"Like I always say, Blackwood, I'm glad you're on my side . . . In any event this young man has, or perhaps I should say had, some training in archaeology. He was showing a couple of TV producers through the excavations under Notre-Dame in preparation for a program about the continuity of the Church in France."

"Doubtless he intended to make clear that the original Parisi were Celts."

"Doubtless, Blackwood. Anyway, he vanished. Turned a corner and when the producers caught up with him, he wasn't there anymore."

"Fascinating!"

"Arguably," Milord Cronin agreed, stealing my favorite word.

"I would be correct if I assumed that there is only one access to these ruins?"

"Yep. And people at the cashier's desk who

recognized him from his TV program swore he never left. . . . So the assumption is that he jumped into a house they had unearthed in the ruins and returned to the third century."

"Arguably where he belonged."

"I suppose that there are more rational explanations. However, no one has ever found him."

I could think of some obvious ones. However, assuming that the Paris police still worked in the tradition of C. August Dupin and Inspector Maigret, they would have thought of them too. The disappearance could be conveniently accounted for perhaps. But the motive was another matter altogether. Murder? Perhaps. Fleeing from the priesthood? Arguably. Or something more sinister and cynical? The basic principle of disappearance was easy enough. You needed a few forged credentials, some credit cards and bank accounts under a new name, a place to come to earth and stay until the police gave up and stopped looking—either because they figured you were dead or had made up your mind not to be found. If, however, you were a celebrity—like a prominent TV priest—it was much more difficult to come to ground where you would not be known. More difficult, but not impossible so long as you had a loyal team of coconspirators and lots of money.

The Church might take the position, especially if there were no ransom demands, that you were dead and that Communists or radicals had killed you. At that point the Church would quietly stop hoping that you'd turn up and begin to hope that you would not.

"So"—Sean Cardinal Cronin bounced from my easy chair, neglecting to replace the pile of computer output which represented the parish schedule for the next six months—"when we get there and you're not busy with your chaperone duties, you can see to it, Blackwood!"

He thereupon departed my study with his best maniacal laugh, a crimson guided missile going into orbit.

On the whole, as Holmes would say, it was a matter not without some interesting points.

"Punk, you really have to go to Paris with Sean and Nora," insisted my sister, Mary Kathleen Ryan Murphy, who was on the phone almost as soon as Milord Cronin left the room. "You owe it to him."

"Ah," I said. "I am unaware of what that debt might be."

I had already committed myself, more or less, to the venture. Family scenarios however, had to be preserved.

"You should stay at the Abbey where Joe and I stayed when we went over with Red Kane and Eileen."

Eileen Ryan Kane, a judge in the Federal Appellate Court, was the number two matriarch in our family.

"The Abbey," I replied, "is in Lake Geneva, Wisconsin."

"No, I mean the one in the Saint Germain district, near the Sour Bean."

My virtuous sister is perhaps the finest woman psychiatrist in Chicago, which is to say the finest of any. However, her geography leaves something to be desired.

"St-Germain-des-Prés," I said, "across the Luxembourg Gardens from the *Sorbonne.*"

"Whatever"—she dismissed my cavils as irrelevant—"it's an eleventh-century convent."

If it were it would be a precious museum. Seventeenth century more likely.

"I don't like convents."

"Don't be ridiculous, it's darling. Right near the Saint Surplus metro stop."

"St-Sulpice," I said.

"Whatever . . . Well, I've told Nora about it."

"Patently."

I did not tell her that *l'abbaye St-Germain* was right around the corner from the *Institut Catholique*—the Catholic presence near the Latin Quarter after theology had been forced out of the *Sorbonne*, St. Thomas Aquinas's university. That information was utterly irrelevant. Besides, what did I know?

So the matter had been settled. The family had once again made sure that I would act right, despite my proclivities not to do so. In fact, I would accompany Sean Cronin to the ends of the earth. I had no doubt that he could get to the aforementioned outer limits without my help, but he would not be able to return unless I were along for the ride.

The phone rang again. Crystal Lane, our resident mystic and youth minister, who answered phones until the Megan (four porter persons with the same name) appeared after school.

"Senator Cronin, Bishop Blackie."

"Thank you, Crystal."

"I'll pray for you while you're away on the trip."

That would not be an innovation. Crystal prayed all the time for everyone. Even she knew about the ill-advised journey. Even before I did.

"Thank you, Crystal," I said with my heavy West-of-Ireland sigh. "I'm sure I'll need the prayers."

"Blackwood, you're a dear," Nora Cronin began.

"Patently."

"Poor Sean needs time away from Chicago."

The word "poor" on the lips of an Irishwoman indicated high praise.

"Doubtless."

"And so do you."

This was simply not true. I never need to be away from Chicago. Even in the winter.

"Perhaps."

"It's very sweet of you to come. I'm sure we'll have a wonderful time. You know everything about Paris."

The Lady Nora thought I was adorable.

"It will do as a city," I admitted.

They had been lovers long ago, adulterous and sacrilegious lovers. Passions like that never really go away. I would accompany them so that they would be reassured that the passions would not escape from the currents in which they had been controlled for decades. I knew well that nothing like that could ever happen. But they didn't.

I had been to the City of Lights despite my pretense that I had not. It had a terrible, blood-soaked history. I knew too much of that history to enjoy my visit. I am not psychic like my friend and colleague Nuala Anne McGrail, but there were too many ghosts—of peasants and queens, of saints and sinners, of innocents and monsters—wandering about. However, the French, with the exception of their politicians, their intellectuals and their clergy, were nice people—just like every other people, though patently not as nice as the Irish.

Truth to tell, I liked sparring with the haughty French hierarchs I had encountered. I looked forward with considerable interest to this delightful amusement.

There was, of course, the interesting matter of the TV priest who had leaped back into the third century.

Fascinating.

2

"**They call this square the parvis,** which means the square in front of the Cathedral. The word comes from the Old French and it is a contraction of the Latin *paradisus,* which means paradise or more literally garden or park. So it is the park in front of the Cathedral. You will doubtless note that it is currently disproportionate. Originally the parvis was designed to match the proportions of the façade. A later architect felt that while a modest park was nice, a larger one would be nicer, more being more."

In front of us the great white cathedral loomed against a September blue sky. It was quite impossible that such a remarkable work should exist. Out of the question. Built by folk that Ms. Barbara Tuchman had assured us were barbarians.

"You swallowed the guidebook, Blackwood," Milord Cronin grumbled.

"I merely remember what I've read," I insisted. "You'll note the spire which was built or perhaps restored in the nineteenth century by another architect who calculated rather neatly what the first such intended. You'll also note the gallery between the two towers, unheard of previously in churches, whence our good friend Quasimodo hurled stones at the citizenry of Paris, on the whole a good idea."

Both Milord Cronin and I were wearing Roman collars and blacks suits. His clerical shirt had a bit of red stitching around the gap for the collar, a low-key reminder that he was after all a prince of the Church. It did the trick because he looked like a Cardinal; tall, erect, white-haired, handsome, with withering blue eyes. Just to make sure that his rank was not missed, he also wore a large ruby ring and an elaborate pectoral cross. He had left all other paraphernalia of office back in his suite in the Cathedral Rectory. For my part, I had remembered to bring my St. Brigid Cross, which my cousin Catherine Collins Curran had made for me. However, I had secured it in my suitcase at the hotel, lest I lose it on the metro. There was thus no way I could be identified as a successor to the apostles. Milord Cronin was pleased to remark that I looked like a priest from the West of Ireland who had never been east of the Shannon river before. On the whole, I thought it was a nice compliment.

The secret of being invisible is to be so commonplace that people didn't notice you when they boarded an elevator where you were hiding in the corner. The little man who wasn't there again today.

"It is the most beautiful church in the world." Nora, a trim and handsome woman with a miraculously unlined face, sighed.

"Until you see *Chartres*," I replied. "Compared to both of them your brother's seat is not much. On the other hand the upkeep is less."

"My cathedral indeed." The Cardinal laughed. "Everyone knows it's Bishop Blackie's church."

"The so-called Gothic style," I droned on, "is one of the great artistic miracles of human history. It exploded almost without warning in the twelfth century and within a few decades reached its zenith. The people that built it were heavily Norman, the folks who a century before were coming up the Seine in their longboats and sacking the city, before Hugh Capet arrived on the scene and made this island his capital."

"They were converts?" Nora whispered, reduced to awe by the astonishing sight.

"Second and third generation . . . The various 'Notre-Dames' which sprang up in Northern France in the eleven and twelve hundreds were patently temples to a Christian spring goddess, a symbol of the mother love of God and the triumph of life over death."

"Oh," Nora said, and then after reflection, "of course!"

"Blackwood is occasionally in error, Nora, but he is never in doubt . . . You look at this place and it kind of restores one's faith in humankind. Despite all our faults and flaws we were able to create such works of sublime beauty and grace."

It was a comment that was most untypical of Milord Cronin, who normally displayed only the hard-edged pragmatism which is required to be an American cardinal—the only alternative being nauseous piety.

We entered the church, which, despite the hundreds of tourists with their flashbulbs, creates its own unassailable awe.

"The Abbott Suger built his abbey up in St-Denis, which was the first big Gothic church—though it's a misnomer because the people that built these places were not Goths or even mainly Franks, and Bishop Maurice DeSully decided that he wanted one of his own.

"They were patently," the Cardinal observed, "a mixture of Celts and Normans, M. l'Evêque."

I ignored his use of my word and my theory.

"Note, however, that none of the later cathedrals were able to imitate the spaciousness created by the two side aisles. In the thirteenth century they compensated for this but the interior is still not as bright as some of the later Cathedrals."

"I like it the way it is," Cardinal Cronin insisted.

Our eyes blinked in the bright sunlight as we left the Cathedral after my tour was over.

"How do they keep it so clean?" Nora asked. "Didn't they have any pollution here?"

"They didn't keep it clean for eight hundred years," I replied. "The Cathedral about which Victor Hugo wrote was jet-black—and also run-down. Then *le Gén-éral* came along and ordered it cleaned. They told him it was impossible, as only the French can say impossible. He repeated the order. You don't argue with a man who thinks he's Charlemagne, Jeanne d'Arc, and Napoleon all rolled into one. So they cleaned it."

"Astonishing!"

"Isn't this parvis place in front of us," the Cardinal asked, "where the archaeological excavations are?"

"In the second century, the Romans occupied this island and built one of their provincial towns, which they called Lutetia, with the usual array of a forum, a theater, and baths. Some of the ruins of that town are beneath the parvis. When the empire became Christian, they also built or perhaps converted a basilica into a church. When the Franks took over and Clovis became king they either rebuilt or expanded the basilica which might have been as long as Notre-Dame. Maurice DeSully, unimpeded by preservations, simply knocked it down. Archaeologists have been reluctant to probe beneath Notre-Dame because its east end is on landfill. You can go underneath the parvis, however, and see third-century homes."

"Creepy." Nora dismissed the idea.

"I agree," Milord Cronin echoed her feeling.

"Me three," I said, though I knew I would be in the excavations before sunset.

Nora, who was not to attend the lunch with *M. le Cardinal de Paris*, pecked us both on the cheek.

"See you at supper. Be nice to the local Cardinal."

"You sure you know how to get back?" Sean Cronin asked her.

"Certainly." She dismissed his fears as foolish with a wave of her hand. "I turn right, and then left, and go down into the subway. I take the Porte d'Orléans train to St-Sulpice. You two are the ones who will probably get lost."

We watched her walk up the parvis and turn right.

"Sometimes," the Cardinal admitted, "I think I made a mistake when I didn't marry her thirty-five years ago, not that I had a chance. If I had, we'd both either be unhappy or dead."

"More likely the latter."

On that cheerful note, we turned and walked towards the official residence of the Cardinal Archbishop of Paris. I looked forward to the encounter with some eagerness.

My expectations were not dashed.

"Of course, *M. le Cardinal*," he informed Sean Cronin, "you have the enormous problem of individualism in America."

If Milord Cronin looked like a Cardinal in clerical black with an edge of crimson at his collar, the Archbishop of Paris in full color with the buttons, *zuchetto* (yarmulke-like skullcap), cummerbund, and socks to match, looked like a Corsican bandit disguised as a Cardinal—short, squat, dark, and dangerous. The fact that he was alleged to be a distinguished philosopher did not change the impression. He was supported at the dinner table by three others who could easily fit the bandito model, one a young, bald auxiliary bishop (who had been presented to us as a theologian) in full regalia, and two scrawny priests who, I felt sure, wore knives under their cassocks.

On the whole, for amusement purposes, they beat the crowd around the lunch table at Holy Name Cathedral Rectory.

The Cardinal, as is the wont of so many European hierarchs, was the sort who told you about your problems since he didn't have any of his own.

"Actually, individualism doesn't exist," I observed.

Everyone in the room turned to stare at me, as if I had appeared from nowhere—or perhaps from a small planet in the area of Alpha Centauri.

"But, *M. l'Evêque*, tout le world knows this to be true, doesn't it? . . ."

"Actually," I continued blissfully, "the word is a label, an artifact under which one may subsume a number of often contrasting and sometimes contradictory developments and ideas. Such constructs may be useful for shorthand conversation and perhaps for undergraduate instruction, but they ought not to be reified as if there is some overpowering reality in the outside world that corresponds to them."

"Actually," Sean Cronin joined the fun, "*M. l'Evêque* Ryan is a quite distinguished philosopher. He has published studies of James Joyce, William James, Bernard Lonergan, and David Tracy."

"All Celts," I said modestly, "like the original fisher folk and hunters after whom this city is named."

"But," my counterpart sweeper entered the combat, "American materialism and consumerism *certainement* . . ."

"In my experience all words that end in 'ism' or

'ization' are also constructs which ought not to be confused with reality."

The reader will doubtless perceive that the word "experience" hinted where I was coming from.

One of the clerical thugs grinned. So there was an ally here.

"*M. l'Evêque* is clearly a radical empiricist."

"No," I said modestly, "politically I am a Rich Daley/Bill Clinton Democrat. Philosophically, as is patent, I am an Aristotelian realist, like the good Neapolitan Dominican who taught across the river a few centuries ago. Actually in my book *Aquinas and James* I develop quite clearly the thesis that James was something of a Thomist."

I was talking bullshit, you say. Well partly. On the other hand, I was in the center of one of the greatest bullshit, you should excuse the expression, cultures the world has ever known.

The conversation continued in this arena for some time. *M. le Cardinal* Cronin, taking pity on the poor French, finally blew the whistle and raised the question of the tragic disappearance of *Frère* Jean-Claude Chrétien O. P. His Parisian counterpart suggested we adjourn to the parlor. One of the knife-bearing clerics joined us, the others took their leave, politely enough, but not quite able to hide their dismay over my little show. As I say, it takes bullshit to rout bullshit.

The young priest who accompanied us to the parlor grinned crookedly and winked. His name he informed me was François, Frankie for short. Studied in America, almost certainly. Doubtless he secretly preferred Coca-Cola or perhaps Bailey's to cognac. There was still hope for France.

Sean Cronin's parlor at the Cathedral Rectory was Spartan but tasteful, the former because of his inclinations, the latter because of the inclinations of the valiant Nora. The Archbishop of Paris's parlor, overlooking the Seine, was both ornate and uncomfortable, Versailles in miniature.

"*M. le Cardinal* tells me, Bishop Ryan, that you might be of some assistance in finding our unfortunate *Frère* Chrétien, no? I have heard from our brother in Cologne that you are skilled at this kind of investigation, yes?"

I almost said something about the little gray cells but desisted, not because it would have been a bit over the top, but because I feared that he had never read Agatha Christie and wouldn't get it.

"I'm sure, *M. le Cardinal*, that the Paris police have made a thorough and professional search."

"True, true, *oui*?" He handed me a tumbler of cognac. "However, they do not understand priests ... François, will you explain?"

"Jean-Claude," said my friend Frankie in American English, California variety, "was a sensation—young, handsome, charming, with curly hair and a marvelous smile. He was a chaplain at the *Sorbonne*. Some of the young people put him on their own radio station. Very soon he had a national television program every Sunday morning. He really was quite conservative, if you understand my meaning, and very pious. Yet, he knew popular music and told wonderful stories. You must understand, Bishop Ryan, that the French are almost genetically Catholic, even those who never go to church or claim that they are atheists. There is in the early life of many of us, especially in the middle class, a priest or perhaps a nun who was important. We tell ourselves that if the Church was like that person, we would still be Catholic. This is mostly nonsense, but there is enough truth in it that a priest, apparently simple and direct, recalls memories of childhood. Father Chrétien was for many of us that priest."

The cognac was golden not only in color but also in flavor. I sipped it gradually and warned the leprechaun who often stole from my liquor glass that I would tolerate none of his effrontery today. One did not drink two glasses of cognac after two glasses of splendid red Rhône after one has just defeated the odds and made a successful trip across the Atlantic.

The Cardinal of Paris waved his hands in protest. "He was really very shallow, you know. He singularized himself. There was question of his orthodoxy, *malheureusement* he did not seem to emphasize all the doctrines the way he should have. Many priests protested that people watched him on Sunday morning when they should be at the Eucharist. We bishops considered it and decided that more harm than good would happen if we tried, at the present time, to bar him from television, no?"

"The odd thing about Jean-Claude," Frankie continued, "is that he would have given up the program without complaint. He was an innocent, Bishop Ryan . . ."

"Call me Blackie."

Frankie raised his eyebrows and went on. "His important work he thought was with the young people in the Latin Quarter. He was a national celebrity who didn't know what a celebrity was. We have some videotapes and you'll see what I mean. He was absolutely unaffected. Moreover, he was slight of build and boyish, almost like a child. So people young and old, men and women adored him, each, one presumes, for their own reason."

"Fascinating."

"Some priests called him a 'pretty boy' with the obvious negative implications. Priests are very envious, you know, ah, Blackie."

"His real name is Blackie," Cardinal Cronin observed. "His nickname is Blackwood."

"Like Leonardo DiCaprio in *Titanic?*" I asked.

"Only more so."

I noted that the leprechaun had defied my instructions and disposed of most of my cognac. I put my hand over the top when Frankie offered me a refill.

"We investigated him very carefully," the Cardinal entered the conversation again. "Since his ordination he had been a chaplain to a convent of contemplative nuns in the Latin Quarter. That seemed suspicious, but nothing definite was ever proven. We had to move ourselves very cautiously in this matter, *M. l'Evêque*, as you will surely understand. The Dominicans were very proud of him. We did not want any trouble with them. However, Rome raised repeated questions about his orthodoxy. They were afraid he was confusing the simple faithful."

"They always are," I agreed with sympathy.

Milord Cronin snorted.

"We did not want a crisis. We felt it was better to move gradually. We ordered him to leave the convent where he was chaplain and move into the Dominican priory of St-Jacques. He seemed docile and asked only for a few days so that things might organize themselves."

The Cardinal threw up his hands.

"Then he disappeared."

"In truth," Frankie took the narrative away from the Cardinal, "he was always docile, humble, self-effacing. A committee of theologians reviewed his work and found him completely orthodox though they recommended that he emphasize transubstantiation in the Eucharist. He did that, but in such a way that the most conservative people in France accused him of heresy."

"He was not a heretic." The Cardinal sighed. "M. le Nuncio compared him to St-Vincent de Paul. Yet he was a problem . . . as are all priests who gain public attention."

"Bad thing, attention"—Sean Cronin sighed hypocritically—"except when it is focused on us who are successors of the apostles."

The Cardinal of Paris sighed in agreement. Frankie caught my eye to make sure that Milord was being ironic.

"France2 Television was planning a major program on Notre-Dame," Frankie continued. "They wanted Jean-Claude to narrate it, an idea which offended all the architects and historians and archaeologists in France. He knew nothing about these disciplines and could not have cared less. Yet he had a wonderful sense of television setting. He suggested a scene in the parvis, third-century pagan Paris and the lives of the people there as they gradually became Christian. It would have had tremendous appeal. He was showing the producers the crypt on the week after Easter when the trees and flowers were blooming. He walked a little ahead of them as they took notes. They looked up and he was gone. They thought he was around the corner. He was not. No one has ever seen him since."

I shivered slightly. I glanced at Sean Cronin. He had shivered too. It was the sort of event that he would not have tolerated in Chicago. See to it, Blackwood.

"There were no other people in the crypt?"

"A few early-morning tourists. The police ques-

tioned them, of course, and the clerks at the door.
Everyone in France knew *Frère* Jean-Claude. They
would have recognized him."

"The disappearance solved *M. le Cardinal*'s problems, didn't they?"

The Cardinal exploded. "They made worse problems. The media accused us of abducting him. It was
not impossible. Some priests do odd things. We did
all we could to find him . . ."

"We discovered," Frankie went on, "that Jean-
Claude missing was even worse than Jean-Claude
alive. People brought bouquets of flowers to the entrance of the crypt, which, of course, was promptly
closed. There was a novena of prayers for his safety
all over France. He was hailed as a hero and maybe
a saint. Students from the Latin Quarter marched
on the Cardinal's residence. The government hinted
broadly that we were not cooperating fully."

"That is what the socialists would say!" the Cardinal spit out the words with withering contempt. "Yet
they did not like him. They feared a resurgence of
Catholic spirit in France."

"Sort of things the Leftists would do." I sighed.

"The weeks have turned into months," Frankie
added. "We thought the media would forget about
him. And indeed, they pretty much have. Yet the flowers still appear each morning. They are promptly
swept up, naturally."

"Now they claim miracles!" the Cardinal sputtered.
"A young pretty boy works miracles!"

"His relatives?" I asked.

"He did not seem to have any. His parents died in
an auto accident when he was a child. He was raised
by the Dominican sisters. There was a sister, an actress I believe, but she died some time ago of tuber-

culosis, a few months after his ordination. I believe her name was Jeanne."

"He was trained here?"

"No, in Rome. At the Angelicum, of course. He lived in the Dominican house at San Clemente. On the Via Irelandesi."

Something clicked in my head. You can't trust your Irish Dominicans. Or any Irish for that matter. When someone slips into the Lutetia of Constantine's time and you learn that he's associated with the most fey people on earth, you wonder . . .

"Was not that unusual?"

He shrugged. "There was construction at the French Dominican house. They sent him to the Irish and forgot him. That was easy to do in those days. Jean-Claude was a very nondescript person, a little boy, how do you Americans say it, tagging along with the big kids."

"And now," *M. le Cardinal* threw up his hands—"he works miracles."

It was agreed that Father Frankie and I would meet at the entrance of the crypt the next morning to visit, so to speak, the scene of the crime. He gave me a stack of four videotapes.

"What do you think, Blackwood?" Milord Cronin asked me as we found ourselves at the *gare d'Austerlitz* after taking two trains we should not have taken. I thought it was arguable that we would ever return either to our hotel on *rue* Cassette, not to say North Wabash Avenue.

"I think that we should not wander this city without the valiant Nora minding us."

"Don't tell her."

"No way."

"I mean about *Frère* John Claude."

I hesitated because I didn't have any thoughts. An idea was tickling the back of my brain, but it was too unformed to be of any help.

"I think his disappearance solved the problems of a lot of people and created new ones for them, which they might not have anticipated. Perhaps it solved some problems for him, though he sounds like he might have been too simple to be aware of the problems."

"Will he go away eventually? Celebrities don't have much of a shelf life these days."

"I don't think so. The French have a way of hanging on to the people they think are saints. Joan of Arc for half a millennium."

"They'll need miracles, won't they?"

"Go long on it: there will be miracles. There always are."

That evening Milord Cronin and the virtuous Nora left for a dinner tour on the Seine. She overruled his plan to take a taxi.

"We just ride down to St-Michel on the metro and pick up the RER there. It'll drop us by the Eiffel Tower right next to the wharf."

That settled that.

I retired to my room, which it seemed to me was undersized even for a sixteenth-century French convent, and watched the tapes of *Frère* Jean-Claude Chrétien.

His French was too colloquial, too rapid, and too accented for me to catch more than bits and pieces of what he was saying. It was not, however, necessary to understand his exact words. The young man was simply enchanting—open, transparent, unselfconscious, happy. One knew almost immediately that his faith was deep and authentic. He said the rosary with fervor that somehow was not sweet or falsely pious. In fact, he was not pious at all in the ordinary sense of the word. He was too exuberant, too witty, too modern to be called pious. Perhaps he defined by his words and his joy a new meaning for the word "piety." In his loose black turtleneck sweater and black jeans he was not a new image in France. French clergy, including cardinals, had been dressing that way for years. Somehow for Jean-Claude it was neither a protest nor an affectation. It was simply who he was—a priest. He wouldn't wander around like I do in a Bulls jacket under the pretense that color meant a lot.

The "pretty boy" charge was false. He was indeed attractive in a boyish way, sparkling blue eyes, short curly hair, fine teeth and a neatly etched face. However, his gestures and his tenor voice were strong and masculine. Such traits, of course, don't guarantee heterosexuality in a man. But they provide no support for the thesis that he was gay. Perhaps he was, but surely the church authorities had searched, perhaps half-hopefully, for evidence and found none. Presumably the Paris police had done the same thing.

Jean-Claude was a very dangerous young man. In another era he certainly would have been burned at the stake. In our more enlightened days, he would be shipped off to Africa or some such place (perhaps Antarctica would be better), an assignment he would have accepted with meek obedience. The Church and particularly the clergy and the hierarchy could not long tolerate a man like Jean-Claude Chrétien.

The Cardinal had ridiculed, with more than a little insecurity I thought, the idea that Jean-Claude might be another Vincent de Paul. I knew M. Vincent, to paraphrase Senator Lloyd Bentsen talking to Dan Quayle, and Jean-Claude was no M. Vincent—at least as that saint was played by Pierre Fresnay.

However, he might have been something even more dangerous to *M. le Cardinal* and the French Church—his simplicity and humility and deep faith suggested a male, twentieth-century version of Thérèse of Lisieux.

3

The entrance to the **crypte** *archeologique du parvis de Notre-Dame* was indeed covered with flowers. On some of them were little notes to Jean-Claude asking for blessings and favors.

One note thanked him for a miraculous cure.

Like I had told Milord Cronin, the miracles would surely come.

I wondered what Jean-Claude, wherever he might be, would think of these phenomena.

"So what did you think of him?" Frankie asked me at the bottom of the steps. I wished that I could stop thinking of this nice young priest, now in a sweatshirt and jeans, as a Corsican knife wielder. Sometimes my imagination is truly weird.

"Enchanting is not a word I often use, Frankie. Somehow it fits. He is magic!"

"Is or was?"

My friend Nuala Anne, if she were present, would have an instant and unerring response. Not being fey, I didn't know.

"My best guess would be that he is still alive . . . What was he like?"

"Nice guy. Really nice. Yet you'd hardly notice him. Little guy that smiled a lot, but didn't have much to say. The kids at the *Sorbonne* thought he was great, but they couldn't quite say why. Just that he seemed to understand everything. Then he goes on television, same guy, but now he's suddenly magic, like you say, Blackie. No one ever noticed him. The red eye of the camera eliminates everyone but him. He doesn't change. We see him for the first time, *tout le monde* as we French put it."

"Anneberg school?" I asked, having placed his Southern California accent.

"Got it, Blackie, a real Trojan from Southern Cal."

"*M. le Cardinal*'s media maven?"

"Kind of. Not a bad guy, for a Corsican."

Ah, good guess. I suppressed a yawn. My virtuous morning sleep, a protest against jet lag, had been disturbed by the laughter of a group of giggling young females, seemingly in the courtyard of the hotel. However, the courtyard was empty. The concierge, the ineffable Bernard, assured me that the damsels were students at the music school of the *Institut Catholique*, next to the hotel. A bishop, I thought with a sigh, must tolerate the youthful exuberance of Catholic students who studied music.

"Come on," Frankie went on, "let me show you the place."

He introduced me to the two young women at the ticket counter as "M. Blackie, *un détective américain*." They twittered appropriately.

It dawned on me for the first time, doubtless because I was suffering from jet lag, that I would need my own translator. I could read menus and newspapers and catch what people were saying if they talked slowly enough, but I could not ask them questions and catch the nuances of what they were saying. As good a guy as Frankie seemed to be, he still worked for *M. le Cardinal de Paris*.

Anyway, I tried to talk to the two twitterers. *Certainement* they had recognized *Frère* Jean-Claude. Did not everyone in France know who he was? He had smiled at them and signed two of the brochures of the crypt for them. The police had taken away the brochures to check the fingerprints but had not returned them. *Père* François replied that they needed them for evidence and promised they would get them back soon. The two women insisted that they were relics of a martyr.

Second-class relics but who cares.

Malheureusement, they had not seen him depart. How would it have been possible to miss such a man? *Naturellement* there had been some other visitors, a few American tourists with cameras. None of them looked at all like *le petit Frère* Jean-Claude. How was he dressed? As he was always dressed, black jeans, black sweater, black beret. How could one fail to recognize him? Surely his friends came dashing after him. Where was he? They rushed around the crypt again. Still could not find him. *Certainement,* they ran out with them. Some other tourists might have come in, they didn't remember. Everyone was terrified. Then the police came. They were horrible, but are not the police always that way.

I did not doubt that they were telling the truth as they remembered it. I was also pretty sure that in their excitement—and fear—they had not remembered everything.

Frankie then took me on a tour of the crypt. It was a rather disappointing experience. I personally would rather tour city streets swarming with human beings than investigate so-called monuments which are deader than the tourists snapping broken-down walls with their cameras. However, if one has to probe into the distant past, into third- or fourth-century Lutetia, I would prefer to explore damp and dark caverns with various rodent creatures roaming around. Alas, current archaeological theory seems to require that excavation become underground museums, clean, well lighted, sanitary, heated or air conditioned depending on the season, and protected by fences and, on occasion, walls.

Dullsville.

We explored from landings which circled the excavations of the remains of Lutetia. We observed foundations of medieval chapels, a trace of the foundation of the Cathedral of St-Étienne, which Maurice DeSully had torn down, quay walls, an occasional cellar, even partial multiroom medieval homes and an occasional street pavement. We also pondered remnants of walls of the Hôtel-Dieu, the vast hospital which once pressed in on the cathedral, a giant place of suffering which burned down long ago.

Again dullsville.

Or horrorsville.

If they had tried to reconstruct some of the third-century homes, I would have been delighted. Perhaps television would have tried to do just that for the now abandoned program. As it was, all that really remained were cleaned and polished walls of rock and stone.

Did I know how *Frère* Jean-Claude had managed to disappear? There were a number of different ways that he could have done it, one in particular. He would have needed some help, but perhaps no more than one person. Had the Paris police thought of this exit strategy?

I had had occasion to observe that police forces tend to be uncreative about locked-room mysteries. They don't encounter them very often. They usually respond by accusing the duped witnesses of lying, behavior which makes it all the more difficult to learn the truth. Unable to explain an impossible phenomenon, they endeavor to explain the motivation for what has happened.

Frère Jean-Claude slipped by the two women at the ticket counter. Perhaps through inattention they had not noticed him. Or perhaps they were part of the conspiracy. He had dashed by them, perhaps by some trick distracting them, then rushed up the stairs and into a waiting car driven by confederates. Perhaps he had been kidnapped and eventually murdered by co-conspirators who had deceived him. Or perhaps he had deliberately disappeared.

One would think the latter scenario more likely. Why had he disappeared? Church and State had investigated his life thoroughly and found no motive. What more could they do? Were not urban police always busy? Would not the media soon forget this stupid little priest? They reckoned without the faithful.

Alas, they didn't have his fingerprints. How would they have the fingerprints of a priest? The case would remain theoretically open so that should he reappear they could claim they had been looking for him all along and were not at all surprised that he had reappeared. Nonetheless, they did not expect him to reappear.

Nor did they expect the flowers and the miracles of faithful followers who had been mesmerized by *Frère* Jean-Claude's transparent goodness.

My theoretical explanation was twisted and convoluted. Possible, *oui M. l'Evêque,* but not likely. But why, that was the question.

Looking back on the disappearance, I could have answered that question even then if I had been alert.

In retrospect the answer seems obvious. I do not do very well on jet lag.

"Any help?" Frankie asked me when we had climbed back into daylight.

"Not much," I said with perhaps some lack of total honesty. "He was a priest, was he not?"

"Certainly. He was ordained at San Clemente by an Irish bishop five years ago. Sometimes religious order priests here use 'brother' to emphasize their humility and poverty over our supposed pride and riches. I find all that stuff silly. Jean-Claude had been Brother Jean-Claude through the seminary. He probably took it for granted. I suppose it made some of the kids feel closer to him. I am sure it added to his appeal on the TV screen."

Irish bishop, was it? Some of them were pretty dangerous too. Shitkickers, in the words of my nephew Peter Murphy, son to my sister Mary Kathleen, father to my grandniece Katiesoo.

"A very brief career in the priesthood before he disappeared," I observed to Frankie.

"I often wondered whether he would die young. He seemed like a bursting rocket or a meteorite. Brilliant but short-lived. One would not notice on the TV screen how frail he seemed or how exhausted at the end of a broadcast."

Frankie had led me to an outdoor café at the opposite corner of the Cathedral. He ordered two pernods just the way Inspector Maigret would have. I compromised by changing my order to Bailey's.

"No wonder we French have liver problems, huh, Blackie?"

"Heaven forfend that I make any judgments in the matter . . . Was Jean-Claude naïve?"

"That's a good question. Did you think so when you watched the tapes?"

"I'm not sure. He seemed transparent. Yet one needs perhaps not only virtue but a sense of the scene to generate that impression. I would not think he did it with full deliberation. However, I would suspect that he was not unaware of what he was doing."

He pondered that.

"Sounds right. He could be very elusive. When the theologians were questioning him about his beliefs, he was quite orthodox in his answers, but one wondered if he was giving the answers that he knew they wanted . . . No, that isn't quite what I mean . . . he was quite disarming and well aware that he was disarming."

"Like Joan of Arc or Bernadette?"

He almost spilled his glass of anisette and liquorice, a foul drink if there ever were one.

"Damn it, Blackie, that's perfect. Wise as a serpent and as prudent as a dove. That's the way he was. Transparent, yet opaque when he wanted to be. Innocent and yet somehow profoundly shrewd. Does that diminish him, do you think?"

I beat my leprechaun before he could vandalize my Bailey's and turned to the glass of ice tea that one can find everywhere these days, even in the shadow of *Notre-Dame de Paris*. Such is the power of American cultural imperialism.

"Saints tend to be that way, even the delightful Thérèse."

He grinned. "Good comparison, though I think Jean-Claude was a bit more ingenious than she was."

"Different era, different spirituality."

"Fersure . . . I saw a lot of him because I work the television beat for *M. le Cardinal* . . . I remember when he got the orders to leave the convent where he had worked since he came back from Rome. Tears came to his eyes, but he said, 'of course, Frankie, I will do it. It is God's will.' "

"I haven't heard that phrase for a long time."

"Nor have I. He didn't have to go to the priory of St-Jacques though that's a nice enough place these days despite the grimy neighborhood and all the theologians. I told him that we could find him other smaller and more quiet places where he could lead a quiet life."

"And he thought about it for a few moments and said he did not want to go against God's will."

"Exactly."

"Do you think the new assignment would drive him to disappear?" I asked.

"Surely not!" he said, sipping his coffee. "Why should it? St-Jacques is a new building and ugly but not a bad place to live in. Like all religious orders, the Dominicans are hard on their own till others are hard on them. Then they rally like the Old Guard did for that bloody butcher Napoleon."

"Suppose that he wanted to disappear. Suppose that somehow he escaped from the crypt, what would he have done next? Would he have had a car waiting for him?"

"I never thought of that . . . Well, if I wanted to disappear, I would duck into Notre-Dame, take the secret tunnel from there to Ste-Chapelle, disappear in the crowds crossing the Pont St-Michel, and take the metro or the RER from there to wherever I wanted to go."

"Aha!"

"You want to see that tunnel?"

It would, I thought, have little impact on my investigation, if that was what I was doing, but it might be fun.

"Did *Frère* Jean-Claude know about it?"

"Sure, he wanted to film part of the program from there, not giving away the secrets, of course, not that there is all that much of a secret anymore."

"There are keys?"

"And he had them because I lent them to him so he could take the TV people down there. I don't know whether he ever did, however."

"And you never got the keys back?"

"Sure I did, but he could have made a copy, couldn't he?"

I paid the waiter for our drinks and tipped him far more than a Frenchman would.

"You believe *Frère* Jean-Claude made a copy of your key?"

He considered that as we ambled over to Notre-Dame.

"If he were planning to disappear, he might. Ste-Thérèse might not have done it, but, like you say, different era, different spirituality. Still I can't imagine why he would want to disappear. He didn't want to leave the convent. He stalled a little like he did when there was something he didn't want to do, but he was determined to do what his superiors wanted. . . . And then he disappeared."

"Patently."

"The transfer didn't seem to bother him very much."

"Indeed?"

"Not as much as the inquisition before the theologians. He seemed mostly his usual happy self."

"You had seen him weep before?"

He frowned, shook his head, and said, "No, damn it, I had not . . . *Merde!*"

"Arguably."

So we had a motive. Whether it was the *real* motive was not immediately clear. It did seem a disproportionate response to the problem.

I will not detail the route from Notre-Dame to Ste-Chapelle. It was dark, dusty, and appropriately spooky. An occasional bare lightbulb flickered dimly. The powerful flashlight that Frankie had found inside the door was a big help. I suspected that the light had been left for those who had the keys and could show the chosen few through the tunnel. It went under the parvis, the *rue de la Cité*, the *Boulevard du Palais*, the *Conciergerie* (where the prospective victims of the Guillotine waited either death or the Scarlet Pimpernel) and into the royal chapel. It had been the model for St. James chapel of the high-school seminary which Milord Cronin and I had both attended and at which I had instructed young men on the wonders of Latin. With little success, I might remark.

The designs of both buildings were strikingly similar, though the art work in Ste-Chapelle was much older and more expensive and the stained glass more beautiful (though not much more). However, the spiral staircases tucked into tiny enclosures were exactly the same.

Why bother with an imitation, I wondered. Still the chapel at Quigley, as the seminary was called, was indeed striking if derivative.

"We got in free," I said to Frankie, coughing the dust out of my lungs. "Do the cops know about this tunnel?"

"More or less, but they leave it alone."

"So if our good friend wanted to slip away, he

wouldn't have needed an accomplice in a car? He would just have had to walk briskly into the Cathedral, go down the stairs into the crypt, traverse the tunnel, escape into the crowds here, walk out with the tourists, cross the bridge, and catch a train—any train—at St-Michel?"

"He could have gone to the *Cité* station of the metro, but he might have thought that was too close to the parvis."

"Indeed," I mused.

"I cannot believe that he would do that. It would simply not be like him. Why?"

I agreed that was the problem. It would be the problem for some time. Was he still alive? That depended, did it not, on who were his accomplices.

My theory might be all wrong.

"I have a list of people you should see. His friends, students who were close to him, his TV producers, the prioress at the convent. I'll call them if you want to make appointments with them and trail along as a translator."

"That would be demanding too much of your time. You make the appointments. I'll find a translator who has nothing else to do."

"Good idea," he said, relieved that he would no longer have to report back to the Cardinal on my doings. We shook hands.

"You're good at this sort of thing, Blackie. . . . Do you really think you'll find him?"

"I haven't failed yet," I said immodestly, and then added, "there's always a first time. . . . It is one thing to find him or find what happened to him and quite another to promise to bring him back."

He nodded. "Gotcha!"

I wondered if he did.

4

I crossed the Seine on the Pont-Neuf, which didn't look very new, walked in a direction which I thought was east but which was patently west, and ended up at the *Musée d'Orsay*. I realized that I was lost and turned off the *quai* and into the Left Bank. As luck would have it I came upon the *Boulevard* St-Germain, hesitated, and, doubtless through the intervention of my over-worked guardian angel, turned left. Shortly I came upon the intersection of the *Boulevard* with the *rue* Bonaparte. This was an important spot, I realized, because on one side of the street was the famous *les Deux Magots*, frequented by such illustrious writers as Jean-Paul Sartre, Ernest Hemingway and, doubtless, though I was not sure, your man Jimmy Joyce. It would be appropriate to lunch there so I could say I had sat at the same table as . . . a claim which would cut no ice with my siblings or my nieces and nephews.

Across the street was the famous church of *St-Germain-des-Prés*. I could not recollect why it was famous, so I opened my trusty guidebook.

"For more than fifteen centuries a church has stood on this corner, which in Roman times was a pasture (*prés*). The first church, built in A.D. 452 by Merovingian king Childebert, was repeatedly destroyed by invading Normans and finally rebuilt to last in 1163. The Romanesque western gate tower is faintly reminiscent of the great abbeys on the outskirts of Paris. During the Middle Ages, *St-Germain-des-Prés* (named after St. Germanus (A.D. 496–576) bishop of Paris,) became a focal point for Easter fairs, with hundreds of stalls, performing theater troupes, and dancing bears. (None of this has changed today save the dancing bears, which have been replaced by street musicians of the imitation Dylan school.)

"Inside the church is an altar dedicated to the victims of the September 1793 massacre, a shameful chapter of French history, when Paris was ruled by a bloodthirsty mob called the *sans-culottes* (because they wore linen trousers instead of aristocratic knee breeches). In 1793, after a mock trial on the weekend of 2–3 September, almost two hundred prisoners sequestered in the church were led into the courtyard (at the corner of what is now *rue* Bonaparte and *Boulevard* St-Germain), where they were stabbed and hacked to death by hired killers. Ministers of Louis XVI, his father confessor, and the Swiss Guards were slaughtered. The carnage was followed by an auction of the victims' personal effects. The skull of René Descartes, the seventeenth-century mathematician and philosopher, along with the body of John Casimir, a seventeenth-century king of Poland who was abbot of St-Germain, are buried inside the church.

"Today, however, the edifice is best known for its evening concerts of classical music. It also provides a cool place to meditate on muggy summer days."

Hacking people to death in church, nice people. However, they did it again in 1870 when Communards killed the Archbishop of Paris, with children participating in the murders.

Well, that was a long time ago. I had not checked in with God either at Notre-Dame or at Ste-Chapelle. I would check in with him here and ask him why he permitted such atrocities—and all the other dehumanization which had marked the erratic history of our species. I didn't expect an answer.

At the door of *St-Germain-des-Prés*, a woman sat on the steps begging. I stopped in astonishment. She was not a Rom as the gypsies call themselves, nor an old woman, nor an obvious drug addict. Quite the contrary—she seemed inescapably middle-class. She wore a black skirt with floral prints, a white blouse, and a beige sweater. Her clothes were clean and so was her face. Her blond hair was neatly combed. Her pale skin was unmarked. She seemed neither embarrassed nor ashamed of her plight. Rather she was sad and resigned. Perhaps twenty-three or twenty-four, a student most likely at the *Sorbonne*.

What was her story? An AIDS victim rejected by her family?

I reached in my pocket. Blessedly, my wallet with its indispensable credit cards was still there. Then I remembered that there were no francs in it. I searched the pockets of my Chicago Bulls windbreaker (a memorial to better times). I found a crumpled-up two-hundred-franc note (the leprechaun who steals my drinks also crumples all my cash): $30.00. Last of the big-time givers.

I handed the crumpled note to her. She did not look at it. Instead she looked up at me and smiled. Her lifeless face shone for a moment.

"Merci, M. le Curé."

I stumbled into the darkness of *St-Germain-des-Prés*. On another day I would contend with the Deity about children hacking archbishops to death. There were more urgent matters.

I am well aware that I amuse You. I suspect that we all amuse You, but I am one of those who knows that. I promise I won't tell anyone. Nonetheless, how is it that babies, infants, children, dogs, and young people know that I am a priest? I am wearing blue jeans, a Chicago Millennium tee shirt, and my Bulls memorial jacket. I am covered with dust. I never look prepossessing and especially not today. Yet she unerringly smelled priest. How can this be? Do we really have a special smell. Moreover, she had the effrontery to label me as a curate, the lowest possible form of clerical life, ranked in the old days when we had such in America by the engineer, the mother superior, the cook, the housekeeper, the director of religious education, the chairman of the school board, the director of liturgy and, should there be one, the pastor's dog. How can this be?

Am I supposed to do something about the poor child? Like what? This is not my parish, nor my diocese, nor even my country. Still, I am supposed to do something about her. . . .

Ah, hire her as my translator. *Bien*. Not a bad idea. You do have a sense of humor. Thank you.

I had read in the always informed if not always accurate *Economist* magazine that middle-class French kids had to beg in the streets because the rigidities of the French socioeconomic structure had yet to be shaken up by a French version of Margaret Thatcher. If she really was poor, she'd jump at the offer of a job.

"Does *mademoiselle* have English?" I asked her at the door.

"But of course, *M. le Curé*," she said in a tone of voice which suggested that only a stupid American priest would ask such a stupid American question. However, the gentle smile which spread across her face suggested that I was too kind to dismiss as a stupid American fool.

"We might have lunch."

She pondered for a brief moment. Patently I was not a dangerous person.

"But of course," she said as she struggled to stand up. I extended my hand.

"Merci, M. le Curé."

Her judgment about my harmlessness was not altogether accurate. "The Clan Ryan," Milord Cronin once suggested with more wit than charity, and more wisdom than wit, "is like the Catholic Church. It has this incorrigible propensity to take people under its wing. Once it has done so, it is loath to let go, even if the protégé would rather not be under the wing anymore."

We waited for the light to change and walked across to *les Deux Magots*.

"Where Jean-Paul and Simone dined," I said.

"He was a terrible man," she snapped, "and she was a fool. . . . Also Hemingway and that very strange man James Joyce . . . You are Irish, *M. le Curé*?"

"Irish-American."

"I am Celtic too. My whole family. We have Celtic stones by our home."

Everyone is Celtic these days.

Her English was quite good, a little artificial and stilted but infinitely better than my French. God would not have sent a translator who did not speak serviceable English, would She?

We found ourselves a table under an aquamarine umbrella.

"What is your name, fellow Celt?"

"Marie-Bernadette," she said in a tone of voice which strongly suggested that neither name should be used by itself and that one should not even consider calling her Bernie. "I am from Valence. On the Rhône. South of Lyon."

"Languedoc, if I'm not mistaken."

"The place of heresies, eh? But we are all orthodox Catholics these days, *M. le Curé.*"

"Isn't everyone in France since you chased your Huguenots to America and Ireland?"

"That was terrible," she agreed. "And how does one call yourself, *M. le Curé?*"

"Call me Blackie."

I cannot resist the temptation to respond that way. It suggests Ishmael and Ahab and the white whale and Boston Blackie and Black Bart and the Black Prince. The comparison, of course, is comedic because I am the antithesis of all such images.

"Blackie," she said, accenting the last syllable. What a funny name! *M. le Curé Blackie!* I like it! . . . I suppose you wonder why I beg?"

"You don't have to tell me . . . You're a student?"

"Pas du tout. Jacques-Yves and I received our licenses last year."

Only later did I realize that the young man's name was not Jackie.

"And who is this Jackie?"

"My boyfriend," she said with a dismissive wave of her hand, as if he were not very important. Such dismissals, I have come to understand, in fact represent the exact opposite.

"And how long have you known him?"

"That's the kind of question priests ask all the time." She dismissed the young man with another wave. "We grew up together."

"And you both graduated from the *Sorbonne?*"

"Non, the *Institut Catholique,* we are both musicians, which is why we *must* beg. I have done it so often that

I no longer feel shame. Not so much, anyway."

Aha, a predecessor of the damsels who disturbed my resting of my eyes that morning.

"And why *must* you beg?"

"Do you know the unemployment rate for young people in France?" she asked as she attacked the seafood soup that came with our meal.

"Twenty-five percent?"

"*Bien.* And for young musicians?"

"Fifty percent?" I guessed.

"Almost twice as much as that all over France. In Paris?" She snapped her fingers, "there is no work at all. *Pas du tout.* It is very serious. We study hard at school, we have great hopes, we graduate, and there is nothing for us, not in Paris, not in Valence, not anywhere. It should not be this way, but it is. We want to work, but there is nothing, except twenty-five hundred francs a month from the government after our twenty-fifth birthday. One can barely stay alive on that. One can never think of marriage or children or a home. We think it will always be so. What can we do? There is no hope left." She shrugged her shoulders as only a French person can. "We are young, however, and we continue to hope."

She grinned defiantly, and then added, "We will not give up hope."

She was very like one of the pretty young women in an Eric Rohmer film. Except that she did not take herself quite as seriously as they do. Maybe beggars can't.

"So you beg to stay alive?"

"Only when we have to. We band together and crowd into the same apartment, we barter, we trade, we buy food that is a day too old, we pawn our precious belongings, some of us reclaim the abandoned towns in the country and grow food. I sew. Jacques-Yves works as a carpenter. Only for our friends. They do things for us. We play music on the metro stations and even on the train—Bach duets on the metro!"

She laughed at the folly of it all.

"The government chases us. They want to collect taxes. But we dodge them. In a way it is fun, *M. le Curé,* an adventure we will talk about when we have grandchildren and are rich and famous. We do not permit ourselves to think that we will never have grandchildren or will never be rich and famous. Then we have to beg and we become sad and ashamed."

"Bach duets?"

"*Oui,* I play the viola and Jacques-Yves plays the violin. We like to think we are quite good, but we do not know really. We give a concert today at the *Institut.* Our friends will come and give us some money. That is why I beg, so I can reclaim my viola from the pawnbroker. Jacques-Yves's violin is too expensive to risk. His parents are music teachers. My parents sell books. Both are respectable families. They would be humiliated if they knew we begged. But even in Valence we would have to beg and that would be worse."

They could make beds in hotels like the Algerians in our hotel. No, perhaps they could not. Perhaps all those jobs were taken. They could come to America. Was there room in America for young, as yet unproved, immigrant musicians?

"You have enough money now to reclaim your viola?"

A faint tinge crept from her face to her neck.

"Only because of your generosity, *Père* Blackie. I was afraid I would have to borrow one. That would be even more shameful than begging . . . *Merci beaucoup!*"

It should not be that easy to bring such a wondrously happy smile to a young woman's face.

"You could start a revolution. Young French people have a history of doing that, don't they?"

"Fill the streets of the Latin Quarter with protesters? March on the Hôtel de Ville? Bah! That does not work anymore, if it ever did. All the government cares about is stealing money from the people. The Left is worse than the Right. M. Mitterand did not care about us. Neither does M. Chirac or M. Jospin. Politics are a waste of time. France is an immoral country. That is why we must beg. It is foolish to think that we can make it moral. We must be moral ourselves, even if it is hard."

In the United States we would judge her a Catholic school Catholic. Fine. That's what I needed.

"Was it not always this way?"

"*Pas du tout! Le Général* was not immoral. Did he not even pay his own electricity bills when he lived in the *Elysée*? These men make the people pay the electricity bills for their mistresses! Bah!"

The sentiment was historic in France. However, the conviction among the young that nothing could be done was new. What happens to a country which so abuses its young that they have no hope? When its young people must beg to stay alive in the midst of affluence?

"I need a translator for a task in which I am engaged," I said cautiously.

"Most French people," she replied as she wolfed down her salmon, "have English."

"Yours is better."

"I studied it very seriously at the *lycée* because I wanted to visit America. Now that is of course impossible."

"My task requires precision both in what I say and what the other person says."

She sipped more of her white wine. I topped off her glass.

"I could find many excellent translators among my friends."

"This task," I continued carefully, "requires discretion and integrity."

"Integrity?" she lifted a Gallic eyebrow.

"I sometimes am a detective."

The little brat giggled.

"A *tec*, *M. le Curé* Blackie! But that is very funny! You always solve the mysteries?""

"I work with a special kind of mystery, Marie-Bernadette, the locked-room variety."

"I know those," she insisted, "I love them . . . May I have some chocolate ice cream, *s'il-vous plait*?"

"My very thought."

"*Merci* . . . And you solve these locked-room mysteries?"

"*Mais certainement.*"

Her brown eyes widened.

"All of them?"

"So far."

"*Formidable!*"

I ordered the chocolate ice cream.

"If you wish to be my translator, you must promise on your honor to tell no one what you learn. Ever. Except Jacques-Yves, of course."

She waved her hand to dismiss again this young man, who, I was beginning to believe, was a most fortunate young man.

"*D'accord.*"

"And you must promise that he will tell no one. Ever."

"D'accord!"

"The work will last a week and I will pay you for the week," I calculated quickly, "four thousand francs."

A hundred dollars a day—a bargain for what I expected.

"That is far too much," she insisted. "I could not take it."

"Marie-Bernadette, when I tell you what my mystery is, you will perhaps think it is not enough."

"Is it dangerous?" she said, her eyes glowing with enthusiasm while a large chunk of chocolate ice cream hung perilously on her spoon. She was still young enough to hunger for excitement and adventure, never having experienced the accompanying terrors.

"I don't think so."

She pondered my offer so that she would not appear to rush into it.

"Four thousand francs is too much, *Père le tec.*"

"I determine whether it is too much, *Mademoiselle la* translator."

She giggled again.

"Very well, I accept. Who has disappeared in the locked room?"

She waited expectantly.

"Eat that spoonful of ice cream first."

"*Bien!* . . . Now who is missing?"

"You should be able to guess."

She frowned and thought for a moment. Then her eyes grew large and her fair skin turned ashen.

"But of course, *Père* Blackie! *Frère* Jean-Claude . . ."

"*Précisément, Mademoiselle* Marie-Bernadette. Do you wish to continue on the job?"

"How could I not, *Père le tec!* It would be wonderful if we found him! He was a delightful, holy man. They have tried to take him from us. We must get him back!"

"They?"

She dismissed the question with a somewhat larger wave of her hand than poor Jacques-Yves rated.

"The Church, the government, all those who do bad things to us ... Do you work for *them, Pere* Blackie?"

"I work for myself and for my boss, who is certainly not one of *them.* I want to find the truth about *Frère* Jean-Claude. When I find it I have no obligation to anyone. However, if someone has harmed him. I promise you they will not get away with it."

Big words from the little bishop. Was I trying to impress this fragile child?

Probably.

"Bien," she said sadly.

"You knew him?"

"Certainement! Jacques-Yves and I went to his Mass every Saturday evening. Our whole house watched him on Sunday. Jacques-Yves and I went to his scripture lecture every Tuesday evening. He was so holy and so happy. We all loved him, even those who were atheists. If there were more priests like *Frère* Jean-Claude, *tout le monde* would be Catholic!"

"Would he have disappeared of his own will?"

"No, no, no! They kidnapped him and killed him because he was so good. They were afraid he would tell us who the bad ones were."

"Had he begun to do that?"

"In his last four or five weeks he began to preach against immorality in high places. He told us stories about *le Général* who paid for the food when he had guests to dinner. He said that we all should be as honest."

"Did he mention the premier or the president?"

"Oh, no, *Frère* Jean-Claude wouldn't have done that. He never mentioned anyone. But the comparison between *le Général* and our recent presidents was obvious, was it not, *Père* Blackie?"

"Perhaps . . . You say that he was not political?"

"None of us are. Politics is a foolish waste of time in France today. He was talking about morality."

The French State, which valued itself beyond all other realities, might disagree.

"He was one of us," Marie-Bernadette went on, "Only a few years older than Jacques-Yves and myself. We all knew politics is only a game that the rich and powerful play."

"You two were close to him, Marie-Bernadette?"

"We all thought we were close to him. He even came to our little concerts and prayed for us. We loved him. . . . And"—she began to cry—"they took him away from us because he dared to suggest that they were immoral."

"Indeed."

"Is he still alive, *Père* Blackie?" she dabbed at her eyes with a tissue. "Will we find him?"

"I don't know, Marie-Bernadette. I'm not sure. I think he disappeared of his own free will. . . . More ice cream?' "

She nodded, still mourning for her missing hero.

I ordered two more dishes of ice cream and two cups of tea.

"You mean," Marie-Bernadette said, "he left us deliberately? I cannot believe that."

"I mean that he disappeared deliberately. I don't know why or what happened after that."

I explained my theory of how the disappearance might have been accomplished. Marie-Bernadette listened thoughtfully. We polished off our second dish of ice cream, though the ever-present leprechaun stole most of mine.

"You are a very good *tec, Père* Blackie. Probably because you are a very good priest who understands people, even silly weeping beggar girls."

"In Paris, when Notre-Dame was built, all the wandering minstrels were beggars. You and Jacques-Yves are part of a great tradition."

She brightened and squared her shoulders. "*C'est vrai.* Now I must recover my poor viola . . . where do I begin my work tomorrow?"

"I'll come to your concert."

"How wonderful!"

She told me the address of the music school, which I knew very well since it was the place next to our hotel where the damsels prevented me from reading the fathers that morning.

I bid her farewell and walked down the *rue* Bonaparte, by St-Sulpice, and finally, by a bit of luck, found *l'abbaye* on the *rue* Cassette.

I pondered on my way the idea that some obscure French intelligence agency had decided more or less on its own that the young TV priest was a threat to the State. They might have kidnapped *Frère* Jean-Claude and murdered him.

Nonsense! This is France, not East Germany or Bulgaria.

Nonetheless it would not be the first time something like that had happened in France.

It might be, I thought uneasily, that the venture would be a lot more dangerous than I had promised Marie-Bernadette.

5

"I have hired a new lay member of the Cathedral staff," I informed Milord Cronin when I found him and *la bella* Nora in the small, flower-decorated bar of our hotel.

They were sipping tea and smiling happily in the contentment of their chaste but passionate love. They had walked the *Champs-Elysées* to the *place Charles DeGaulle* and then turned back towards the river to the Eiffel Tower. Foolishly violating all prudence, they had taken the elevator to the very top and offered me Polaroid photos to prove it.

"Great experience, Blackwood," Sean Cronin had exulted. "Exhilarating!"

"Doubtless"—I had sighed—"though I would not expect your good sister to tolerate such risks."

"Blackwood, like your sisters say, you were born old."

My siblings' comment was not necessarily defamatory.

I had ordered a Bailey's in preference to Jameson's (which the worthy bar actually carried) lest I further impair my already damaged sleep cycle. Then I had told them of the new staff person.

"It's on your budget," the Cardinal insisted firmly.

"Arguably not."

"What does this person do?"

"I believe we could call her a beggar, though perhaps we could also call her a minstrel."

I thereupon told them the stories of Marie-Bernadette, Jacques-Yves, and *Frère* Jean-Claude.

"The poor dear things." Nora Cronin sighed, more loudly than I usually do. "You have to do something for them, Blackwood."

Which was her equivalent of "See to it, Blackwood!"

"Don't worry about them, Nora. Blackwood always has a high card up his sleeve. Usually an ace. . . . It was ingenious to hire her as a translator. She'll be eager to find out what happened to our young friend."

It was hardly necessary, I thought, to enlighten them about my conversation with the Deity in the church of *St-Germain-des-Prés*.

"We should attend their concert, Sean," she informed Milord Cronin definitively. "They sound like sweet children."

Thus it was settled. Before we went round the corner to *Le Périgord* for supper we would drift into the music hall of the school next door and listen to the "sweet children"—a fair description of two lost souls who would somehow survive, I told myself, because of their goodness and love.

As for the card up my sleeve, Milord Cronin underestimated me. It was *always* an ace, usually the ace of spades.

So at 5:30 we entered the small, dusty hall and settled into a seat in the back row, so we could be inconspicuous as Milord Cronin put it, in the absurd belief that a handsome white-haired, broad-shouldered cleric six-foot three-and-a-half inches tall with a crimson fringe on his clerical shirt could possibly be inconspicuous. Everyone in the room glanced at us as if we were visitors from a distant star system.

Perforce I had removed Catherine's silver Brigid pectoral cross from safekeeping and managed to look like I was either an auxiliary bishop to this prince of the church or his court jester or arguably both.

Marie-Bernadette and Jacques-Yves sat on the raised platform nervously tuning their instruments. She wore a white blouse and a long, black skirt, he a dark suit and a white shirt with a discreet tie. Their clothes were old and slightly shabby but neatly pressed and clean. They both seemed fragile and very young.

One might doubt Marie-Bernadette's Celtic genes, there could be no doubt about her boyfriend's. He was short, dark, with straight black hair that seemed to end just above his eyebrows, flashing blue eyes, and a gentle smile, especially when he looked at her. Pirate, IRA gunman, precinct captain, undertaker, commodity trader—he could have been any of these in Chicago. Here on the Left Bank he was a violinist and a lover. *Mademoiselle la* translator was clearly in charge of the duo, but she treated him with respectful veneration.

Really Celts? Or just current fashion? The collection of peoples with similar culture that we call Celts spread all over Europe after the last ice age and probably still are the population base in many regions (definitely in Northern Italy). As an Irish scholar at an English university wrote a few years ago, anyone is Celtic who wants to believe that they're Celtic. For the Irish, of course, it's not faith but fact.

"Blackwood," Nora whispered to me, "they're simply adorable. God sent you here to help them."

See to it!

The hall was half-filled, a scattering of older people, faculty doubtless, and several dozen younger folk, per-

haps members of the commune where the two per-
formers lived, searching for ways to give them money
honorably. The photocopied program announced that
four duets would be performed—one each by Bach,
Mozart, Debussy, and Messiaen.

Precisely on time, our two young friends caught
each other's eye and began to play. They were indeed
good, much better than I had hoped. Not great, not
now. But perhaps they could be with more training.
Eventually with such training they would prove more
than good enough to earn a decent living in Chicago
and play eventually with the Chicago Symphony (the
best in the world, as everyone knows). More than
that? God knew.

Their duo was enhanced by the intensity of their
lifelong love, which they spoke to one another as they
played. I sighed. There was grace in the small hall and
the two young people radiated it as the viola and violin spoke to one another.

At intermission, after enthusiastic applause, a young
man and woman passed among the audience with two
battered paper boxes in which we were supposed to
make our contributions. The diminutive redhead who
worked our side of the hall hesitated at the sight of
the two clergy, though I'm sure she saw only one of
us.

Milord Cronin, with characteristic flair, motioned
her towards us, put three thousand-franc notes into
the box, and gestured with his hand to indicate that it
was from the three of us.

Inconspicuous, right?

Well, there was still one Renaissance prince around.

Almost as much as I had offered Marie-Bernadette
for a week's work. I didn't think she'd have any trouble believing that my boss was not one of *them*.

After the concert I presented *M. le Cardinal* Sean Cronin and *Madame sa soeur* Nora Cronin to Marie-Bernadette who in turn presented Jacques-Yves to them and to me. I was solemnly identified as *M. l'Evêque* Blackie. She did not seem at all penitent that she had once confused me with a curate.

Milord turned on all his considerable charm for the occasion, as I had assumed he would. The two awed children were soon smiling and laughing and blushing with his praise for their playing. Sean Cronin might not know a whole lot about the delicacies of string duets, but he did know how to make people feel that they had been brilliant, a talent rare enough in most priests and almost nonexistent in hierarchs. It was altogether vintage Cronin.

We bought several copies of the disk of their music which was offered for sale in the lobby of the hall.

"Nice kids," he said to me over our white Bordeaux later in *Le Perigord.*

"Simply adorable," *Madame sa soeur* agreed.

"Do they have any talent, Blackwood?"

"A lot. How much it would be hard to say until they had a couple more years of training."

"Could you get it for them? Say an Edward P. Ryan scholarship at the American Conservatory?"

"Arguably. However, it would have to be an honest grant. Skilled musicians would have to vet their work and approve their promise."

I pointed at their CD.

"Completely level playing field?"

"Hardly."

He nodded his approval.

"Let me know if my name would be any help."

"The question remains whether they would want to leave France and their families behind. However cruel their country may have been to them, it is still France. They're small-city provincials with strong family and neighborhood ties. It would be hard to leave."

"Are they sleeping together, Blackie?" Nora asked. "Not that I think it would be terribly wrong if they were."

I had wondered that myself.

"Whatever is between them," I said, "is both chaste and permanently faithful. The rest may safely be left in God's hands."

"Well, we must work it out for them, especially since you probably won't be able to solve this mystery without Her help. See to it, Blackwood!"

Obviously.

6

"All that money last night," *Marie-Bernadette* asked me shyly the next morning as we walked across the Luxembourg Gardens towards the Dominican house near the *Sorbonne*, "was from *M. le Cardinal*?"

The sky was a dour gray, but it only made the autumn flowers of the vast Garden more glorious. Hemingway is alleged to have said that he kept his sanity by walking across the Gardens. Poor dear man, he should never have moved away.

"Oh yes."

"He is very generous."

"Patently."

"I want to say that he should not have done it, but that would not be gracious."

"It would not."

"So I will not say it. Will you tell him, *Père* Blackie, that we thank him very much?"

"*Certainement* . . . He is not one of *them*, Marie-Bernadette."

"*Mais non!* You see that in his eyes. He has suffered much but he loves."

A fair enough evaluation of Sean Cronin.

I had given her the agreed-upon week's salary in advance. She accepted it hesitatingly but gratefully.

"It is perhaps too much, is it not?"

"When this case is over, it may appear perhaps too little."

"Would it be wrong to share some of the money with our friends who need it more than we do? We must all be good to one another, must we not?"

A lump rose in my throat.

"It is your money for you and Jacques-Yves to do with what you want. It would, however, be primitive. Primitive Christian, that is."

She laughed.

"We try to be good Catholics . . . What did you think of my boyfriend?"

No dismissive wave of the hand this time?

"He seems a nice enough young man," I said in a tone of indifference, "the sort that would almost always do what the woman in his life wants him to do."

She threw back her head and laughed, the first burst of laughter I had heard from her.

"He says that is his destiny! I do not think I am *too* bossy."

"We Celts tend to like strong women."

"*C'est vrai* . . . Nevertheless, do you approve of Jacques-Yves?"

My approval was mandatory. How best to grant it?

"You are a most fortunate young woman, Marie-Bernadette. Don't ever let him go."

She laughed again, greatly pleased.

"*Pas du tout, mon père,* I will never let him go. I love him so much. I cannot remember a time when I did not love him. He is my love, my life, my everything. . . . We are both *bourgeois*, as you can tell. It is very hard on him that he is not able to give me a better life. But I say that he has given me himself and that is all that matters, no?"

"Patently."

During our interviews I asked the questions in English and Marie-Bernadette translated them into French.

As far as I could tell, accurately. Then she translated back into English what the other person had said. She was generally quick and smooth. When she didn't know the English word she said something in French. I fear that I picked up some French vocabulary and syntax which would affect my American when I returned home. She worked very hard and must have suffered many headaches in the course of our investigation. She never complained, however.

What right did the Clans Ryan and Cronin have to intervene in their lives? I asked myself. Why should we have the power to alter their destiny, for better perhaps, but also arguably in the long run for worse?

The answer was obvious. Not being God we can't assume Her role. However, if you can help people that need help, then you help them. What happens next is up to them and to God.

Thus reassured, we left the Gardens behind and skirted the *Sorbonne* and its swarms of chattering young people.

"They all look so young," Marie-Bernadette observed.

"To one of your advanced years, they must seem very young indeed. I have noted that the young are younger each year."

She giggled.

"You are very funny, *mon père*."

I explained to her that the good Frankie had made us four appointments at the Dominican house of St-Jacques, with the Provincial, Jean-Claude's former novice master, and two of his classmates. We would doubtless like some of these men and dislike others. However, we must restrain our emotions and seem to believe that we agreed with all of them.

"*Mais certainement!* Is that not what all we professional *tecs* do?"

She had accoutered herself for the role, blond hair tied up in a knot, makeup discreetly applied to her lips, a severe if slightly out-of-fashion (skirt too long) navy blue suit, a large purse—a mother superior of a modern religious order, tolerating the new ways but still convinced in her heart of hearts that the old ways were better.

Inside St-Jacques she was a woman transformed into the role her garb demanded. She was haughty, demanding, impatient. Was she not the translator for *M. l'Evêque* Jean-Blackie Rhine? Was he not a very busy man? Did he not demand punctuality and precision for those he had come to interrogate?

At the Cathedral of the Holy Name in the City of Chicago (Richard M. Daley, Mayor) such a posture would have guaranteed a hilarious reaction. However, in Paris, which was after all where we were, it worked wonders, even if it interfered with my ordinary persona of utter ineffectuality.

Once our first appointment began with the local Dominican provincial, however, she changed again. Now she was the competent technician, *Mademoiselle la* translator, diligently and carefully doing her work, with an eye on both participants to make sure she was doing it properly.

The net effect was charming, a little girl who was eager to please and very able. God had wisely chosen the right Parisian waif to be my interpreter.

Père Duchamp, the provincial, poured us some tea, offered us some cookies (of which I took several and she took none) and asked her which *lycée* she was attending. She replied without the slightest hint of dismay that she had received her license from the *Institut*

Catholique. Father Duchamp lifted his eyebrows in a Gallic sign that he was impressed.

"We have, do we not, Bishop Rhine, a most difficult and a most serious problem?"

He raised a sheaf of documents, doubtless the dossier on *Frère* Jean-Claude, and let it fall back on this desk, a crowded, dusty desk in a crowded dusty room, from which a single dirty window looked out on a rather desolate courtyard. I reminded myself that, if not in this house, in one of its predecessors, the greatest philosophers and theologians in Catholic history had once worked. I personally was a follower of St. Thomas, though via the Transcendental Thomism of Bernard Lonergan and his ilk. The Angelic Doctor himself would have been delighted with us, though many of the Dominicans who had intervened between his time and ours would not have the slightest idea what we were talking about. Some of them, for that matter, had burned Thomas's works at Oxford.

So I should feel a little more awe in this place, especially since *Père* Duchamp looked like a slightly less rotund version of the Angelic Doctor, with his bald head and his black-and-white robes. At first I did not trust his baroque geniality, but Marie-Bernadette seemed to like him, so I suspended judgment.

"I am delighted"—he raised his hands in a gesture of cheerful acceptance—"that a man of your reputation and intelligence has initiated a, how shall we say it, independent investigation. It may be that we are all too close to the matter. For my part, I will confess that, while *Frère* Jean-Claude has caused us considerable inconvenience, I miss him. He was authentic, of this I have no doubt—unusual perhaps and at times maddening, but a flash of brilliant light that illumined all of us and brought great glory to our order, despite the problems with Rome."

"Ah," I said.

"I wish I could turn on the television this Sunday and see his youthful, glowing face. As hardened by administrative responsibilities as a provincial must become, he made me smile, and laugh and hope. As you may imagine, Bishop Rhine, there were other reactions within this house and within our order."

"Ah," I said again, determined to permit him to play out his routine.

"Alas"—he sighed and shook his head sadly—"we will never see him again."

"You believe he is dead then?"

"Is that not obvious? Brother Jean-Claude was a good Dominican. He would not have left us without an explanation. Indeed, he was such a good Dominican, if I may say so, that he would not have left us without seeking my permission."

"Do you believe that he was murdered?"

"Again, Bishop Rhine, I must say that Jean-Claude was a good priest. He would never have committed suicide."

"Except perhaps for the good of the Church?"

I don't know even now why I said that. Perhaps it was a reflection of the cliche that a certain high prelate (not Milord Cronin!) would never lie save for the good of the Church.

My question startled Father Duchamp.

"I had not thought of that." He rubbed his smoothly shaven chin. "There are certain notions in French literature which might encourage . . . Bossuet, more recently Bernanos. . . . But those melancholy spiritual themes would not have affected Jean-Claude. He was always so cheerful, so uncomplicated, so, if I may use the word, boyish."

"Who would have killed him, if indeed he was murdered?"

He sighed again and lifted his shoulders in melancholy resignation.

"We French are a paranoid people, Bishop. Within this house there are many theories, all without any of the empirical verification which you call for so frequently in your work. Perhaps the Royalists who felt that he was about to betray them, perhaps the Socialists who felt he would not betray the Royalists. Perhaps the police or the military who saw him as a revolutionary threat . . . I believe none of these theories, however."

Marie-Bernadette was not only translating this conversation, she was scribbling notes. Possibly she would earn herself a bonus. Arguably, if all things arranged themselves well, she could become a member of my North Wabash Avenue Irregulars.

"And what do you believe?"

"I personally believe he paid a heavy price for his sudden, unexpected and immense popularity. He was such a good man and so, how shall I say, effective in his goodness that he frightened many people in our society. They had to destroy him."

The provincial's personal beliefs amounted to nothing either new or useful.

"And the police?"

A dark frown creased his round, bland face.

"The police? Bah! Certainly they know what happened. It is *incroyable* that the Paris police with all their resources do not know what happened to him. Oh, yes, Bishop Rhine, they know. They have concluded that it would be too dangerous to permit the rest of us to know. Those in highest authority also know. They agree with the decision of the police. They hope that the French people will soon forget about our Jean-Claude."

"The flowers and the alleged miracles?"

Père Duchamp turned and stared out the window at the empty courtyard as if in deep thought.

Then he turned back to us.

"I think they have miscalculated. Our Jean-Claude was not simply another foolish priest who would soon be forgotten. A saint? I do not know. A priest that all of France loved? This is clear. Those who are responsible for his disappearance and those who have covered it up are now certainly very nervous. They do not wish you well in your investigation, Bishop Rhine."

"It would not be the first time. . . . Might he be alive and imprisoned?"

"Perhaps. However, those who took him from us would fear the possibility of escape. No, it is more likely that they would have killed him immediately, the day of his disappearance."

Père Duchamp filled the room with a miasma of paranoid suspicion. He might very well be right. After all, his explanation was not unlike that of the good Marie-Bernadette. Nonetheless, I needed first of all to know more about the elusive friar.

"What was he like, Father Provincial?"

He lifted the dossier again.

"Ordinary, Bishop Rhine. Completely ordinary. There is nothing in his records to indicate that he would climb to such heights so soon. We did not mark him for further studies because he did not seem to have the aptitude or the intelligence for intellectual work. He had a reputation for piety of the traditional

sort, serious but not very deep. He was pleasant and
self-effacing. A good, honest, cheerful young man, but
without any depth. He would have perhaps have been
better suited as a curé in a rural parish. However, he
believed that he had a Dominican vocation and he
persuaded us of the sincerity and the validity of that
belief. Before he was ordained in Rome, the elderly
priest who was the chaplain at the Convent of the
Transfiguration died. We promised the nuns, who are
cloistered sisters in the Dominican tradition, that we
would send them a replacement. I visited our Roman
students shortly before ordination and proposed this
assignment to Friar Jean-Claude. He was delighted
with it. I told him that he could also work with the
students at the University, which made him very
happy. He seemed even younger than the students."

"So he never lived here at St-Jacques."

"I don't believe so. Perhaps he would have been
less happy here."

"I see . . . No question about his sexual orientation?"

"Certainly not!"

A gay priest might be less a problem in a convent
of elderly nuns than in an all-male house. On the other
hand, it might not be wise to let such a man associate
freely and without supervision with students.

There was a memory in Paris still, I was sure, of a
great theologian and cardinal who was also a student
chaplain, who died in a house of prostitution. You had
to watch student chaplains.

You had, in fact, to watch everyone.

"Did he seem happy when you saw him in Rome,
what was it, six years ago?"

"Yes, I had just become provincial. He made little
impression on me, to tell the truth, a hardworking,

somewhat exhausted provincial lad with a good heart and not much seriousness. I have noted here"—he shuffled among his papers and found a single sheet— "that he seemed a bit worn, doubtless from his studies. However, I remember that when he returned to Paris he seemed in fine health and has remained so . . . Had remained so."

"He was then no problem for you until the television appearances began?"

"None at all, Bishop Rhine. We heard from the chief chaplain at the University that his work with the students was most successful. The prioress at the convent praised him as a fine preacher and a sensible confessor. . . . here she has written that he 'is a deeply spiritual man for one so young.' "

He put aside another sheet of paper.

"Did that surprise you?"

"Perhaps it should have, but it did not. I was not, in truth, watching him too closely. It did not seem to me that close observation was necessary."

So you have this nice young priest, shallow but industrious and pious. Why should you watch him closely? What reason was there to expect that he would soon become a national celebrity?

What reason indeed?

"There were negative reactions immediately after the television began?"

"After the first week. Complaints from priests who told us that he was stupid, that a priest should never sing on television, that his recitation of the rosary was inappropriately pious and sentimental, that his doctrine was weak, that there was insufficient concern for social justice in what he said, that he was immature . . . But you are familiar with such complaints about priests who suddenly become famous, are you not, Bishop?"

"Oh yes."

Some of them had indeed been made about me, though they made no impression on Milord Cronin.

"I must confess that I did not watch the first program. I did not even know that he was going to preach on television. I watched him the next week and, candidly, I was delighted. I was even proud of him . . ."

"Surprised?"

"Yes, but not unpleasantly so. He was one of our own. He was doing good work. There were more letters and then a call from the Cardinal's office."

"Oh? From Frankie?"

"No, no, Frankie was always most supportive. He was trained in communication, you know, and he recognized excellent communication when he saw it. In fact, it was one of the auxiliary bishops. He wanted to know if I was aware of Jean-Claude and if he had our permission to preach on television. I asked if his preaching was inappropriate. I was told that there was no such implication. They merely wanted to be certain that I knew about it."

He laughed so bitterly that Marie-Bernadette looked up from her notes in surprise.

"They were letting you know that they didn't particularly like a television rival for *M. le Cardinal*?"

"Precisely. I wouldn't be surprised that they made the first complaint to the Nuncio. He called me after the third broadcast to express his astonishment that one so young would be permitted to appear so prominently."

"And you said?"

Pere Duchamp's shoulders slumped.

"I taught theology in a seminary in West Africa

before I was elected provincial. I had never dealt with
these people before. I was astonished at their resentment. I have no ambitions for anything but to return
to Africa when my term is finished. So I defended
Jean-Claude, though in truth I hardly knew him. I said
that I found no harm in his preaching. I said that I
had discussed him with the chief chaplain at the University and he strongly supported him. If there were
specific charges against him I would, of course, consider such charges. Needless to say there was nothing
specific because he was doing nothing wrong and saying nothing wrong."

"Except effective and popular preaching, which
many can consider a grave sin indeed."

"As you know," he said with another sigh, "the
broadcasts continued and their popularity increased,
as did the complaints, including now an embarrassed
inquiry from our General in Rome."

"And then?"

"Then I read through his dossier and invited him
over for brief discernment. He seemed quite unaware
that he was already a celebrity. He felt that the TV
broadcasts were only a brief interlude. He said that he
saw no harm in them, but he would be happy to stop
them if I ordered him to. I could not in conscience do
that. I appointed an informal group of our wisest men
to report to me on Jean-Claude. They reported back
that there was nothing unorthodox or dubious in his
programs and at the present time there was certainly
no reason to take action against him."

"At the present time" is the classic dodge of eccle-
siastical authority which wants to cover itself.

"No dissent?"

"One of the six men thought he was too young, but
found nothing wrong with the contents of what he

said and did. I sent this report on to the General who seemed quite satisfied with it."

"And *Frère* Jean-Claude?"

"As God is my witness, Bishop Rhine, he was quite unaffected by it all. He had not changed. It was almost as though he was unaware of what was happening. He seemed frail, but then he always seemed frail. He told me often that the broadcasts were of no importance. He promised that he would give them up immediately if I asked him to."

"Most extraordinary!"

"By that time," he said, gathering together the papers and putting them back into their folder, "I began to suspect that he was indeed extraordinary. However, you must understand, Bishop, that he still did not seem extraordinary. Naturally I watched him every Sunday, with, if I may say so, considerable spiritual profit. Then Rome intervened. Through *M. le Cardinal*. The Holy Office. Or the Congregation for the Defense of the Faith as they now call it."

"Or the Inquisition as they used to call it."

He chuckled bitterly.

"Précisément."

Marie-Bernadette did not bother to translate that.

"I have heard stories about what they did to some of our men before the Council—*Père* Chenu, *Père* Congar . . ."

"In the end *M. le Cardinal Congar.*"

"Only when he was dying. . . . I could not believe that they were thinking of doing the same thing to poor Jean-Claude. It was . . . Excessive!"

Swatting a fly with a howitzer.

"So there was a hearing?"

"In the Cardinal's house. Most of the theologians were unfriendly. Very conservative. One or two of our own men who resented Jean-Claude. An intelligent Jesuit who defended him brilliantly . . ."

"Quid mirum!"

We both laughed.

Marie-Bernadette looked up, puzzled by the Latin.

"He means, my dear," said *Père* Duchamp, "that there has been a historic rivalry between us and the Jesuits and that even now it is a little unusual for one of them to stand up for us."

She smiled and nodded.

"You have seen the proceedings of the commission, Bishop Rhine?"

"I have heard descriptions of them, but I have not seen them."

"They are comic, but eventually boring. I have excerpted a few pages for you."

He handed a manila folder to me across his desk. Naturally, I dropped the folder. Marie-Bernadette, striving to hide an utterly inappropriate grin, gathered the papers up and put the folder in her large purse.

"What happened then?"

"The Cardinal, who I am sure understood none of the investigation, appointed the Jesuit to write up the report. Astonishingly he sent it on to Rome, assuming no doubt that, given our historic rivalry, the Jesuit would condemn Jean-Claude. Instead he praised him."

"The Holy Office backed off?"

"How do you call it? A strategic retreat . . . I knew eventually they would be back, that they would say that at the present time it was unwise for *Frère* Jean-Claude to continue the broadcasts. The order would come through the General and he would be very embarrassed, but we would have no choice. I would tell Jean-Claude."

"And then?"

He seemed surprised.

"He would obey. He was an obedient priest."

"Just as he was prepared to obey your order to leave the convent and move here to St-Jacques?"

"That order came again from the General. Doubtless the Congregation for Religious Orders had become involved. I told Jean-Claude and he agreed with the change."

"Readily?"

"I would say so. He seemed, how should I say it, hurt, but he did not protest. He did not ask the reason. I suspect by that time he knew there was pressure and understood the reason. He asked for a week to put his work in order. He even moved some of his books—mostly pious tracts into his new room."

"Then he disappeared."

"Yes, Bishop. Then he disappeared."

"Do you see any connection between his disappearance and the order to leave the convent?"

"How could there have been? If I had told him that he should give up the television program or his work with students or if I forbade him to preach, it was most unlikely that he would walk away from us. He would have promptly obeyed because that was the kind of priest he was. But disappear over a change of residence? That makes no sense at all!"

Indeed it did not.

I thanked him for his helpfulness. He wished me success in my investigation and led us down to a parlor where I would interview *Père* Leroy who had been the Director of Formation when Jean-Claude was in what used to be called the novitiate. He bowed politely and shook hands with Marie-Bernadette.

"What did you think of him?" I whispered to her as we waited for *Père* Leroy.

"He is a very good priest and he did all that he could for poor Jean-Claude. But *they* were too strong for him."

Perhaps they were. Still none of it made sense. Why would Jean-Claude give up to his enemies before he had to?

7

I instantly did not like **Père** Leroy. He was a tall, broad-shouldered, handsome man with wavy black hair tinged with silver, combed straight back from his forehead. He strode into the parlor with his black-and-white robes trailing behind him like they were a royal train. He was genial, outgoing, charming—the kind of priest in which the religious orders abound, who seem to want to overwhelm you with their membership in the clerical brotherhood, whose membership card I had turned in long ago.

More important to my dislike than this "hail-father-well-met" style, he ignored Marie-Bernadette. Indeed, he dismissed her with barely a nod of the head. You don't ignore anyone if you're a good priest, especially not a woman, and more especially if she is an appealing, not to say beautiful, waif like *Mademoiselle la* translator. There is something wrong with your hormones if she doesn't make you smile.

This conversation would not arrange itself well. However, I would remember my own solemn advice to Marie-Bernadette and strive to be professional.

"I'm delighted to meet you, Bishop. I am, of course, familiar with your work. I hope Father Provincial has asked you to speak to us here at St-Jacques before you return to America. I am, as you doubtless know, prior here, and I want to reinforce that invitation."

"Ah," I said.

He sat down on a couch across from the chair on which I was sitting, both pseudo–Second Empire and dilapidated at that, with a flurry of arranging the flounces of his black-and-white robe.

I was back in my standard uniform of black jeans, black clerical shirt (*sans* collar) and Chicago Bulls windbreaker.

(Marie-Bernadette had looked askance at me when we began our hike across the Luxembourg Gardens. Doubtless before the day was over she would remonstrate with me.)

"Well," he continued, "we have a pretty little problem here, do we not? I am not disappointed, between us, that Friar Jean has disappeared. He was an appallingly ignorant and shallow young man. However, he became an overnight celebrity and then, just when his popularity began to wane, elected to disappear without a trace. My own suspicion is that the police have known where he is all along, but have told no one until they are confident that the media and the people have forgotten him and they can reveal that Jean is somewhere with his woman."

Which revelation, it seemed to me, would lead the French media vultures, if anything worse than their American counterparts, to swarm all over him once again.

"You think it is a woman?"

"What else could it be?" he said waving his arms in a theatrical gesture. "*Cherchez la femme*, as the old saying tells us."

"Ah? Do we know who *la femme* is?"

"I think Father Provincial's worst mistake with this man—who believe me, Bishop, is a nonentity, a man who barely exists—was to appoint him to a convent of elderly nuns where he had his own apartment with

his own private entrance. In such circumstances it is
simple to arrange a love affair."

"Indeed."

"You ought not give a young friar with so little ma-
turity an opportunity like that, especially when he is
working with young women, many of whom would
like to seduce a priest just to prove that they can do
it, especially when that priest becomes famous, *n'est-ce
pas?*"

Marie-Bernadette repeated these chauvinist comments in a guarded and neutral voice. So soon had
she become a professional.

"Do we have any idea," I rephrased my question,
"who this lover might be?"

He waved his hand negligently.

"I'm sure the students could tell you, as they undoubtedly told the Paris police. I would not be surprised if they are *en cohabitation* in some attic right here
in the Latin Quarter."

"They haven't left Paris?"

"He's not smart enough to think of that."

He was demolishing Jean-Claude's character with
the confidence of someone who had the inside story
and was merely repeating what all the insiders knew
to be true.

It did not follow that he was wrong, however. I too
had wondered about cherchezing *la femme*.

"What would they do for money?"

"I'm sure he earned much money from the television. Father Provincial should have required much
stricter financial reports from him. Father Provincial
is a wonderful man but everyone in the province
knows that he was in Africa too long. He has really
made a terrible mistake with this ambitious and empty
young man."

Ambitious and empty, shrewd but immature. Could be? Perhaps.

"You were his novice master, were you not?"

"From the very beginning I suspected that he did not belong in the order. He was too bland, too much the *bourgeois*, too conventionally pious, if you take my meaning. In these days we Dominicans need strong, vigorous *men* who can appeal to the men of France and the world, not an effeminate little fellow whom women want to mother and protect. I voted against him, but I was overruled by the council. I appealed to the man who was then provincial and he lacked the courage to support me. I think that he probably realizes now that I was right. So do many of the others. It is all most unfortunate."

So perhaps in the next election, Father Prior would finally be elected Father Provincial.

"Do you suggest that Friar Claude perhaps leaned towards homosexuality?"

"Certainly not," he replied, nervously shifting on the couch and shifting one leg over the other. "Rather, I think he was lacking in any sexuality, too weak to care for women and too bland to really be a man."

"I see. That's a very interesting analysis."

Marie-Bernadette did not give the slightest hint of the fury she must have felt.

"You really don't need me to tell you these things, I'm sure, Bishop. A man as sophisticated as you has doubtless understood them already. The only problem is why the police have not acted. Whatever the reasons, I'm sure that these atrocious displays over at the crypt will lead them to change their strategy."

Would the police actually sit on the story for devious bureaucratic reasons of their own? They might but would not some disaffected cop leak the story to

the scandal journals? Perhaps, however, only some of
the very top cops knew the whole story.

"It would help if we knew the identity of the
woman. That might force the police to take action."

"Ask around in the student scene. You'll find out
who she is. She would certainly brag about her con-
quest."

"Indeed . . . Tell me about his background."

"He is from Grenoble. Attended a very ordinary
lycée and the *École Normale* there. Wanted to be a
primary-school teacher. Then decided he had a Dominican vocation. Absurd."

"Family?"

"His parents died in an auto accident when he and
his sister were children. There was an inheritance
which paid for their education. The sister became
some kind of actress. She visited him occasionally
when he was in formation. A vapid and very ordinary
young woman. I am told that she died subsequently
from a variety of tuberculosis which does not respond
to antibiotics. I believe he buried her here in Paris.
Without church services. She was an unbeliever. If
any of their inheritance remained, it never came to
our order. I took pains to be sure of that. Tragic, of
course. In truth, I'm not sure that Jean-Claude might
not have the same inclinations. He has never looked
healthy."

"I have watched some of the TV tapes, he seems
quite animated. . . ."

"Yet those affiliated with the television industry tell
me that he was on the verge of collapse after many of
the broadcasts. He paid a price for his animation."

Don't we all.

"No other family besides the sister?"

"None that I know of. I would remember because

I went over his records very carefully when he was in formation. He was an empty man with an empty past. We should never have admitted him into the order and never ordained him. We are paying the price now of those mistakes. There will be a heavier price to pay when the full story is told."

I thanked him profusely. He left the parlor confident that, like the obviously sensible person I was, I shared his interpretation of the story of Jean-Claude.

I turned to see my translator, her eyes blazing, her back stiff and erect on her chair.

"I'll say it for you, Marie-Bernadette: *Merde!*"

She blushed, relaxed and then laughed.

"Did my face really say that, Mr. Bishop?"

"That and a lot more. . . . Were there ever any rumors about *Frère* Jean-Claude and women?"

"Many women admired him, *naturellement.* Some tried to seduce him. Either he did not notice or he ignored them. His mind was elsewhere. He did enjoy women, however. He liked to talk to them and joke with them. But he encouraged no one to forget that he was a priest."

I nodded.

"However," she continued thoughtfully, "that terrible man is right that such an affair might explain his disappearance. I do not want to believe it. Yet it might be true."

"No rumors in the *milieu?*"

"None at all. That terrible man is right when he said that a woman who succeeded in the seduction of Jean-Claude would not want to keep it a secret. Otherwise what would be the point?"

What indeed.

Our next visitor was a lank, bearded friar in lay garb—torn jeans, a dirty sweatshirt, and running shoes.

He was *Père* Herbert, a doctoral student in Semitic languages at the *Sorbonne*. Not to put too fine an edge on things, he smelled. One suspected that the smell was deliberate, as though he sprayed it on every day to prove that he was a radical.

It was thirty years too late for that pose.

"I went through the novitiate and seminary with Jean-Claude," he admitted, in a tone that implied it was an experience of which he was certainly not proud and which he would rather not acknowledge. "We were ordained at the same time and came back here to St-Jacques at the same time. I did not know him very well, however, not that there was much to know. His piety did not advance beyond Ste-Thérèse and his theology, such as it was, would have been appropriate before the Great War. He was not relevant."

"Indeed?"

The young priest bent over and rested his chin on his fingertips. His gray eyes suggested not so much revolutionary radicalism as contempt.

"He was totally middle-class and reactionary middle class at that. He was not concerned about the multinational corporations or the environment or global warming or AIDS in Africa. He knew of these problems or at least he had heard of them. It was not so much that he didn't care about them as that he was incapable of comprehending their *actualité*."

Everyone in St-Jacques seemed only too eager to talk about Frère Jean-Claude, even if what they wanted to say about him made him sound like several different men.

What would multiple narrators have to say about you, Blackie Ryan, God whispered and thus shut me up.

"He was unaware of the serious problems of our time?"

"He did not even understand the question of the hermeneutic circle, if you can imagine that."

"And surely never heard of Jacques Derrida?"

"Hardly . . . Of course he achieved a certain celebrity among his fellow *bourgeois*. Alas, poor man, he paid a heavy price for it."

"By disappearing from the face of the earth?"

"Oh, *that!* No, no. I'm sure that he has not disappeared. He is with his Royalist friends. They realized that his popularity was in decline. So they spirited him away to one of their châteaux where he is eating good food and drinking good wine and receiving adoration from elderly women. . . . No, no, no. What I meant was that the strain of his essentially false position had taken its toll on his health. I encountered him one day on the *rue* St-Jacques and noticed that he walked very slowly, his head down and his shoulders sloped. I asked him whether he was in ill health. He replied only that he was very tired. Thus I was not altogether surprised at his disappearance."

Pere Herbert was the kind of man who gives academic snobs their bad name.

"Tell me about these Royalists."

He grimaced. "In French politics, we always have the Royalists. They are small in number though the larger bourgeoisie population has a certain fondness for dukes and barons and marquises. At certain critical times they become very active and because of their money and their prestige they attain some influence—during the Vichy years of the war and when de Gaulle came to power. They mistakenly thought that *le Général* was one of them. They were dismayed to discover that while he was a reactionary, de Gaulle was a re-publican reactionary."

"Whom do they want to restore as king?"

Father Herbert sneered.

"There are many different factions and candidates—Bourbons, Orléanists, Bonapartists. Jean-Claude's friends support the heir of Louis Phillipe, the Duc d'Orléans, who reigned between 1830 and 1848, between the last of Bourbon kings and the last of the Bonaparte emperors. He styled himself 'King of the French' and purported to be a *bourgeois* monarch, if you can imagine that."

"Incroyable."

"Precisely! However, the Baron and Baroness de Vendôme are rich and attractive young people and very pious. In the present confused state of French politics they thought that Jean-Claude was a heaven-sent leader who would restore the old faith and some of the old ways to France, a kind of modern day Jeanne d'Arc, if you will."

"Friar Jean-Claude was close to these people?"

"Has no one told you? He preached a retreat for them at one of their châteaux in the Loire. Very effectively, one hears. Tears, it is said, cascaded themselves down the pretty and powdered cheeks of *Madame la Baroness* . . . It is all absurd, naturally. The Royalists may be amusing in their own little eighteenth century way, but they are uneducated and irrelevant. The quality of their realism should be obvious from the fact that they placed their hope on such a frail reed as Jean-Claude."

"Indeed."

"There is now, of course, the problem of the miracles in the parvis."

For a man who was uninterested in his *confrère,* he certainly knew a lot of the details.

"Oh, yes."

"The rabble thinks he is a saint and a martyr. What will the Royalists do with a living martyr on their hands?" he said, permitting himself a snide little chuckle.

"Kill him?"

"Oh no, no. They are not, poor things, evil people. They could not kill anyone, especially a priest. They probably will pray for another miracle, a political one . . . It is an amusing little incident, is it not?"

"Arguably," I admitted.

This time Marie-Bernadette was the first one to mutter *"merde."*

Our last Dominican, Friar Marcel, was very different from his predecessors. He was a smiling, quiet, young man of about the same age as Jean-Claude. He had known Jean-Claude since the novitiate and admired him greatly, though he thought he worked too hard and read too little. His blond hair was trimmed short and his Dominican habit seemed part of his physical being.

"Where do you think Jean-Claude is?" I began.

He frowned, pained at the difficulty of the question.

"If he is dead, he is in heaven. If he is still alive, he will return soon with the answers to all our questions."

"Which of those outcomes do you anticipate?"

"I do not know, Mr. Bishop. I believe that I had the honor to be his closest friend. He seemed to relax with me. Yet he was also a mystery, perhaps more of a mystery when he relaxed."

The French generally called me *"M. l'Evêque."* However I found Marie-Bernadette's translation of it as Mr. Bishop charming.

"He was this way when you were in Rome?"

"In truth, I cannot remember. It seems so long ago. He did not live in our house there, you see, but with the Irish. . . ."

"A very difficult people."

"Jean-Claude found them fascinating. They appealed to the mystic side of his personality."

Beware of your Irish mystic. He is at least three-quarters mad.

"So."

"Nor have we lived in the same house here. I had looked forward to his return because I thought that life in that convent would put a strain on any man's sanity, especially one as delicate as Jean-Claude."

"Indeed."

"Just so. Yet he seemed happy and worked very hard with the students who loved him, is that not true, *mademoiselle*?"

"*C'est vrai,*" Marie-Bernadette agreed.

Friar Marcel could not take his eyes off *Mademoiselle* my translator. It occurred to me that she was under some circumstances a very beautiful young woman. Indeed almost any circumstance when one had become familiar with her face and her body.

Fortunate Jacques-Yves.

"I am a student at the *Sorbonne,* you see," Friar Marcel continued meekly, "studying sociology. Jean-Claude and I would run into each other frequently and sometimes have a cup of tea at a café. We did not seek each other out, yet he seemed happy to see me, though you could not be certain about him. Many people say he is transparent and I see what they mean. He appears to hide nothing when he preaches or teaches. Yet beneath the transparency there is opacity, no? The serious component of Jean-Claude which many believe is not there."

"But you do?"

"Mais oui. His piety is authentic, simple perhaps and somewhat old-fashioned. In addition to the piety, however, there is something else, deeper, richer and ultimately charming. I only see flashes of it on occasion, a quick, knowing smile, a mischievous glow in his eyes, a hint that he is saying that we both understand that there is more to him than the wonderful preacher we see on the television screen."

"Fascinating!"

"I always find him so. I sense that he gives me such hints because he wants me to see this aspect of him, but he does not want me to know it too well. With this implicit condition, I naturally agree."

"Can you provide me with some sense of the content of this deeper and richer Jean-Claude?"

My translator inserted "more charming," perhaps to hint that she had remembered Marcel's phrase better than I had.

Such is the way they are.

"I have thought of that all morning, Mr. Bishop, as I waited to see you. I do not say that he is acting in, if you will, his public face. No, no. It is very authentic. But in his private face he laughs at himself and at the folly of the world. In truth he makes me think for a moment of François Villon."

"What could poor Jean-Claude have in common with that charming rake of a medieval poet!"

"Sweetness and sadness combined and laughter over both."

"Ah!"

This was a view of Jean-Claude at which no one else had hinted. To the extent that it was not a fantasy of this somewhat romantic young man, it made our search far more interesting.

"You understand what I say, Mr. Bishop?"

"I think so."

"He did not consider the television broadcasts important, not nearly as important as his work with students. He would roll his eyes and smile with that sly, ironic smile that apparently no one else ever saw. Yet he believed in what he was doing. Television was serious, but not important, if you understand."

"He had no sense that he had become an overnight celebrity?"

"He would laugh at it and then tell funny stories about the people at the television station. Not mean stories, funny stories."

"I understand."

"I hope you find him alive, Mr. Bishop. I valued greatly those conversations over tea on the *rue* St-Jacques. Once we even walked in the Luxembourg Gardens."

As we finally left the priory of St-Jacques, I said to Marie-Bernadette, what did you think of Friar Marcel?"

"He was *très* sweet, no?"

"And this extra dimension of Jean-Claude?"

"I saw it too, as *Frère* Marcel saw it. But he saw that he saw it and I did not, *n'est-ce pas?*"

Then she laughed.

"That is very French is it not?"

"Right out of a Rohmer film."

"Do you think I am a character in a Rohmer film, Bishop Blackie?"

I might have said that I think all young women like her in France were Rohmer characters. Instead, however, I said, *"Mais certainement!"*

"*Incroyable!* . . . Marcel at least noticed I was there. That *Père* Leroy, who pretends to be so manly, is certainly gay though he doesn't realize it and *Père* Herbert, the smelly snob, is capable only of autoeroticism."

Rohmer would have loved that line.

"And *Père* Marcel is heterosexual?"

"But of course. So was Jean-Claude. . . . There was mystery in him, as *Père* Marcel said . . . We saw it but we didn't see it. Yet it was what was most attractive about him . . ."

"Any hints that maybe he would be capable of arranging his own disappearance?"

She thought about it.

"*C'est vrai.* That one that we saw but did not see might have chosen to disappear."

Matters had arranged themselves so that the plot had thickened. How very French.

8

"So, Marie-Bernadette, what did we learn today?"

"I learned that being a *tec* is more difficult than playing the viola . . . Does it not exhaust you, Mr. Bishop?"

So now I was Mr. Bishop! The child was an imp.

"I never noticed . . . But what did we learn about Jean-Claude?"

We were sitting in an outdoor café on the *Boulevard* St-Michel eating *jambon et fromage* and sipping hot chocolate—the best in the Latin Quarter, Marie-Bernadette had assured me. Arguably she was right. The *Sorbonne* was two blocks away and we faced it on the *place de la Sorbonne* where the students and the police had fought during the pointless riots of 1968. Scores of students milled around now, lost in either thought or conversation. Not a revolutionary in the lot, I was willing to wager. Revolution had failed for the last time. All revolutions fail, someone had said, but the failures are different. In the distance the great dome of the Pantheon loomed implacable against the gray sky. On the whole, I thought, the Latin Quarter did not compare with Michigan Avenue.

Marie-Bernadette arranged her plate and cup and spoon in a neat row, logical environment a prelude to logical disquisition. She was reveling in her new role as a *"tec."* I noticed that she was wearing a thin ring, not an engagement ring exactly, nor a wedding ring exactly. Nonetheless, it represented, I would be willing to bet, a permanent commitment.

"We have learned that he is a transparent and zealous, if not too intelligent, young priest whom his provincial was willing to defend against *them*, that he is shallow and empty and not really virile or manly, that he is an irrelevant tool of foolish Royalists and had no sense of the important issues of our time, and that he has about himself a certain appealing aura of romantic mystery. . . . Is that good, Mr. Holmes?"

"Excellent, Ms. Watson . . . And you conclude?"

She sighed, a veritable Celtic sigh.

"Each says something important about him, *n'est-ce pas*? Yet, we combine them and we know less than we did this morning. . . . Still, Bishop Holmes, the sexual thing was interesting, was it not?"

"In what way?"

"Did not those who were not heterosexual despise him and those who were rather like him, especially Friar Marcel?"

"And from that you conclude that he was not gay?"

"*Mais oui*, but I never thought he was. . . . Were not Friar Herbert and Friar Leroy caricatures of gay men? Most of them are not that way, unless they deny that they are . . ."

"*D'accord.*"

"There is a special sexual chemistry in Friar Jean-Claude that I do not understand. He appeals to both men and women but not like most men do. . . . There is a charisma . . . I don't know what I mean, Mr. Bishop."

Neither did I. However, she was probably right. In addition to his piety and his simplicity, the young priest's sexuality was an important part of his appeal to the French TV audience.

What, if anything, did that have to do with his strange disappearance.

"Is celibacy very difficult, Mr. Bishop?" my interpreter asked as we crossed the Luxembourg Gardens again.

"For those who are happy in the priesthood, it is usually no more difficult than marriage, which is not very easy."

"Priests do find women attractive?"

"Oh, yes."

"I thought so. . . . It would be strange if they did not, *n'est-ce pas?*"

"Very strange."

"Especially if a woman finds a priest attractive?"

"Arguably."

"I wonder about Friar Jean-Claude. Many women admired him. I saw some students who tried to seduce him. He hardly seemed to notice."

"That's usually the best strategy."

"Yet he liked women. . . ."

"Bien sûr."

"You have more French than you admit, Mr. Bishop. . . . He liked them very much. When he smiled at me, I felt beautiful."

The little imp had seen through my act. I knew a lot of French catchphrases, *n'est-ce pas?* And I could catch the flow of a conversation. I could not, however, either join the conversation or be sure of its nuances. Nonetheless, it helped that I had a sense of what *Mademoiselle* my translator was putting in English before I heard it.

"You should feel beautiful all the time, Marie-Bernadette."

She waved away the compliment.

"I feel somehow that a woman might be involved, Mr. Bishop."

I pondered that notion—which I myself had also suspected and then something which became a suspicion only as I expressed it.

"Arguably . . . However, not in the usual sense of involved."

"Oh," said my translator, too polite and too respectful to ask what the hell that meant.

Search for the woman, but not as a lover?

When we approached our hotel, Jacque-Yves, dressed in his dark suit, was waiting for us. Marie-Bernadette's pace picked up, not so much running for her lover (which would not have been proper) but forcing her employer to walk faster too.

They kissed each other lightly, but with a hint of controlled intensity.

"Good afternoon, Mr. Bishop," Jacques-Yves said, with a polite bow. "We would like to give a presentation to Mr. Cardinal."

"Most young people call him Cardinal Sean," I said. "Doubtless he and his sister are in the bar waiting for me."

Waiting for Blackie, waiting for Godot.

M. le Cardinal and *Madame sa soeur* were indeed sitting in the flower festooned bar, sipping their late-afternoon tea and discussing the Eiffel Tower to the top of which both of them, in defiance of all right reason, had ascended.

"Marie-Bernadette, Jacques-Yves!" he greeted the shy young folk in accordance with his custom of never forgetting a name. "Come in, sit down! I hope Blackwood hasn't been working you too hard, Marie-Bernadette. The young women around my rectory complain about that all the time!"

Two falsehoods. The Megan and Crystal Lane never complained, rather they simply ignored me. Moreover, it was my rectory, not his. Whatever canon law might say.

"You both look like you need a sip of cognac," he continued, waving away their protests.

He had the good grace to order a glass of Bailey's for me.

"Cardinal Sean," Jacques-Yves began hesitantly, "Marie-Bernadette and I are very grateful that you came to listen to us last night and that you encouraged us in our work. We wish to make a presentation to you."

He placed an audiotape on the table.

"Jacques-Yves," Marie-Bernadette continued, "and I are Celts . . ."

"Obviously," Milord agreed genially.

"And we are very interested in Celtic music."

"Shows excellent taste."

"In the summers we have visited many places where they create Celtic music, old and new."

"Brittany," Jacques-Yves found his tongue again, "Gallicia, Manx, Scotland, Wales, and of course Ireland."

"Of course."

"We have collected many pieces and arranged some of them for our instruments, the violin and the viola."

"We have recorded some of them and hope soon to produce a disk," Marie-Bernadette took over. "Until then we would like you to have a tape."

"Hey," Milord enthused. "Great! Nora has brought a tape player along and we'll listen to it this evening. Thank you very much! Really great!"

The two young folk, enormously pleased by his enthusiasm, blushed modestly.

Of Milord Cronin someone (arguably me) once remarked that he was definitive proof that the Irish had
the Blarney Stone not because they needed it but because they deserved it.

"Cute kids," *Madame* Nora said when they had bid
us a shy good-bye. "You have sound instincts, Blackwood, at picking your North Wabash Avenue Irregulars. I presume she is a member already."

"Patently."

I must call the rectory and have Crystal put an
NWAI sweatshirt in a FedEx box before the day
ended.

"You ought to work out a deal to bring them to
Chicago. They won't have to beg to stay alive there."

"Chicago, Richard M. Daley, Mayor." I corrected
him.

In my room before I rested my eyes, I phoned my
brother Packy, who is involved in a small and what
the media call a clout-heavy law firm. I presented our
problem to him.

"Yeah well, it's a tough one, but some of our mutual
friends might be interested and they will go along and
see if they can push it through, maybe tilt the playing
field, know what I mean?"

"Certainly," I said. That was a lie. I never knew
what Packy meant. He spoke a dialect of American
that was the lingua franca of City Hall.

"We may have to pick up a few markers, you
know? Still there's a lot of them left on the table and
all our mutual friends know that."

"Precisely."

"Yeah, well, my best to our mutual friend."

"Naturally."

The last named mutual friend was arguably Milord
Cronin. I had no idea who the others might be.

Then I called the good Crystal Lane at the Cathedral and asked her to FedEx a sweatshirt and a tee shirt, medium, to *l'abbaye St-Germain*.

"I'm praying for you real hard, Bishop Blackie."

"That is a good work, Crystal. Our present project requires the activation of many good angels."

I was always happy to be assured of Ms. Lane's prayers because I believed that she was clout-heavy with God.

It was now time to indulge in the ancient spiritual practice known as "reading the fathers," a spiritual exercise that was not impeded even by noise of the *demoiselles* next door in the *Institut Catholique*.

9

When the phone rang I awoke with no clear idea of where I was or why. I picked up the phone.

"Father Ryan," I said automatically, expecting an emergency call from Northwestern University Hospital.

"You certain that you don't want to come to supper with us at Maxim's, Blackwood?"

Milord Cronin, bless his heart.

"Only five-star restaurants," I replied.

"Yeah, well, you'll be at *La Tour d'Argent* tomorrow night for Nora's birthday dinner?"

"Patently."

"Good! . . . Incidentally, Nora left the tape of our young friends and her player at your door. She was afraid to knock, lest she wake you up."

"Auxiliary bishops never sleep," I protested, but he had hung up.

La bella Nora's room was on my floor, Milord Cronin's two floors up, thus continuing the illusion that I was a chaperone.

I opened the door, picked up the tape player, and placed it on my desk. I was tempted to go to work immediately, but thought better of it. I should walk a bit and find a *jambon et fromage* to sustain me through the night. I indulged myself in my second Bailey's of the day upon return to the hotel and then brewed myself a pot of Bewley's afternoon coffee when I returned to my room. I congratulated myself that I had not become lost during my brief *passage* through the streets of Paris. Well, only once or twice.

Then I inserted the videotapes of Friar Jean-Claude into the video player and watched once more his magic, this time with the sound turned off.

It was a strange experience. His sincerity, devotion, and enthusiasm were so patent that he could have been reading the day's stock market reports and still captivated viewers. A light seemed to radiate from his young face that filled the screen and then the room. Pure charisma.

One does not spend as many years in the priesthood as I have without developing a certain cynicism about charismatic preachers. Often they are narcissistic charlatans. I dread when one of them shows up at the Cathedral to conduct some pious exercise demanded by one or the other groups of the faithful. It will require days, perhaps weeks, to clean up the mess he will have left in the tender consciences of the faithful.

Even without sound Jean-Claude was patently not one such. He made no neurotic demands on anyone. Rather he shared what he believed with us and invited us gently to believe in the same good news. In the broadcasts after the theologians had reviewed his work, he wore his black-and-white Dominican robes and somehow became more ethereal, more mystical, more enchanting.

Had M. Vincent himself been more magical when he was striving to reform France a couple of centuries ago?

I turned off the TV and pondered. Why did I feel guilty because I was not more skeptical? Had I been taken in by a most plausible charlatan? I took off my glasses and rubbed my eyes.

Was Friar Jean-Claude just a little too good to be true? Or was he arguably a saint? Or was he merely an excellent preacher? Might he become a demagogue, converting his charisma and popularity into weapons for some dubious movement, religious or political? Would not Milord Cronin grow uneasy if he appeared in Chicago? Would not I become suspicious if he descended upon the Cathedral parish?

Or was I merely trying to stir embers of clerical envy in my soul, the kind of envy which put John of the Cross in prison and imposed a daily beating on him?

Saints, or apparent saints, always make people uneasy, especially clergy people who professionally must strive to routinize the charisma.

I rubbed my eyes again and concluded that in Chicago I would watch Friar Jean-Claude closely and make no judgments. It would have been very difficult to find reasons to complain about him. Yet many priests would complain, usually in the dependent clause of clerical put-downs as in, "he's certainly a good preacher, but he's theologically naïve." Or "Poor man means well, but the Cardinal doesn't trust him." The latter comment would be made quite apart from any evidence to support the Cardinal's disapproval.

Next question: had I observed any of that special dimension of mystery that Friar Marcel had observed and the good Marie-Bernadette had remembered when that adoring friar had jogged her memory?

What was it that they had both seen? Some sort of sexual appeal that had impressed, indeed captivated a heterosexual priest and a heterosexual young woman?

I could not honestly say that I had noticed any such

special dimension to his personality as it appeared on the screen, certainly nothing like the appealing and knowing smile that Friar Marcel had reported.

A distinct hint of mystery? Maybe, but my sensitivity to the aura of mystery around people was notoriously deficient. Friar Jean-Claude, on the contrary, seemed innocent of any complexity. He permitted his vision to possess him completely, like he was an inanimate chalice which was possessed by the Precious Blood within it.

This metaphor caused me to remove my glasses and rub my eyes for a third time. There was something I was missing, something delicate, subtle, ephemeral.

Was he laughing at us, at himself, at human folly?

Where did that idea come from?

Enough reflection on the tapes. Friar Jean-Claude had given me a headache. He might also present the first puzzle that was beyond the notoriously prosaic imagination of John Blackwood Ryan.

I resorted to two Tylenol tablets to combat the headache and turned to the transcript of his interrogation by a distinguished commission of theologians, for most of whom I developed an almost instant dislike.

Q. Well, now, Friar, what are your qualifications to be a public theologian in France?

A. None at all, Father. I am a simple priest.

Q. Do you really believe that a simple priest as you call yourself could win such attention from the Catholic people of France?

A. No, Father, I find it very hard to believe.

Q. How do you explain it?

A. I cannot explain it, Father. I'm sure that, like everything on television, it will quickly fade away.

Q. If your superiors should order you to cease these, ah, escapades, would you do so?

A. Certainly!

Q. But you enjoy the attention and adulation?

A. Vanity of vanities and all is vanity . . . Chasing the wind as the scripture tells us.

Q. Ah, Friar, you quote the scripture? Do you have any background in scripture studies?

A. Only the courses I attended at the Angelicum.

Q. And the same in theology?

A. Yes, Father. The courses were interesting and well taught, however.

Q. Ah! And that qualifies you to teach the whole world (*tout le monde*)?

A. I don't try to teach, Father. I just try to tell people how much God loves them.

Q. Do you not think that your Dominican superiors are taking a grave risk in permitting your little entertainments?

A. I never try to judge my superiors' decisions, Sister.

Q. But if you were a superior, would you permit someone like yourself to singularize himself on French television?

A. (Laughs) It is hard to imagine myself as a superior, Sister. I am so unqualified for the job. If I were a superior and those who knew more than I did suggested that a friar like me should not singularize himself on television and scandalize the faithful, I would surely follow their advice.

Q. You are a very clever man, Friar Jean-Claude.

A. Thank you, Sister, but I fear that I am not very clever. If I were, there would be no need to ask me these questions.

Q. What about Jesus, Friar?

A. He is our lord and savior.

Q. It is said that you don't emphasize his divinity on your broadcasts.

A. I believe that he is true God and true man. If I fail to emphasize both, then it is a grave fault in me.

Q. Don't you think that the problem of denying the Divinity of Jesus is the more serious in France?

A. I do not know that, Doctor. I would think that perhaps the most serious problem might be that the French people do not realize how much God loves them.

Q. Do you think that they are obedient enough to the Holy Father?

A. They have great reverence for His Holiness, as I do.

Q. Yet you do not emphasize infallibility in your little presentations, do you? Don't you think it is important?

A. Surely it is important, but I am not a teacher of doctrine, Doctor. I am not clever enough for that. I merely preach about God's love as revealed in Jesus and the Church. That is all that I can do.

Q. You think that's enough, Father?

A. Not for a theology class, Father, but for a television homily, that is often more than enough.

Q. You must forgive a Jesuit's stupidity, but are you trying to tell me that God's love for us is what our holy faith is all about?

A. I have never met a stupid Jesuit, Father. What else is so central to our faith? Weren't the stories and sayings of Jesus all about his heavenly Father's kingdom of love?

Q. It would seem so, Father. What do you think of these questions that are being asked you? A kind of climbing of Calvary?

A. Oh, no, Father. I am pleased that so many wise scholars are forcing me to review what I learned in the seminary.

Q. Do you believe, Friar, that Jesus is really present in the Eucharist?

A. Of course. When we gather round the table Jesus is among us, he comes to us to share our meals with us and to be our spiritual food.

Q. Yet you never mention the doctrine of transubstantiation.

A. I am not so clever to be able to explain such matters, Father, in the short time I have. I'd be happy to interview you on one of my broadcasts and ask you to explain it to the viewers.

Q. I would not venture to singularize myself, Friar, as you do.

Q. The Catholic people of France, Friar Jean-Claude, have the Pope and the bishops and their priests and the Holy Teachings of our Holy Church. How could they possibly need you?

A. I'm sure they don't need me.

Q. Forgive a Jesuit another stupid question, Friar. Why do you think your broadcasts are so popular?

A. I never heard a stupid question from a Jesuit, Father. I do not understand why people watch me on television. Perhaps in my own inept way I tell them the good news which Jesus told us all so long ago.

I threw the transcript across the room and shouted in rage!

The idiotic clericalist bastards!

They were striving to keep the C.D.F. (Congregation for the Defense of the Faith, née the Holy Office, née the Inquisition) happy by doing in Jean-Claude. He had creamed them. With the exception of the very clever Jesuit, they had revealed themselves as small-minded, mean-spirited, green-eyed fools.

Again I thought of Jeanne d'Arc and Bernadette of Lourdes.

Did they see the parallel between themselves and those who tormented the two saints?

Probably not. Still they had doubtless left the inquisition room with a vague sense that they had not quite carried the day the way they had expected. They had tried to please Rome. However, Rome would not be happy with them.

Served them right.

With enemies like that Jean-Claude didn't need friends. However, I was now on his side.

Regardless of the aura of mystery around him, which might or might not be there.

10

Marie-Bernadette insisted that I borrow Cardinal
Sean's ring for our visit to the Baron and Baroness de
Vendôme. Not enough that I don a clerical collar and
my St. Brigid pectoral cross. I had to look like a full-
fledged bishop. I consented to her instructions, but did
not promise that I would act like a "real" bishop.

"They will insist on kissing your ring," she contended. "They are very devout Catholics."

"You did not insist on kissing my ring," I said, par-
rying as best I could her argument. "And you're a
very devout Catholic."

"I did not know you were a Mr. Bishop," she said
primly.

So when the baronial Renault—with the appropriate
coat of arms—appeared at the hotel I looked as much
like a bishop as I ever looked.

Milord Cronin had reported to me that he and Madame Nora had encountered the Chuck O'Malleys at
Maxim's the night before and that they would join us
at Nora's birthday party that evening. He also instructed me to pass on to Marie-Bernadette how much
they had enjoyed their Celtic recording.

Both Charles Cronin O'Malley and his wife Rosemarie Clancy O'Malley claimed that I was their confessor, something of an exaggeration. Yet they were
fun people. He was reputed to be one of the great
photographers of our time, though his efforts to make

me look like a presentable result of Apostolic Succession had proven an abysmal failure. Or so it seemed to me, despite the fact that my sibs and their offspring thought it was "terribly cute."

I had relayed Milord's verdict on their Celtic tape to Marie-Bernadette. She dismissed the compliment with a wave of her hand.

"It is not adequate, but it is all we could do at the present time."

I regretted that I had not bothered to listen to it the night before, so confused had I been by the enigma of Jean-Claude. Since the Vendômes were the only "suspects" today, I would listen to the tape this afternoon.

The chauffeur was a small man with a large mustache and the military bearing of a marshal of France. He bowed to Marie-Bernadette as he ushered her into the car and saluted me. She accepted the bow like she herself was at least a baroness and arguably a duchess.

"They are very rich," she told me after the chauffeur had closed the window between himself and us. "They own many vineyards along the Rhône south of Valence. They are nice people, very formal, very reserved, very well meaning, and very dumb."

She pointed at her head to signify "very dumb."

"Yet you French like to have a few nobles around, *n'est-ce pas?*"

"But of course! They are colorful and they do no one any harm, unlike the Socialists in our government. If they were running the country, the *jeunesse* would have jobs."

"You want to return to the *ancien régime, mademoiselle?*"

"Certainly not. Jacques-Yves would have to fight in their silly wars. I would perhaps starve to death. Or be raped by nobles."

Were her conflicting opinions a contradiction or merely a symptom of French ambivalence about their troubled past?

"They are very military, you know. Henri, the present baron went to St. Cyr where we train officers. His father died at Dien Bien Phu in Vietnam, his grandfather died at Toulon when the English sank our Navy during the Second War, his great-grandfather died at Verdun. Henri is the only one who has not had to fight."

"No wonder they don't have much confidence in the Republic."

"All our leaders are incompetent, arrogant and incompetent, but why should they be different from the rest of us French, *n'est-ce pas?*"

"I wouldn't say that."

"You wouldn't, Mr. Bishop, because you are an American and a good man. But I as a Frenchwoman should say it and do!"

"Ah," I said, routed.

The Paris manse of the de Vendômes was in the Trocadero area, on the Right Bank beyond the shadow of the Eiffel Tower. We turned off the Avenue Foch and down a street of apartments which proclaimed to all, "inside is wealth, but you can't come in to see it."

We pulled up to an elegant doorway. The chauffeur bowed us out of the car solemnly. The door opened before we could reach it and a tall, bald and angular man in some sort of military uniform bowed to us again.

"Monseigneur," he said to me, using a title which conveyed a good deal more in France than in the United States. *"Madame,"* he bowed to Marie-Bernadette, who

once again acted like she belonged in a house of the nobility.

Inside, the house looked like a comfortable, modern version of Versailles—all blue and silver and ivory in what I thought might be modernized Louis XV style.

This could easily be the kind of drawing room in which Marcel, that insufferable and snobbish alter ego to Proust, might forever hope in vain to be received.

"*M. le Baron and Madame la Baroness* will be with you shortly," the butler intoned solemnly, and took his leave.

"Should we sit down?" I asked my tour guide.

"I would be afraid to."

We had rich people in Chicago, even in my parish. Most of them were "New Rich" whose taste did not match their goodness. The Old Rich were the opposite—their taste exceeded their goodness. Aristocracy who combined both taste and goodness hardly existed.

"Which of the pretenders do they support?" I whispered to Marie-Bernadette.

"The *Duc d'Orléans*, of course. None of the others are really serious."

"The Duke is serious?"

"Less unserious than the others. They are all realists, *n'est-ce pas*? But they do not permit realism to interfere with their fantasies or their fantasies to interfere with their realism."

Aha! That explained everything.

Then Barbie and Ken entered the room, two practically perfect blond human beings, impeccably groomed in expensive tailor-made casual clothes and flawless coiffeurs. On second thought, they were a somewhat superannuated Ken and Barbie. Despite her makeup and his outdoor tan they were in their middle thirties.

Nonetheless, I felt myself hoping that I should look so good if I were ever thirty again.

Their manners were perfect—courteous, friendly, dignified without too much dignity, quick, bright smiles, small, casual laughs, eagerness to put their guests at ease. Marie-Bernadette, among whose ancestors there must have been Celtic queens responded to them in kind, beggar from the streets of Paris or not. Mr. Bishop among whose ancestors were sheep thieves, smugglers, and revolutionaries maintained a calm, slightly aloof dignity which none of his clerical *confrères* in Chicago would have recognized. He even accepted the kissing of his ring as though it were an honor to which he was entitled and acknowledged with modest restraint the admiration for the silver pectoral cross created by *"madame ma cousine."*

The two nobles displayed perfect appearance, perfect manners, and, as *Mademoiselle* my translator had predicted, precious little intelligence. Their English was hesitant and formal, but we—well, Marie-Bernadette—decided to let them speak it with a little help from her.

"We were so happy, *Monseigneur,* to learn of your interest in our problem of *le petit* Jean-Claude," the Baron began. "We know of your reputation for solving these difficult puzzles and we know you will solve this one."

Breaking all the implicit rules of dignity and restraint *la petite* Marie-Bernadette announced firmly, "*Monseigneur* always solves his puzzles."

They both smiled faintly, at this breach of good manners, acceptable, *en fait* delightful, in one so young and so attractive. Indeed my translator became more attractive every day as hope deftly slipped back into her life.

"*La petite* Marie-Bernadette," I said trying to sound like I was a prince bishop, though not of Beauvais, "is too kind, but we will do our best."

I almost said with "our little gray cells" but restrained the impulse to sink to the comedy that the scene seemed to demand.

"*Frère* Jean-Claude," the baroness continued, "was a clean wind sweeping away all the corruption which stains our beloved France. We had such great hopes that he would lead a powerful religious revival in France, a modern M. Vincent who would transform this poor country and return it to its old greatness."

With all due respect to St-Vincent de Paul, whose feats are material for legend and whose missions still affected some of the regions of France, he did not transform France as the events at the end of the eighteenth century proved beyond any doubt.

"Now," the Baron said sadly, "they have taken him away from us."

So even the rich nobility feared "them."

I wondered what the proper title for a baron was. Mr. Baron? *M. le Baron? Monseigneur?* Excellency?

"You were very close to him, milord?"

They didn't blanch at that so I must have got it right. Two cheers for the descendent of Roscommon smugglers and ribbonmen.

"Well, yes, I think we were. We approached him after one of his broadcasts and invited him to supper at our house. He did not know who we were, but did not seem surprised at this house"—a diffident sweep of his hand—"in which our station compels us to live. He was a delightful dinner guest. *Très charmant.* He did not preach, he did not demand, he did not moralize. Yet we knew he was of God."

"In a certain way," the baroness said, "he became

our spiritual director. He said many things which helped me to become a better woman and a better wife...."

"We are not naïfs, *Monseigneur*," the Baron added, with a bit of a blush over his wife's revelation. "We know that Duc Louis will not become king tomorrow or perhaps ever. He would not want to be king unless there was a vast moral reform in France. He is more of a democrat than the criminals who run the country. Perhaps even more of a republican than any of the leaders of our evil republic."

"Except," his wife corrected him, *"le Général."*

"Of course. . . . If only he had been able to do what he knew should be done. But there was no moral reform in France then. We were still enjoying our materialism too much. We had thought that perhaps Friar Jean-Claude would have begun that reform. . . . Duc Louis would be for France what Don Carlos is in Spain."

It was madness° to think that in a post-Mitterand France, for all its seamy and sour corruption and its abuse of its young, anyone was willing to sacrifice their own selfishness in the name of moral reform. It was, however, a harmless madness and even a slightly endearing one.

"We invited him to meet some of our friends. He influenced them too, *n'est-ce pas*, Henri?"

"C'est vrai, Constance. There was something magical in his presence. He did us much good."

"He changed our lives." She wrung her hands in sadness.

"Yes, he certainly did that. . . . We miss him very much."

So, they had sought to use him for their own zany

political purposes and he had converted them. My regard for Jean-Claude went up.

"If only he had more time . . ." The baron sighed. "We introduced him to Duc Louis. Afterwards His Majesty, who you may know is a bit of an anticlerical, said to us that Jean-Claude could change France if *they* would let him, but that he was certain *they* would not."

"They" doubtless included the Cardinal who had, according to Frankie when he had made the appointment for us, detested the Royalists and the nobility. "He's a Corsican peasant despite his crimson robes."

"Did you notice any change in his behavior before his disappearance?"

"No," the baron said, trying to think. "He was always very *engagé*, dedicated, tense. There were no signs . . ."

"He was concerned about leaving the nuns and moving to that horrible place on the *rue* St-Jacques. *They* were punishing him for his success, of course."

"He accepted it as God's will, Constance. He did not seem upset."

"No, not upset, Henri. But he didn't like it."

"Perhaps, my dear. You are always more sensitive than I am, though I try hard to be sensitive. . . ."

The transfer to St-Jacques seemed to have been a decisive turning point. Why?

"As someone who never knew him, I find it hard to see him," I confessed, honestly enough. "Some people have suggested that there was a certain aspect of mystery about him, that revealed itself only occasionally, though with great power."

They both seemed mystified.

"I cannot think of any such mystery, can you, Constance?"

"No . . . He was quite transparent. One did not

think that there was anything more than what one saw. . . ."

"He was the most remarkable man I have ever met." The baron spoke slowly. "If he is not found, it will be a great tragedy for all France."

"There were times," Constance said slowly, "when there was a certain smile . . . When he was talking to me . . . Not suggestive or familiar . . . A different kind of smile . . . And as you say, *Monseigneur*, very, ah, appealing. It did not last for more than a moment. Yet it was very powerful."

"I did not notice it. . . ."

"I'm not even sure that I did."

"But if you did," I asked, "what did it mean?"

"Perhaps that we all shared a great joke that we dared not mention because it was too wonderful."

The smile that hinted at laughter again. The smile that Marcel had seen and Marie-Bernadette had remembered and I had not recognized.

"Will you find him for us, *Monseigneur*?" the baroness asked pleadingly, tears in her eyes. "We love him so much. Not for the politics. That is important. Yet not really important."

I sighed.

"I can only believe that he disappeared of his own free will," I said slowly. "No one forced him to do that. I do not know what happened afterwards. However, if we do find him . . ."

"We *will* find him," Marie-Bernadette contended.

". . . We will have to respect his privacy. I'm sure he loves you as much as you love him. You are in his prayers and he must be in yours."

"Every day," the baron replied.

"Always, *Monseigneur*."

In the car on the way back to *St-Germain-des-Prés,* we were both silent for some time.

"A few days ago I was a beggar," my translator said thoughtfully. "Now I visit the nobility in the *Seizième Arrondissement.* Perhaps next week I will be a beggar again."

"Not if we can help it," I said firmly. "Did Jean-Claude often give women instructions on lovemaking?"

"Mais oui," she said. "Very subtly, so that you hardly noticed that he was doing it till after. Women should know that the things they would like to do with their men, but are afraid to, are those things which the men like the most."

More and more surprising was this simple, innocent, and transparent Dominican friar.

Tomorrow we would see his colleagues at the television station, including the two who were with him when he leaped into the third century.

Jacques-Yves was waiting for us at the hotel. He kissed her as he had the day before. For both of them a touch of eternity slipped into time.

"Any success with the nobility?" he asked politely.

"Some," I admitted, somewhat to my surprise. "They were nice people, not intelligent perhaps but rather sweet."

"Everyone is sweet," he said, "if we give them a chance."

It was not true but it was generous.

He kissed her again, presumably just in case he had forgotten to the first time. They were to go next door to the *Institut* for a practice session and then he would take her home to Belleville, perhaps the worst neighborhood in Paris, which, as he assured me, could be very dangerous. Marie-Bernadette rolled her eyes. Patently she thought she could take care of herself but would yield the role of knight-protector to Jacques-Yves if it made him happy. So it is with women: they know that if there really is a protector in a family it is not the man.

I sighed, went to my room, and discovered that the good Crystal Lane had contrived to send me the uniforms of the North Wabash Avenue Irregulars in record time, almost as though she had beamed them across the Atlantic.

The North Wabash Avenue Irregulars, patently an imitation of an earlier organization founded by Sherlock Holmes, is a secret and elite group which helps me out of the troubles in which I find myself when I am trying to resolve puzzles. Mike Casey the Cop is a charter member. Other honorees are such worthies as Nuala Anne McGrail and my niece-in-law Cindasoo Murphy, mother to the earlier mentioned Katiesoo Murphy.

As befits such a discreet band, its uniforms are not such as to attract public attention. Both the tee shirts and sweatshirts are black with North Wabash Avenue Irregulars emblazoned on the back in cardinatial crimson (in honor of Milord Cronin—who is NOT a member) and a drawing on the front in the same color of the rectory of Holy Name Cathedral (located patently on North Wabash Avenue). For sake of contrast the door of the rectory is gilt.

Milord Cronin, perhaps because of disappointment that he is not a member, does protest, "I could walk down Wabash Avenue in my full choir robes and not garner as much attention as those shirts. Who you trying to kid?"

In any event, those who possess them purport to be honored.

I phoned my friend Frankie and managed with considerable difficulty to get through the barriers of staff who did not speak English.

"How did it go with the aristos?" he demanded.

"Like many of the others they revere Friar Jean-Claude."

"Of course they do. His simple piety appealed to simple people. . . . Tomorrow we have you set up with people at the network. You'll find that many revered him and many despised him. Just like the priests at St-Jacques."

"The clergy have no monopoly on professional envy, they just do it better than anyone else."

"If we could teach you presentable French, we might give you a program to replace Jean-Claude and you could say things like that in public."

"Alas, I would disappear more quickly than he did. . . . Tell me, Frankie, is your Lord Cardinal unhappy that the good Dominican friar is off the air?"

"Hell, no. My boss becomes nervous when anyone around him mentions Jesus. Jean-Claude was an embarrassment. Questions were asked by other bishops and then by Rome. Doesn't he have enough trouble without this troublesome priest? Now the troublesome priest is working miracles and that means further distractions. Still *M. le Cardinal* does not put out contracts on people, as much as his Corsican culture would incline him to."

"Would not even stick pins in a doll of Jean-Claude?"

Frankie thought that was very funny.

"I wouldn't put it past him if someone had suggested it, but only at midnight on a moonless night."

No one would have accused Frankie of being too heavily burdened by loyalty to Mr. Cardinal de Paris.

"The truth is, Blackie," he went on, "he was a distraction and an embarrassment to a lot of people, but not enough for anyone to go to the trouble of kidnapping him."

That seemed a reasonable position. It was time for me to list the possible suspects, which is what detectives do in mystery stories if not in real life. It is a ritual which almost never helps.

Then I noticed Nora Cronin's tape player under Crystal Lane's delicate tissue wrappings. I had better listen to the tape. I would surely be quizzed tonight at *La Tour d'Argent* about it.

I flipped the switch and was almost blasted out of my chair. Our gentle violinist and violist had been transformed into mad Celts. While our ancestors did not have such musical instruments when first by foot and then by horse they had pushed their way through the forests and the swamps of post-glacial Europe towards the ocean and beyond, they surely had that music. I closed my eyes and pictured massive blond warriors, beautiful women, chattering poets, and nervous druids chanting such sounds as the sun set in the west and thus unleashed all the demons lurking in the forest.

How did these kids know about that?

The second piece was recognizably Turough O'Carolan, though played with a manic verve that might have shocked your man himself. The third was a lullaby of some sort, rendered with a tender sweetness that would break your heart.

Why were these kids messing with Mozart and Bach when they could play this kind of music? Anyone could play Mozart and Bach. No one, I wagered to myself, had ever tried to interpret Celtic music with their fire and sweetness.

"So that," I addressed the Deity, "is why You had me stumble by *St-Germain-des-Prés* when she was begging? Very clever of You."

For a half hour the problem of *le petit* Jean-Claude slipped back into the crypt of my brain and I listened to the history of the Celts celebrated, mourned, and then celebrated again by two sensitive and powerful musicians. Enchantment, pure enchantment.

I dialed a certain number in Chicago, reached a person who was either Asian or Cajun and tried again.

"Nuala Anne," I was informed by a voice which, as her husband had written, sounded like bells ringing softly over bogs.

"Ah," I said, "how very fortunate! I was just about to call you!"

"Your lordship," she said patiently, "isn't it yourself who just called me?"

"Is it now?"

" 'Tis!"

"So how's your family keeping?" I pushed the button on Nora's machine.

"Isn't me husband writing up a storm and isn't me daughter twice as bossy as I ever was and isn't me little lad a delight altogether, even if he is lazy like his father?"

"And yourself?"

"Meself? I'm not doing much, except preparing for me Christmas special 'Nuala Anne Goes Global.' "

"Sounds exhausting."

"Your lordship, what's that wild fiddle playing? Is there an army of crazy Irishmen in your room?"

"Celtic music," I said.

"Well, I know that, now don't I? Not Irish exactly . . ."

"Gallician, I think."

"Spanish people."

"Arguably."

"Old minstrels from Brittany, are they?"

"Two kids younger than yourself from Provence."

"Mere children!"

"This is your man Turough O'Carolan, I believe."

"Sure don't I know him well enough, but I've never heard him played that way. Brilliant altogether."

Sentimentalist that she is, like all Irishwomen, she wept during the lullaby.

"Wherever did you find them?" she asked between sniffles.

"Herself was begging in front of *St-Germain-des-Prés.*"

"Begging!"

"Twenty-five percent youth unemployment rate. No jobs here for young musicians, especially those who want to interpret in music the whole story of the Celts."

"Like it was back home when me dear Dermot found me in O'Neill's pub."

"France is too old and too stiff to change like Ireland did."

"Are they nice people, your lordship?"

I was always "your lordship." My sometime associate pastor and her brother-in-law was "your rivirence." The archbishop of Chicago was, needless to say, "Cardinal Sean."

"Unbearably sweet."

"Sure, shouldn't we be after bringing them to America?"

I turned off the player.

"That would be a good work."

"Would you be sending me the tape?"

"FedEx tonight."

"Don't I have a little clout in the industry?"

"Clout-heavy is the phrase we Chicagoans use."

"Do we now?"

"You might communicate with me, er, my brother Packy Ryan, who is working in this direction too."

"Tilting the playing field, is he?"

So soon had this Irish-speaking lass from Connemara learned the language of Chicago politics.

"Does the good Packy ever do anything else?"

"Like his brother . . . Now wouldn't these children be grand altogether on me Christmas special?"

"Arguably."

I was inordinately pleased with myself after the call. Then my conscience troubled me. What right did I have to play lord of the manor for these two young people? Might they not be better off following the course of their life that was marked out before I gave Marie-Bernadette the two-hundred-franc note in front of the church of *St-Germain-des-Prés?* What might be the unintended consequences of our meddling in their lives? Did the Ryan Clan and the North Wabash Avenue Irregulars have the right to interfere in their lives?

I always experience such guilt feelings when I succumb to the temptation to do good. On the other hand, maybe my variegated colleagues and I were merely doing what Christians should do.

In any case, I descended to the lobby to arrange that the tape be beamed back across the Atlantic to Southport Avenue in the shadow of St. Josaphat's Church. Such guilt feelings never interfered with the Ryan Clan's determination to help people who we thought needed help—whether they wanted it or not!

11

Who might want to rid themselves of this troublesome priest, I wrote. Lots of people.

1) The French government. Mired in its own corruption and incompetence and fearful of a mass movement, it might have decided for the "good of the State" to eliminate *Frère* Jean-Claude from the political equation. In France the "State" was something sacred. You could do almost anything if you persuaded yourself or others that it was for the good of the State. Neither the Gaulists nor the Socialists could be at ease with Jean-Claude. His influence spanned the whole range of French life from the Royalists to the students in the Latin Quarter, who might, suddenly and without warning, decide that it was 1968 again and take to the streets. Since both groups were outside the political consensus which governed the country (for their own profit), they were unpredictable and dangerous. Moreover, while the anticlericals, always a major element in French political life, dismissed him as a fraud, there were still enough Catholics in the country who found him charming even if they did not go to church too often. Mass movements were dangerous because they might stir up the people. Probably there would not be a political movement around Jean-Claude, but why take the chance? There were several secret intelligence agencies in the country which might dispose of this troublesome priest on their own initiative and would

be delighted to do so if a mere hint came from one of the cabinet ministers. The police would cover up, at least until the media began to sniff the story.

2) The Church. The Catholic institution traditionally was skeptical of saints, especially those who were not under its firm control. And what kind of saint would remain under firm control? All right, Thérèse and Bernadette did not make trouble, but neither had lived very long and neither had a television pulpit. Saints were distracting and, as Frankie had said, embarrassing. Rome, in its present configuration, was suspicious of just about anyone who stirred up the people. True, no one had been able to find any heresy in Jean-Claude's preaching, but someday he might become a heretic and one with a vast popular following. Was it not prudent to prevent that from happening by depriving him of his audience before he turned heretical?

Yet the Church leadership these days did not poison troublesome priests. Rather it leaned on their superiors to shut them up. The Dominican provincial was unfortunately sympathetic to Jean-Claude. However, his Roman superiors could order him to order Jean-Claude to give up his television ministry. The friar himself had indicated that he would obey such an order. Why then kidnap him and hide him in a monastery, especially when the ever-present media might discover what you had done. Why not silence him the traditional way and be done with it? There would be complaints but they would gradually fade. Certainly religious motives would not restrain either the Parisian Curia or the Roman Curia. Jean-Claude should be silenced for the good of the Church. That was enough.

Leaders of the Catholic Church are generally administratively conservative as well as politically and religiously. They would rather decide not to decide "at the present time" than decide. They had therefore bided their time, hoping that Jean-Claude would go away. He did just that, but in a way that made matters worse instead of better. Now there were flowers and miracles. Neither the Vatican nor the Dominican generalate could do anything about either.

3) The Dominican Order. Patently some of its members had grave reservations about Jean-Claude, most of which were rooted in envy. The provincial liked him and approved of what he was doing. However, the provincial was thinking of religion and not of the welfare of the order. A secret messenger might have come from Rome with the verbal order to send Jean-Claude off to a monastery somewhere in the Alps for meditation and reflection "at the present time." Jean-Claude seemed to be the sort of humble friar who would quietly obey such instructions. Why then the charade in front of *Notre-Dame de Paris*? Perhaps because that would make his disappearance less controversial. That was a mistaken judgment as it turned out. However, the order might not have realized just how popular he was. What would they do now that he seemed to be working miracles?

4) Television. Doubtless there was resentment against Jean-Claude in the industry. An amateur, an outsider, he had earned almost immediately a position in the national media which every TV personality dreams of but never achieves. Certainly he had a large audience but in France ratings were not as important as they were in America. To many at all the levels of the industry, the sooner the Jean-Claude phenomenon ran its course—as all phenomena eventually do—the better. The red-eyed camera would eat him alive in due

course, but why was it taking so long? Why was his support so solid?

We will know more about the reaction of inside television personnel to Jean-Claude tomorrow. While they might have resented him, more than likely they would have waited for the red-eyed monster to do him in. They had less to lose than either the Church or the State—unless of course he showed signs of attacking the industry.

5) The Royalists. They might be upset that Jean-Claude was not about to call for the return of the monarchy and for the accession to the throne of Duc Louis. But while they were not terribly bright they could hardly have expected that he would do that. He did seem to represent the possibility of a "moral revival" that they thought was a necessary precondition for the national call for a renewal of the monarchy—as if eighteenth-century France had been a profoundly moral country and Versailles a center of piety and devotion. Why would the Royalists want him to disappear?

6) The students. Jean-Claude was patently popular with many of them. Yet not everyone would be as enthusiastic as Marie-Bernadette and Jacques-Yves. Some students would undoubtedly feel that the only proper reaction to Jean-Claude was to spit on him as Frenchmen and women had spit on priests from time immemorial. Yet 1968 was a long time ago. Today's French students did not kidnap popular leaders and hold them for ransom. Moreover, there had been no demand for ransom. Pending interviews with more students, I would put them at the bottom of the list of suspects.

7) Jean-Claude himself. I was inclined to think that this was the truth of the matter. For reasons of his

own, the friar wanted to drop from sight and, perhaps with the help of others, executed this disappearance with remarkable éclat. I had always suspected that this was the explanation. The others were too far-fetched, too paranoid to be taken seriously. However, this was France, after all, where the whiff of paranoia always floated in the air, like vapor rising from a polluted river. Let us assume, nonetheless, that Jean-Claude had decided to leave behind his influence and potential power. Why? And where was he?

And why had there been no hint that he was planning such a disappearance? Could the transfer from Ste-Catherine convent to St-Jacques, a transfer which he apparently did not like but did not resist, be a sufficient reason for, as Sean Cronin had put it, leaping back into the third century?

Perhaps if he was able somehow to conduct a love affair at Ste-Catherine which would not be possible at St-Jacques. We would have to press the nuns on that issue when we see them tomorrow after our visit to television.

I put aside my preliminary notes, removed my glasses, rubbed my eyes, and thought. Rather, I tried to think. No thoughts came. My analysis was comprehensive enough. It would be expanded as our interviews proceeded. However, I suspected that after further interviews the matter would not, as the French might put it, clarify itself. Jean-Claude had chosen to disappear for reasons of his own. If he did not choose to reappear, we would never know what those reasons were.

I put away my notes, studied the fathers again, took a shower and dressed for the second time that day in my full clerical array, without the ring, however. Chuck and Rosemarie O'Malley were not ring kissers.

Rather they were one of the best comedy teams I had ever seen. They fed each other comic lines, set each other up for jokes, and laughed enthusiastically at each other's triumph. They were a little younger than Sean and Nora and had grown up in the same neighborhood on the West Side of Chicago during the Depression and the War. Chuck insisted at every opportunity that he had wanted to be nothing more than an accountant and that Rosemarie had forced him to become a photographer. He had in fact become one of the great photographers of the century, publishing books, staging exhibitions, traveling to the far parts of the world for photo essays. After they had raised a large family, he and Rosemarie became a team—"She's the quarterback," he said. "Women have to be quarterbacks."

"Point guard," Rosemarie corrected him. Much laughter around the table.

Chuck was a white-haired, white-bearded leprechaun with a face both quizzical and comic. Rosemarie (he never called her "Rosie"—not since she was fourteen years old, though she didn't mind the nickname) was a trim woman with a smooth complexion like Nora Cronin's and carefully groomed silver hair.

Chucky (as his wife calls him) is responsible for the photograph of Milord Cronin which decorates almost every rectory in Chicago—a handsome, happy Renaissance prince with an Irish twinkle in his eye. He is also responsible for the "official" photo of the inconspicuous auxiliary bishop which, as far as I know, decorates only the homes of my siblings and is relegated to the basement rooms where grandchildren frolic. The sibling's reaction is "Oh, Punk, it is *so* cute!"

Despite Chuck's success, they had hard times in their lives. Rosemarie didn't touch the wine at *La Tour d'Argent* and there were stories about serious alcoholic problems several decades before. Yet their love for each other was obvious and happy. They touched each other often, a hand on the other's hand as one told a joke. A gentle jab at the other's arm, a light tap on the shoulder when they were sitting down—the sort of signs of affection that one hardly notices unless one is watching carefully, as this one always does.

They were much less formal with one another than Milord and his sister. I was grateful to God and the angels who seemed to be working overtime currently that the O'Malleys had come to the birthday dinner. Otherwise, it would have risked sinking into morose wonder about what might have been.

I held my peace, as befits an insignificant auxiliary bishop, laughed at the jokes, and ate every bite of food put in front of me.

It was the best meal I had ever eaten in all my life, which covers a lot of good meals.

I also watched every detail of the interaction patterns. I was Chuck's confessor and the cardinal's *éminence grise*. Hence I must be alert. Mostly I laughed at jokes about places I did not know in the "old" neighborhood—Motto's Pharmacy, Kallas's Pharmacy, Fred's Pool Hall, the Ambassador Theater, the St. Ursula softball field, Hansen Park stadium, where Chuck allegedly won a crucial football game before I was born. For a few moments they were all young again, a sacrament perhaps of the world to come in which we will all be young again.

I also pondered the five different varieties of love I had observed during the day—the restrained and tentative love of the baron and the baroness, the intense passion revealed in small signs between Marie-Bernadette and Jacques-Yves, the mature and experi-

enced delight of Chuck and Rosemarie, the deep but
chaste chemistry between the Cronins, and the mysterious love of Friar Jean-Claude for the people to
whom he ministered.

Our God is nothing if not a God of variety, often,
truth to tell, comic variety.

I may even have said that over the dessert wine (no
Bailey's tonight). There may have been riotous laughter from the others as the poor little bishop sallied
forth with his one line of the evening.

They all seemed to know what I meant, which I
thought was remarkable, almost as though I had said
grace after meals. Which of course is precisely what I
did.

Back in my room at *l'abbaye* as I swallowed my melatonin, I reflected that the first four loves were all
healthy human intimacies, even that of the baron and
the baroness, who were groping at least towards something better than they had now, thanks to the elusive
Friar Jean-Claude.

Somehow I had to discover the nature of the
strange, though perhaps not so strange after all, erotic
energy which drove him.

12

"*We must be clear about one* thing, Mr. Bishop," Marie-Bernadette said solemnly, as we began our metro ride to the TV Center on the Avenue Montaigne.

"The French," I mused, "have a passion for clarity which has caused them much trouble. And caused the rest of us much trouble. We could all have done without René Descartes."

She giggled faintly, turned away for a moment from her seriousness.

"I am *très sérieuse*," she insisted.

"As always."

I was recovering from the disturbance to my organism caused by the previous evening's celebrations. Hence I was in a mildly fey mood.

"Mr. Bishop," she insisted with some asperity, "you must listen to me!"

"As always."

"You have no obligation to take care of me and Jacques-Yves when my term as your translator is finished. Sometimes I think that you do not need a translator and that it suits your purpose to pretend you don't understand what the other person is saying when indeed you do."

"Defamation," I said to this highly accurate charge.

"You distract me from my point."

"God forgive me."

"Which is that we can take care of ourselves. We do not want American pity! Is that understood!"

"Pourquoi?"

"Because we are French and one takes care of one-self!"

"What would Friar Jean-Claude say to such an arrogant French rejection of help?"

The air went out of her balloon of arrogance, not a very healthy balloon anyway.

"He would say that I was a little fool," she said sadly.

"I'm sure that's not what he would say."

She sighed and tried again. "He would say that we must all give help to those we can help and accept help from those who would help us, *n'est-ce pas?*"

"Patently.... Incidentally your review of the history of the Celtic people through their music was outstanding."

She dismissed the record with the imperious wave of her hand which she reserved for unimportant matters—like Jacques-Yves, for example.

"It is an exercise, nothing important. We are serious musicians."

"*D'accord.* And that is very serious music. Anyone can play Mozart. I doubt that there is a duo anywhere in the world that has such a command of the Celtic tradition."

She looked at me, tears in her eyes.

"Is that really true?"

"Oh, yes."

"*Merci,* Mr. Bishop. I will tell Jacques-Yves. It will make him very happy as it makes me very happy."

One good work for the morning. Now everything was in the hands of the clout-heavy Packy Ryan and the equally clout-heavy Nuala Anne McGrail—different kinds of clout patently.

Later in the canteen of France2, where we were discussing the disappearance of Jean-Claude with the two producers who had accompanied him into the crypt, Sarah, a Jewish woman in her middle forties with an achingly lovely Middle Eastern face, buried her face in her hands.

"You must excuse me, Mr. Bishop. I cannot forgive myself for what happened. If I had been a little quicker, he would not have disappeared. I know that. God will judge me for that."

"You don't believe in God, remember, Sarah?" replied Pierre, her somewhat younger colleague, a hulking Norman with a shaved head, black sweater and black jeans.

"I believe in whatever he believed in, Pierre. . . . He was a few steps ahead of us, Mr. Bishop. He turned the corner at the far end of the crypt. We paused to stare at the parlor of a third-century Gallo-Roman house. Then we turned the corner and he was not there."

"At first, we were not worried," Pierre carried on the story. "Jean-Claude loved the occasional practical joke—there was something of the young boy about him. We assumed that he was hiding on us. We walked to the entrance of the crypt and asked the clerks at the door if they had seen him leave. They had not. Jean-Claude's face was known everywhere in France at the time. Nonetheless, we ran up the steps to the parvis. He was nowhere to be seen, only a handful of tourists that early in the morning."

"Then we went back down," Sarah continued, dabbing at her tears, "to the crypt and searched everywhere. We could not find him. So we called the police."

"They were arrogant and insulting," Pierre told us, "like French police usually are. Clearly, they said, the friar had chosen to disappear. There was nothing more to be done. Only that night, when the story appeared on the evening news, did they bother to become concerned. Then it was much too late."

"Were they not, however, correct?" I probed. "Surely it must have been Friar Jean-Claude's own wish to disappear. No one could have come into the crypt and carried him off."

"We searched everywhere inside the crypt," Sarah replied. "There are little alcoves and half-opened walls into which he might have jumped. However, he was in none of them. . . . It is almost as though he jumped back into the third century."

I noted that my young aide shivered at the possibility.

Absurd, I reassured myself. He had hidden from his friends and then slipped out when they were outside looking for him. Cleverly done, perhaps too clever by half.

"Were there others in the crypt while you were searching?"

"A few people, mostly tourists. Americans one would think," Pierre answered. "None of them looked at all like Jean-Claude. He could not have disguised himself so that we would not recognize him in such a brief period of time."

"Did he do his own television makeup?" I asked.

"Not at first," Sarah replied. "Very soon, however, he became quite professional and insisted on doing it himself."

"Insisted?"

"He was a perfectionist, Mr. Bishop. He said that if he were preaching for the Lord, everything should be done as well as it could possibly be done. He did not want his face to interfere with the face of God, which he thought was what our makeup people were doing."

"He was always quite meek," Pierre said with a hint of exasperation in his voice. "Yet he had a way of assuring that we did things his way. He was more gentle about it than other talent. Yet quite determined."

"Not that we minded," Sarah insisted. "We all loved him here. He was a saint if there ever was one."

"There were some upstairs"—Pierre gestured towards the higher floors of the building—"who were furious at him. They don't like religion and they don't like priests and they don't like amateur talent which takes over the system. . . . But what could they do? The public had spoken. They had to wait till his popularity faded, as does that of all talent."

"Were they capable of doing anything to accelerate that process?"

"They are not nice men, Mr. Bishop." Sarah shook her head dolefully. "Naturally, we thought that they might be responsible, especially since the police seemed so unresponsive, almost as if they had been told not to search too carefully. Yet to what purpose? He would fade before the year was out, or so they thought. Why take any risks when they were not necessary?"

"Did you think he would fade?" I asked bluntly.

The two producers looked at each other for a moment.

"We weren't sure," Pierre said slowly. "Our surveys suggested that his ratings were very strong, solid.

At least it would have taken longer than it did for most talent. Years, *bien sûr*."

"So it seemed to us," Sarah agreed. "He worked very hard, Mr. Bishop. On the air he seemed so innocent, so casual, so spontaneous. Anyone who knows our medium knows that you can only seem to be spontaneous if you have practiced many, many times. We could go through at least four takes before he was satisfied. He was very apologetic—blamed the mistakes on his own ineptitude. When he was ordered to wear his Dominican robes—which were very effective by the way—he was careful to make sure that they flowed the proper way. He permitted no disarray."

"His late sister, he told us, had been an actress and she had always insisted on perfection. She would haunt him if he did not do the same."

"Not as transparent as he seemed?"

"No, no, Mr. Bishop. He was utterly transparent, but he was a professional. That is a virtue, *n'est-ce pas*, Pierre?"

Pierre hesitated.

"You couldn't help but like the fellow. He was a good man, a good friar, a good priest. I never doubted his authenticity for a moment and yet . . ."

"And yet?"

"I couldn't help but wonder at times whether there was something we didn't see, something that wasn't obvious, something . . . well hidden in his personality."

"Pierre!" Sarah protested.

"If there were not," said the hulking Norman, "would he have disappeared so suddenly? . . . Mr. Bishop, we had an idea for a series on *Notre-Dame de Paris*. We asked him to be our narrator. He was enthused by the idea. Notre-Dame, he said, was both

France and the Church. He was in good spirits when we went into the crypt. He removed a notebook from the briefcase he always carried—both disgracefully *bon marché* by the way—and was jotting down notes and laughing as he always did when he was excited . . . Then suddenly he wasn't there anymore."

My translator shivered again.

"I ask you, Mr. Bishop," Pierre continued, "a man that disappears like that has something hidden in his personality, *n'est-ce pas?*"

"I think we all agree that he was an unusual person," I replied cautiously. "Why did he want to disappear and so dramatically?"

"One possibility," Pierre glanced hesitantly at his colleague, "is that he had contracted AIDS. . . ."

"Pierre!" Sarah protested.

"Certainly there are treatments . . ." I suggested.

"Not for a man as well known as Jean-Claude. Moreover the shock to the Catholics of France . . . No, no! He disappeared because that was all he could do!"

"He was not gay!" Sarah argued hotly.

"There are other ways of getting AIDS," Pierre said, now defensive.

"It is absurd!" Sarah argued. "He was a perfectly normal heterosexual male. He liked women and women liked him. . . . Women know when men enjoy them!"

"I wonder," Pierre said thoughtfully. "He was a strange one."

"Saints are always strange, Pierre."

"There was something about him, something mysterious. Wonderful too, but mysterious. . . . Are saints always mysterious, Mr. Bishop?"

"Arguably . . . However, do you not think it possible that Friar Jean-Claude was looking for a way to disappear, found himself out of your sight for a moment, and seized the opportunity?"

They were silent for a moment. They regarded me with surprise. Even my loyal translator frowned at me.

"It is not impossible . . ." Sarah admitted. "But why?"

"Why indeed?" I said mysteriously, hinting perhaps that I knew the answer when I certainly did not.

I had some ideas about how he might have disappeared, though it would have required quick work. Perhaps he had done it before. A quick change of costume, a hasty touch of makeup, and then he was someone else, equally nondescript but apparently quite different. Like the postman in G. K. Chesterton's story—someone that everybody had seen but no one recognized, a sweeper perhaps in his white clothes. Yes that was a possibility—or something like that. A trick that he could have done almost anywhere, but chose to do in the crypt because the opportunity was perfect and the result perfectly mysterious. Risky? Yes, but it could have been explained as one of his little practical jokes if he were caught. It could have been done. Why, however?

Sarah was wrong about gay men, especially those who for one reason or another wish to remain in the closet, as a priest well might. Some of them can deceive women if they want to.

"That is the issue, isn't it?" I said, continuing the conversation. "Perhaps he was tired of being Jean-Claude and wanted some other kind of priestly work. Perhaps the Dominicans are cooperating with him. Perhaps he has departed to a monastery whose abbot is sheltering him. Perhaps he fell in love with a woman and fled with her. Perhaps the pressure of those who were opposed to him was too much to resist. Maybe he felt he needed some time off and discovered that he really didn't want to return. *Pour moi*, the 'why' is more important than the 'how.' "

Marie-Bernadette brought more coffee for the two television people and two cups of tea for us. She was paying me the highest compliment possible, imitating me.

"He was always," Sarah said slowly, "a little unpredictable. He prepared in detail for everything he would say on camera and then, even after the taping had begun, change it completely. . . . Remember Christmas, Pierre?"

He rolled his eyes. "How could I forget it. Our superiors asked him to talk about renewal for men and women of all faiths or no faith. That didn't bother Jean-Claude. He had nothing against atheists or infidels. So he prepared a discreet Christmas message which would please everyone and offend no one. . . . He never wanted to offend. Then, five minutes into the program, he began to sing Christmas carols, with great simplicity and fervor. It was contagious. Even the atheists in the studio staff were singing with him. So did *tout le monde* all over France. Our superiors were furious until our phones were overwhelmed by favorable reactions."

What, I asked myself, would have happened in the days of Bishop Sheen in America if he had suddenly and mysteriously disappeared?

"A *tour de force*," Sarah agreed. "He was always quite unpredictable, which perhaps is why so many people loved him."

"So," I pursued the point, "the strange manner of his disappearance could not have been a complete surprise when you reflected on it?"

"No," she said hesitantly, "it is the sort of thing he

might have done on impulse. But he would have come back. Perhaps something happened to him. . . ."

That was always a possibility. He had fled somewhere seeking help or sanctuary or love or something and had been betrayed.

"Who would want something to happen?" I asked.

"*They* would," the TV colleagues replied as one person.

They again.

"And who are *they*?"

Pierre responded with a Gallic shrug which was the functional equivalent of the Irish sigh. "The government, the police, the priests . . ."

"The Communists," Sarah continued, "the Royalists, the people upstairs, perhaps the Arabs . . ."

"I see," I said with a sigh, though I didn't see at all.

Marie-Bernadette gathered up the paper cups and took them to the trash bin. I shook hands with the two producers and promised to do my best to find Jean-Claude. They didn't look too hopeful.

"Are you going to rerun any of his tapes?" I asked on sudden inspiration.

They glanced at one another uncomfortably.

"It has been discussed," Sarah said.

"The men upstairs do not want to do it," Pierre explained. "But many pressures are brought on them. I think we will do it."

Jean-Claude talking from the grave. Eerie. All those who did not like Jean-Claude alive would like him even less dead. They might, however, have to put up with him on occasion.

Pierre took us up on the elevator to the top of the building to the office of *"M. le Président"* of the station.

"We were not much help," he said sorrowfully. "The truth is we miss him so much, Sarah perhaps more than me. He was the light of our life."

Not what one expected to hear from an experienced television journalist, especially in France.

"I would assume that Mr. President will not want to see us," I said tentatively.

"He is a terrible man, a puppet, a popinjay. He will try to intimidate you."

"No one intimidates Mr. Bishop," Marie-Bernadette said confidently.

Arguably her assertion was true. She had not, however, seen anyone who really tried.

"Did the network take any steps to find Jean-Claude after he disappeared?"

"Ha! They did nothing. They seemed to hope that he would not be found. Some of us tried to ask them to offer a reward. They said that was a matter for the police and dismissed us. They try to pretend that he never existed."

In the United States a TV network, hungry for ratings, would already be presenting reruns.

Mr. President kept us waiting forty-five minutes in his outer office. His decorative secretary frowned disapprovingly at this odd duo who were disturbing her careful shifting of files of paper.

"Mr. President is a very busy man," she said.

"Doubtless," I replied, heading off any conflict between her and the stalwart Marie-Bernadette.

Finally, we were ushered into his inner sanctum with the solemnity of a sacristan entering the sanctuary where the Blessed Sacrament was exposed for adoration. I had already begun to dislike Mr. President intensely. His appearance did not warm my heart towards him. He was a little fellow with thick, slicked-back black hair, a tiny mustache, a high voice, a perfectly tailored pinstripe suit, and blue shirt with a white collar and a tie which suggested membership in an elite English regiment. One sniffed heavy cologne as soon as one entered his office.

He did not ask us to sit down. He stood behind a massive oak desk with the Eiffel Tower and river traffic on the Seine behind him, waved his hands at us and yelled that he was a very busy man and had nothing much to say about Friar Jean-Claude who had been a serious problem to the network. Obviously he was a hypocrite who had run away with a lover.

Marie-Bernadette tried frantically to translate for him. He cut her off, told her she was a stupid child, and continued to yell.

I sat down in an enormous chair across from his desk and motioned my translator to sit in a similar chair.

I waited till he had stopped yelling, glanced at my watch and then began to speak slowly and confidently, as though I had no doubt that he could understand English if I did not rush through it.

"Sir, I am not accustomed to being treated with such disdain. Nor do I accept your right to insult a member of my staff. You will either talk to me as one civilized human being to another or I will end this conversation and you will have to face the consequences."

He collapsed into an enormous desk chair and sputtered, in English, "You can do nothing to me. I am not afraid of you."

Ah, but he was afraid of me, a harmless little auxiliary bishop. Now wasn't that interesting?

"That is imprudent of you, sir. I can destroy you with a simple phone call."

"I am not afraid of priests, especially American priests." He sniffed. A line of sweat appeared at his hairline.

"Not even of one who could call the bureau chief of the *New York Times* and suggest a front-page story which would raise the possibility that this network collaborated in the kidnapping of a celebrated TV priest?"

"You cannot prove that," he gasped, all the fire and vinegar going out of him.

"You know the media well enough, sir, to know that no smoking gun is required. The evidence nonetheless is persuasive: *tout le monde* knows that you and your masters had grown uneasy over the enormous popularity of Friar Jean-Claude, that you did nothing to try to find him when he disappeared, and that you are resisting demands that you present reruns of his tapes. It would make an interesting story in the American media. Think of the attention when our media discover the TV priest who disappeared into the third century while his network stood by complacently."

I confess that I am not a little pleased with myself when I cook up something like that out of the blue.

"You wouldn't dare!"

"Oh?"

"We would say that Jean-Claude was a homosexual and had run off with a lover!"

"How long would you sit in that cavernous chair after you tried to put such a spin on the case?"

I avoided Marie-Bernadette's face. She should not be admiring such nonsense, but neither should she burst into laughter.

"Very well"—he waved his hand negligently—"I will consent to answer your questions."

"Prudent of you. . . . I will put them in English. My aide will translate them into French and you will reply in French. . . . Is that clear?"

"Why is it necessary? I speak excellent English!"

"It is necessary because I say it is necessary. . . . My first question then is what can you tell us about the disappearance of Friar Jean-Claude?"

"I know only what the police tell me," he said with the usual French shrug. "He disappeared in the crypt under the parvis of Notre-Dame. The police are convinced that, with the help of two of my producers, he slipped away and was carried off by someone in a car, a woman most likely, and is either dead or with that woman. They have tried a thorough search and have not found him. What more is there to say?"

"When did they stop the search?"

"I understand that the case is still open."

"That is not what I asked."

"I think it became a routine matter for them after the first week."

"Did that not surprise you?"

"The police are very busy these days with all the crime in Paris."

"You were not disappointed in his disappearance?"

"We felt that his popularity would decline very quickly and he would leave. There were already some signs . . . When such an end to his fame was inevitable why would we want to take chances?"

His head was framed for a moment against a large white excursion boat on the river—Mephisto with a white halo.

"Why were you eager to end his run?"

"We are under many pressures here. Not all France is Catholic, nor is all of Paris. Many Jews, Moslems, atheists, anticlericals were very angry at us for spreading such pious nonsense. Intellectuals were becoming very critical. The relevant people in the State were asking embarrassing questions. Even the Church was not happy at the attention to this man, whom many considered a heretic. I do not pretend that we did not feel relief at the end of the series. . . . You must understand that, if the silly priest became the leader of a mass movement, we would be blamed."

"It is about time for people to take to the streets again, is it not?"

"Précisément!"

"You think your two producers were part of the plot?"

"Certainly not! They are not intelligent enough to devise something that cunning. They are skilled at what they do, nothing more. They had fallen under the foolish priest's spell, of course. Many people here had. But his disappearance was the act of a master-mind of evil—which is what I thought he was all along."

"I see. . . . You don't expect him to return?"

He waved his hand as if chasing off a pesky bug.

"He will not be back. He is probably dead or some-where very far away. I do not know why he disap-peared or how. *Hélas*, Mr. Bishop, I do not care. I believe you are wasting your time, but that is not my concern.

I thanked him briefly and we took our leave. As we stepped out the door, I glanced back and saw that he was wiping sweat off his face. Served him right.

Next to me, *Mademoiselle* my translator was trying to suppress a giggle.

"Quiet, witch," I ordered, "or I will have you thrown into the Seine."

My warning had no effect. The giggle became a laugh as soon as we had slipped into the corridor out-side Mr. President's office. She suppressed it quickly when we bumped into Sarah at the elevator.

"I brought you something, Mr. Bishop," Sarah

whispered, holding a thick manila folder against her chest.

"Indeed?"

"This is the folder in which Jean-Claude kept notes for his sermons. He usually locked it in a drawer of his desk. He was working on it just before we went to Notre-Dame. I did not want the cops to pry into his secrets. So I hid it. I know I can trust you with it."

She extended the folder cautiously in my direction.

"You have read it?" I asked.

"Oh, no. I did not want to violate his secrets. Perhaps you will burn it if there is nothing in it that will help the search for him."

"I will honor his privacy," I said solemnly, "and yours."

We walked out of the lobby and onto the street. Low clouds had quickly raced across the sky. In Chicago that would mean rain, arguably for several days. On the fringe of the Eurasian landmass, it did not necessarily mean that at all.

"If I am not being presumptuous, Sarah, might I ask what your Jewish family and friends thought of Jean-Claude?"

"Did *he* tell you there was Jewish opposition?"

"Something of the sort."

"A few intellectuals perhaps. Most of us admired him too. He was very much like one of our best rabbis."

13

"Bon . . . You were joking sûrement, were you not, Mr. Bishop?"

"Perhaps," I said as I devoured the pasta at *les Deux Magots.*

Marie-Bernadette had insisted we walk from the *Châtelet* metro station back to the hotel because I needed the exercise. Then when we had come to the intersection of *rue* Napoleon and *Boulevard* St-Germain, she had further insisted that I needed some lunch.

"You will order Jacques-Yves this way for the rest of your life?"

She had laughed happily.

"Mais certainement! How else do we keep men alive except we tell them what they should do?"

It was safe for me to walk into the St-Germain district as long as I had a human Seeing Eye dog to lead me. Nor have I ever turned down the opportunity for a bite to eat at midday. Then she began to quiz me about my *demo* with the Mr. President of the TV network.

"You do not know the Paris bureau chief of the *New York Times,* do you?"

"Their phone number is in the book."

"So you really do not know him?"

"No, but I do know those who know him."

"The Americans would not be interested in the story of *le pauvre* Jean-Claude, would they?"

"Very interested."

"Yet you made up your threat, ah, ad libitum?"

"Arguably."

"What if Mr. President had refused to answer our questions?"

Our questions, huh?

"The point is, *Demoiselle* my translator, that he would not have refused once we had frightened him with a plausible threat."

"I see," she sipped her glass of white wine. "You were making, how do you say it, *la escarpé?*"

"Bluff."

"Yes, you were making the bluff, *n'est-ce pas?*"

"Arguably."

"D'accord."

She half understood that it's only really a bluff when you're not sure it will work.

After we had finished our ice cream, she led me across the street to the church where I had found her begging a few days ago.

"I must pray," she informed me. *"N'est-ce pas?"*

So we prayed. A few tears formed around her eyes. She brushed them away with the back of her hand.

"*Merci,* Mr. Bishop," she said as we walked up the street towards St-Sulpice. "Even when I'm back there begging again I will remember this great adventure."

"Fergedaboudit," I said.

"Pardon?"

"Even if I wanted to abandon you and Jacques-Yves, Sean Cardinal Cronin, Cardinal Priest of the Roman Church, wouldn't permit it."

She did not reply.

Her thoughts, I realized, were confused, uncertain, but increasingly hopeful. At least she didn't argue that her future was not our concern.

Inside the hotel, I instructed her to wait downstairs. I must bring something from my room which would be useful in our interview with her student friends that was scheduled for a half hour from now. I searched around the room for some time before I discovered that the leprechaun who is responsible for hiding my possessions had lifted my North Wabash Avenue Irregulars shirts and hidden them under the bed. I retrieved them and, unable to find the box in which they belonged, carried them downstairs over my arm.

"It is *juste*," I told her, showing off the improvement of my French vocabulary, "that you should have the uniform which is appropriate for your job."

"Pour moi?" She exclaimed. "North Wabash Avenue Irregulars! Like the Baker Street Irregulars of M. Holmes! *Magnifique!"*

"That's the Cathedral rectory where Cardinal Sean and I live."

"But of course!" she modeled the shirt against her chest. *"Très jolie!"*

"Actually it's remarkably colorfast," I noted, "yet it is wise to wash it in cold water."

"Of course . . . May I wear it today?"

"Why not?"

She dashed off to the women's room of the hotel and came back wearing the sweatshirt. I assumed that her blouse and tee shirt had been jammed into her purse.

"My cousin Catherine Collins Curran designed it, the one who made my Brigid pectoral cross."

"I may keep it?"

"No, we'll take it away when we send you back to begging at St-Germain. Actually, that's the current model. Catherine designs a new one every year."

"*Merci*, Mr. Bishop," she said pecking at my cheek, "Jacques-Yves will love it."

My considered opinion was that Jacques-Yves would love everything that his love wore.

I was not sure that I was up to the task of coping with an adoring daughter. Then, in my mind, I thanked the One-In-Charge for having put her at the door of St-Germain with her hand out for alms. Your ways, I informed Herself, are indeed wonderful.

Her friends in the café at *la place de la Sorbonne* joined in her excitement as she explained in French too rapid for me to comprehend that I was a detective as well as a bishop and that like *M. le Curé* Holmes I had a group of helpers that were called the North Wabash Avenue Irregulars instead of the Baker Street Irregulars. They were all greatly impressed, especially Jacques-Yves, who beamed over his love's animation and the color in her face.

As well he might.

They wanted to know what *Avenue Wabash du Nord* was like. I tried to describe it, though I doubted I could bring that part of Chicago alive for anyone who had not been there. I did make a mental note that in the next edition of the North Wabash Avenue Irregulars shirts one would read *Les irregulars d'Avenue Wabash du Nord*.

Things always sounded better in French.

The group, two young men and two young women besides Jacques-Yves and Marie-Bernadette, listened attentively and respectfully, save for one young woman, slim and pretty and a couple of years older than Marie-Bernadette, whose name apparently was Chantal. She smiled at me wickedly as if to say that I didn't look much like either a bishop or a detective.

D'accord, I thought. But that's part of the game.

Then, first things last, Marie-Bernadette sailed off in another long and rapid announcement in French that I was going to find Jean-Claude for them and she translated for me so that I would hear the exact nuance in French.

However, our conversation was in English. Marie-Bernadette did not think it appropriate, it seemed, to try to translate her friends' conversation.

"Do you really think you will find him, Mr. Bishop?" Chantal asked me skeptically.

"Mr. Bishop never fails to solve a mystery," Marie-Bernadette announced proudly.

"Never?" Chantal considered me with her eyebrows lifted dubiously.

"There's always a first time," I admitted.

"It would be wonderful to have him back," said a bearded youth, undoubtedly a pirate or a revolutionary. "He was an amazing man, *n'est-ce pas?*"

"But, Teddi," the other young woman protested, "what if he doesn't want to come back?"

"Yes, Mr. Bishop," Jacques-Yves asked respectfully. "Would you make him come back if he does not want to?"

"Mais non," I said firmly. "If I find him, he's still perfectly free to make his own decisions. I'm not a cop. . . . However, do you think he is still alive?"

Silence all around the table.

The young people stared at their beer bottles. I checked around the table to make sure I had names right. There were of course Jacques-Yves and Marie-Bernadette. Three of the other four had American-sounding nicknames.

Teddi—Law.

Chantal—French Drama.

Billi—A short lad with glasses and red hair. Psychology.

Tessie—Black hair, brown eyes, an expression of incurable melancholy on her face. Some kind of scientist.

Save for Chantal they all were approximately the same age as Jacques-Yves and Marie-Bernadette. They were what we would consider graduate students, though it was not clear that they were enrolled in any classes. They were but a short step from becoming the perpetual students of Russian fiction or the Committee on Social Thought of the University (of Chicago). They seemed mildly impoverished, save perhaps for Chantal, whose jeans and blouse hinted at designer origins. None of them appeared to be particularly unhappy.

Tessie was the first one to answer my question.

"He must be dead, Mr. Bishop. Otherwise, he would have come back long ago. He would know how much we miss him."

"I don't think so," Billi said. "Psychologically he was a very interesting man. Complicated. He liked to pretend that he was mysterious, that there were parts of his life that it was necessary to hide. I suspect his disappearance is part of the aura of mystery he cultivated."

"Merde!" Chantal ground out a cigarette. "He was not intelligent enough to be mysterious. You intellectuals see in him the complexity you like to imagine in yourselves. He was a typical French peasant."

She turned to me. "I was the only one of this little group, *Monseigneur,* to be immune to his charm. He was a nice man, *oui,* and doubtless sincere in his piety. However, he lacked depth and intelligence. I am astonished that *tout le monde* was fascinated by him. It would not have lasted. We French are very cynical. When we watched him on TV, I laughed, while 'les enfants,'" she gestured at her friends—"silently worshipped him."

"She made fun of him," Marie-Bernadette said in mild disapproval. "We are all Catholics, of course, but only Jacques-Yves and I are believers."

In France you could be a Catholic and not be a believer.

"I am an atheist, *Monseigneur*," Chantal announced. "However, I keep my options open." She grinned mischievously.

In France you could also be an atheist and call a bishop by an old-fashioned title.

"The first pain in her chest and she will call for the Holy Oils," Teddi said. "She is a weak-minded atheist."

"I do not exclude that possibility!"

"Were you surprised when he disappeared?" I asked.

"It was not like him, Mr. Bishop," Marie-Bernadette said sadly. "He was so good to us. The students thought that he was the only one in this whole terrible city that cared for us as human beings. We felt let down. I personally thought that he would never let us down. But he did, *n'est-ce pas?*"

"You must understand, Mr. Bishop," Tessie said, her face growing more melancholy, "that he was for us like the sun rising in the spring, a burst of light in our lives. We should have known that darkness always extinguishes the light."

"Ah."

"*They* got him," Teddi said with a touch of bitterness in his voice. "In France they always get the ones who bring a little hope."

They again.

"Was there a woman in his life?"

From five of the six there were instant denials, though *Demoiselle* my translator was cautious in her denial.

"He was too much a priest," Tessie insisted, "for women even to think about going to bed with him. *Très* cute, but not to be touched, *n'est-ce pas?*"

"Nonsense, *chérie!*" Chantal exploded. "He was an adorable little fellow. I myself had fantasies about seducing him. It would have been delightful, though he is not my type."

"No one is your type," Teddi said.

They all laughed.

Chantal could say outrageous things with such charm that no one seemed to be offended. Her smile at the end of her outbursts hinted that she was speaking half in fun.

Only half?

"No, no, Chantal," Billi protested. "You do not understand. Women know instinctively the difference between a man whom one may seduce and one whom they may not, even though they may enjoy their little private fantasies. You would no more have wanted to destroy *Frère* Jean-Claude in the real world than would *la petite* Marie-Bernadette."

"Perhaps," Chantal replied, as she lit another cigarette. "Perhaps not."

"Most of our lives are very difficult, Mr. Bishop," said the local delegate from the North Wabash Avenue Irregulars, "We have hope still because we are young. Yet often we worry about what it would be like to be poor all our lives and to die in the street as penniless beggars. *Le frère* taught us that we should never quit and never cease to smile, *n'est-ce pas?*"

"He never said those things to us," her true love agreed. "Yet we came to believe that God loved us and that seemed to be enough."

"D'accord," said the melancholy Tessie.

Billi offered yet another psychological insight.

"Tout le monde identified with the poor man. The strain must have been terrible. It is quite understandable that finally he wanted to escape from it all, no?"

"We are not angry at him," Jacques-Yves said. "If he felt the need to leave us, then he should have. It would have been impossible to say good-bye."

"Précisément!" Billi agreed. "The strain would have been too much on both sides.

Chantal quietly puffed on her cigarette, her eyes seeing something far away. Perhaps.

"Yet you all think he is dead?"

Silent agreement.

"Were there any hints that he might leave you?"

"He left us immediately after *la Pâques*—Easter to you, *Monseigneur,*" Chantal said, as from a great distance. "He had worked very hard at that time, of course, both for the nuns and for the students. He looked completely exhausted on the TV that week. Did I not say to you, *chérie*"—she nodded at Marie-Bernadette like the latter was her little sister—" 'your friend needs a vacation'?"

Marie-Bernadette nodded solemnly.

"It did not seem right to think of *le frère* on a beach in swim trunks. I said I thought he looked fine. Yet I worried about him . . ."

"No other hints?"

None apparently.

"Did he have any special friends here at the *Sorbonne?*"

"He had the ability," Teddi spoke slowly, "to make

all of us think we were special. . . . Anyone who came to talk to him. But it was never said that he had a special group."

"Or a close friend," Tessie added. "He seemed to appear out of aloneness and return to it."

"A hellish existence," Jacques-Yves said, "though I never thought of it that way."

"Do you suffer from being alone, *Monseigneur*?" Chantal asked. "Are you ever like Bernanos's *curé de campagne*?"

"A pastor of an American parish with three hospitals in its boundaries and a cardinal to keep happy has the opposite problem—no solitude. So he never notices that he is alone, except on Sunday afternoons when the football games are over."

"*Touché!*" Chantal came back from wherever she was and smiled.

The others all laughed. I hoped I had made my point.

"So there is no one else to whom I might talk?"

"*Monseigneur, le pauvre* Jean-Claude was exhausted, stressed out as you Americans would say," Chantal assumed the responsibility to speak for all of them. "He ran away to escape the pressures. We all agree that he was *très sensitif*. He had to run. Perhaps he planned to come back. Most likely he would have come back. Then something *mauvaise* happened . . . You will not find him because he is not to be found."

She glanced around the table. There was no disagreement. I ordered another round of beer. Much to my surprise they had a pint of Guinness inside.

I had heard a similar analysis several times during our search. I did not believe it for a minute. It made no sense to separate his disappearance from the crypt and his disappearance from the world, unless you wanted to because you loved him so much, to excuse what was a heartless trick on all those whom he had captured in his vision of a God who loves. There was no sound reason to postulate a *mauvais* influence which came into play only after he had slipped out of the crypt.

I said as much to the group when the new supply of beer had arrived and fought off their expressions of disgust at the sight of my swamplike pint.

Suddenly they were voluble. I had touched a tender spot.

"Maybe he felt he had no choice!"

"You do not understand his psychology, Mr. Bishop!"

"Perhaps it would be more difficult for us if he had stayed and collapsed before our very eyes!"

"He never wanted to hurt anyone!"

"Why should he be as sad as we are!"

"Merde," Chantal said again, grinding out another cigarette. "Is it not more likely that for some reason he lost his faith in what he was preaching. Could he not have discovered that life wasn't quite so simple as he preached that it was? Maybe he ran because he was frightened of what he had learned and how terrible it would be to tell *tout le monde* that he was a fraud!"

"Chantal!" Marie-Bernadette exclaimed.

"I do not want to disillusion you, *chérie*. But there is evil and suffering and tragedy in this world. Jean-Claude did not seem to realize that. Then suddenly perhaps he discovered it. So he had to flee. *Monseigneur* is correct. When he disappeared from the crypt, he intended to disappear completely. It does not matter whether he is dead or not. We will never see him again."

"Arguably," I agreed.

"Priests do lose their faith, do they not, *Monseigneur*?"

"No more often than a couple of times a day."

"If you do find him, *Monseigneur*, you will truly respect his choice?"

"Certainement!"

"Then he will not come back. We should mourn him and get on with our lives. Perhaps he was a trick, perhaps he was a grace. I do not know. Yet he is gone forever, *n'est-ce pas*?"

"I think you go too far, Chantal," Billi intervened. "There are some moments of crisis in human life when the only choice is to escape. Jean-Claude needed to escape. Perhaps he will never come back. Perhaps he will."

"If he is still alive," Tessie said grimly.

"Our pain is so great, Mr. Bishop," Marie-Bernadette said softly, "that we can't even talk sense about him. So we cannot be of much help to you."

"D'accord," said Chantal, "I miss him too, even if I did make fun of him."

We chatted about other things. Drizzle began to seep from the gray skies. They all shook hands with me. Jacques-Yves and Marie-Bernadette led me back to *l'abbaye* and then departed hand in hand.

14

"*Is it yourself, now?*" **Nuala Anne** asked when I picked up the phone. I had been resting my eyes and had no idea where I was.

"Arguably," I murmured.

"Didn't I think it might be?"

"Indeed?"

"And haven't I been listening to that tape you sent? And doesn't me daughter want to dance to it?"

"High praise," I said.

"You're not telling me that them French fiddle players are younger than I am, are you now? And meself not twenty-six yet?"

"Woman, I am," I said, getting into the flow of the peculiar brand of English with which this Irish-speaking woman from Connemara addressed the world. "Not that much younger, however."

She sighed loudly, a much richer and more expressive sigh than I can possibly manage.

"Is she gorgeous now?"

"All Celtic women are."

Another sigh. "Doesn't your lordship have a clever tongue now? They're Celts that's for sure. Only our kind can play that way, and usually only the crazy ones. . . . They aren't crazy, are they?"

"Not when they're not playing their fiddles."

"Where did they learn it?"

We were proceeding in typical West of Ireland (and

Chicago political) fashion—circling round a subject until we got to the point at the end of the conversation.

"They learned their fiddle playing in their home in Valence down on the Rhône River, near Avignon—"

Nuala Anne interrupted me to sing something about *"Sur le pont d'Avignon."*

"I suspect they decided they were Celts when they studied the big stones behind their homes. Then they went on a tour of the Celtic countries during a couple of summers . . ."

"People are born with that kind of music in them, aren't they now?"

"If you say so, Nuala Anne."

"Your French people don't appreciate them?"

"I don't think they know about them."

She sighed again. "And do they have jobs?"

"Jacques-Yves is a part-time carpenter and Marie-Bernadette is a beggar."

"A beggar, is it!" Nuala shouted.

I explained the situation for young people in France and described how I had met Marie-Bernadette in front of *St-Germain-des-Prés.*

At the other end of the line, wasn't herself weeping?

" 'Tis worse than it was in Ireland when I was a kid. And now don't they want us all to come back. . . ."

"That's not likely to happen here. Ireland has a young economy and a young society. This country is very old."

I waited while she dried her eyes.

"Well," she said, "I'm making no promises, but I'll see what I can do for them. I'll talk to a few people around and to some of the lawyers and try to work something out."

I thanked her.

I interpreted her circuitous message to mean that she would work something out, come hell or high water. It would be interesting to listen to a conversation between her and me, uh, my brother Packy.

I went back to resting my eyes. When the phone rang again it was Nora Cronin.

"It is the most beautiful church in the world, Blackwood, incredible. The sun was still out when we got there. Heaven must be a little bit like that."

"Better heated, I trust."

"Sean went to his room and collapsed."

"Resting his eyes."

"Reading the fathers," she said.

"Same thing."

"Where are we eating tonight?"

"We ate last night."

"That was twenty-four hours ago."

"As a precaution I asked the concierge to make bookings at a place called the Odeon, right near the theater of the same at seven-thirty."

"Good, we'll see you in the lobby at seven."

There was no point in trying to review the data from today's ventures. That could wait till after supper. There was also something I should look at, something which I had left in the hotel room before we went over to *la place de la Sorbonne*.

But my eyes were too tired to read it.

Only in the shower did I remember that it was Jean-Claude's confidential file. It would have to wait, since predictably Milord Cronin would be hungry.

It was eleven before I opened the Jean-Claude file. It was dated on the Saturday before the First Sunday in Easter. Apparently he kept a file for each TV program. I glanced through his notes. The first set was a preliminary outline. The theme seemed to be that

every day is Easter because every day we rise from
the dead as Jesus did. Every day is a gift of new life.
He had finished three and a half versions of the theme,
all on computer output. The final version was only
half-finished. He must have left for the crypt before
he had completed it.

He worked systematically. On each of the first three
drafts he had crossed out words, lines, sentences and
paragraphs as he wrestled with the tough question of
whether Easter meant new life for those suffering the
final agonies before death. He said, as we must, that
for them especially new life is coming.

The tone was not philosophical but simple, and direct—the approach of a man of faith who had to fall
back on faith in the face of evil.

He had worked very hard on his drafts. He could
easily have gotten away with the first draft. The incomplete version, however, was polished and smooth.
It had been a long time since I had worked that carefully on a sermon. However, I was Irish and inexcus-
ably glib.

I put the computer output paper back in the folder.
I would return it to Sarah as a keepsake of a priest
whose transparency on the tube was the result of per-
sistent effort. As a veteran newsman had said to me,
"the secret of this business is sincerity. Once you learn
how to fake that, everything else is easy."

Then I noticed several single sheets of paper folded
neatly into the pocket of the folder. However, *Frère*
Jean-Claude's handwriting, though small, was neat
and clear. I hesitated before I began to read. It was
after all personal, something he had not intended to
leave on his desk. Yet he owed all the people who
loved him an explanation for his bizarre behavior.
Would I show it to *la petite* Marie-Bernadette? Perhaps.

First I must read it.

My hands grew sweaty and my stomach knotted as I read. Later, after we had solved the case, I showed the last will and testament of Jean-Claude to Marie-Bernadette and she translated it into good English.

There were many separate entries, spread perhaps over time though none of them were dated. The inks were of different shade and color, as though he had grabbed whatever pen might have been available.

It was a mistake for me ever to become a priest. I've known that for a long time. Now I am captured in the priesthood. I must leave it, but somehow I don't want to. I hate being a priest, but I like it too. What am I to do?

The pressures increase. I grow careless. I am so tired and so confused that I make mistakes. One of them might be fatal. The world must not know of my hidden life.

I believe absolutely nothing. Yet when I preach I believe everything I say. How can this be? Am I a hypocrite?

I pray to God, whom I doubt every day, to give me a sign of what I should do. Perhaps he has already given me that sign.

I watched myself on TV last night in my hidden self. I thought that the young man was charming and had worked very hard on his sermon. Perhaps he is a fool, but a sincere fool. However, how is it possible that so many people listen to him and accept him as a teacher. I was tempted myself to believe him.

I was not meant to be a priest. I became one because of pride and folly—and perhaps a sense of guilt. Why

*cannot I simply walk away from it like so many priests
do. It would create a national scandal, almost as much
as if I am found out. How did I permit myself to become
a TV preacher? The true answer to that is that I enjoy
the attention, the challenge, the excitement. It is my vanity
that trapped me. O vanity of vanities and all is vanity!*

*I cannot merely leave the priesthood. I must disappear
completely. I can do that of course. Perhaps without much
trouble. That will hurt many people that I love and who
love me. It is better that way than any other way. The
Church will be happy to see no more of me. Similarly the
government. And the TV industry. As for those I love—
I have helped them all a little bit, I think. They have no
right to make more demands on me. They will miss me,
as I will miss them. But they will forget about me. God,
if he exists, will have to take care of them. And if he does
not exist, and I don't think he does, then nothing matters
anyway.*

*A young man to whom I had talked for several hours
said at the end of our conversation that he wished all
priests were like me. I was, he said, his ideal as a priest
and, if he became a priest, he wanted to be one like me.
I almost wept. He will, I hope, never find out the truth
about me. He must never learn that I lusted after him
while we talked. The crooked lines of God are ironic,
almost comic lines.*

*Bodies attract me, challenge me, fill me with desire.
Women's bodies, men's bodies, any body to hold me in its
arms in my lonely bed here at St. Catherine's. Could I
sneak someone in here? That's a blasphemous thought! I
will never do that. Yet I dream of taking the clothes off
a body and playing with it all night and loving it forever.*

An ugly evil fantasy which shows just how depraved I've become. Dear God, if You are listening or even there to listen, I am sorry. There are too many young bodies available to me.

Since I have become a priest, I have desired more than ever to touch and fondle the breasts of women. Is that what ordination does to one?

I am getting desperate. This charade cannot continue much longer. I must run, I must escape, I must disappear. Oh, God, why did I ever do this?

I grow careless. I left these pages on my desk at St. Catherine's. What if one of the nuns should read them? They would not know everything, but they would know enough to know that I ought never to have become a priest and that I should leave now. Poor Father Provincial would die of shame if he knew what a worthless follower of Dominic I am.

Why am I careless? Why do I cross the boundaries between my two lives with so little regard for prudence? Do I want to be found out for the false priest, the hypocrite that I am? Do I want them to know how empty are the fine words I speak to all of France every week? I do not need to be a psychologist to answer that question.

The Christmas program was a huge success. If I believed in the Holy Spirit, I would think that he whispered in my ear to abandon my script and sing. The managers were furious, the producers delighted and all France rejoiced. I admit that I reveled in the triumph. I have become vain. I enjoy success. I love the acclaim. Now I am exhausted and depressed. I must take action soon.

Despite my firm intentions I am still a priest, still living my double life. I must leave. Let Pâques be the last broadcast of Frère Jean-Claude. *He has done enough good in the world. I must now disappear. Immediately. Otherwise I will go mad.*

As I plan my disappearance I realize that it will not be easy. Part of me, the priest part, wants to continue to be a priest, even though I am living a lie. I do not want to give up my friends, my colleagues, my students, even the silly Royalists who are now more interested in each other than they are in restoring the Duc. Poor people. I am determined to give them all up, lest something terrible will happen. Yet it is not enough that Frère Jean-Claude *simply disappear. That is not quite enough. He must disappear dramatically. And definitively. Should he jump into the Seine in his Dominican robes? No, someone would doubtless risk their life to pull him out of the water. I must think about this. I must act before I become insane.*

I have fantasized for some time about Henri and Constance making love. I played God for the two of them by intervening in their sexual life with my instructions, much to their embarrassment. I gave Constance more hints, quite direct and vivid, than I gave Henri. She blushed but did not seem shocked. She is at just the age when a woman's sexual needs become strongest. She phoned me later in the week to thank me quite frankly for my suggestions. Our lives will never be the same she said. I am a woman now. You will only improve at it, I said. Can it be that there are still innocents in France? Of course there are. There always will be. Now I have soiled my good work by intruding myself into their bedroom in my imagination and watched them enjoy married love. I am ashamed of myself. Yet the delicious images persist. I watch him gently but with increasing firmness arouse her so that she screams for release. I see him enter her and begin to thrust, slowly then with wild passion. I can almost hear her repeated cries of pleasure.

Forgive me, if there is anyone there to grant forgiveness. I am happy that I was able to bring joy to their sterile lives. I regret that even in my mind I trespassed on their privacy.

There must be someone to forgive. Otherwise why would we want forgiveness?

Do you exist? I think not. I have never seen you or touched you or felt you. Well, sometimes I think you're present but that may be wish fulfillment. Intellectually, I have no reason to believe. Yet much of the time I act like I do believe. Why? Habit, perhaps. My family was devout. Intelligently devout. My parents may have had questions. They may have at times been very angry at priests. But they were firm believers. Did I absorb their belief before I had a chance to think for myself? I am a priest because of my family, that much should be clear. When I play my priest part, I talk and act as if I believe—with the nuns, with the students, with the people who see me on the tube. In those times I do believe. I feel that unquestionably you are a God of mercy and love like I say you are. Only when I have time to reflect do I feel doubts, and then after the doubts certainty that the universe is cold and lonely. I know then that I am a hypocrite and a fool. Then I preside over the Eucharist in my unsteady bumbling way and I know that you are. I don't believe but I know.

Eh bien, if you exist, what must you think of me? I am a faker, a hypocrite, a coward, someone playing the

*role of a priest who does not believe. My sacramental acts
under such circumstances are sacrileges, are they not?*

*I do no deliberate harm to those who hear me. Perhaps
because I strengthen their faith I make them happier. I
smile at them. Is that not a good work? Because my intentions are good, will you forgive me my hypocrisy?*

*I tell people that you cannot help forgiving us. Should
you exist, then am I included in your forgiveness?*

I should not be, but I know that I am.

*That is the most terrifying thought. I am in the hands
of a reality that knows all, sees all, understands all, for-
gives all. I cannot escape that reality because it will never
let me go.*

*And now, God help me, I think that the last paragraph
will be a good line for my next broadcast.*

Bon. Do you want me to say that I love you?

What choice do I have?

*I am near madness. I am filled with fear and anger
and sadness and lust. When I escape the lust will diminish, I think. But I must escape. Soon.*

*Tomorrow we begin our plans for the series on Notre-
Dame de Paris. Poor Victor Hugo, he did not understand, did he? Notre-Dame is France and France is
Notre-Dame. Both are incurably Catholic. I could do
wonderful commentaries in the series, objective history
blended with piety. I would believe what I was saying,
at least when I was saying it. If only I could be the kind
of priest I pretend to be. If only it were all so clear and
simple as I make it in my broadcasts. If only God were
nothing but mercy and love.*

Maybe he is.

Perhaps I should postpone my disappearance until the series is finished. Then vanish from the face of the earth!

I can't believe I wrote the words just above. More vanity and now combined with folly. All the signs are there that it is time to leave. Perhaps tomorrow. With some luck there should be opportunity. There is risk in doing it this way. I find that I love risks. I have an almost sexual hunger to take chances. I have never recognized that quality in myself before. It explains many things. I shall wait till tomorrow to see what happens.

Soon we will go down into the crypt beneath the parvis of Notre-Dame. Frère Jean-Claude will join his ancestors of sixteen hundred years ago. A melodramatic exit perhaps. I relish the challenge. If it doesn't work, I can claim that it's another one of my practical jokes. Poor Pierre and Sarah, I will frighten them. God, if you exist and if you are listening, help me to have the courage to make my escape. And help those who have foolishly loved me to heal the wounds I have caused. I love them all. I love You too.

Please forgive

Thus it ended, an incomplete sentence.

I put the papers back in the folder with trembling fingers and sat at my desk for a long time, unable to think coherently about what I had read.

Such terrible agony.

Was it necessary?

Was there not too much self-dramatization in his pain? Could he not have found a confessor or a spiritual director or a superior, perhaps his wise and sympathetic provincial, with whom to discuss his crisis of faith? Why did it have to be completely internal? What was there about his agony that he could not have shared?

I shook my head. There are only a limited number of ways a priest can give scandal. All of them are old, even familiar. Why did Jean-Claude think that he had invented a different one?

We all, however, must follow our own spirit. Jean-Claude had to wrestle with his own demons by himself. Patently he was a nervous wreck. His fear of a fatal mistake was surely valid. He had left the cries of his heart in a folder on his desk at the station. So anxious was he about his disappearance that he had forgotten to take it with him. After he had slipped into the third century—or more likely into the crowd of Parisian tourists—he might have remembered that the little diary was still on his desk. Fortunately for him that Sarah had refused to read it and had hidden it until she gave it to me.

Or had he perhaps left it behind deliberately as an attempt at explaining his decision, an apology from beyond the grave?

No, that was unlikely. He gave too much away that would provide clues to the searchers.

I knew that melatonin would not put me to sleep this night.

I tried to organize my thoughts.

Jean-Claude was alive. He was hiding somewhere, perhaps even in Paris. Should I try to find him? If he wanted to be left alone, to escape from the trap in which he thought he had been imprisoned, should I not respect his freedom to control his own life? What good would come of finding him? Was I merely trying to keep my record of solving crimes? If I continued the search, would I simply make matters worse for everyone?

My first instincts were to abandon the whole matter. Yet my second instincts said that somehow Jean-Claude was not at peace. He had indeed escaped physically, but had he in fact escaped emotionally? Might he still need healing?

Why should he seek it from you, John Blackwood Ryan?

No reason, except that I'm here and I know the truth. Perhaps others would come to know the truth. Surely there was some speculation already in that direction, though most of those who cared thought he was dead.

And perhaps he was. Perhaps there was still a murder to be solved.

That was unlikely, but not impossible.

The truth should be known by at least some of those who mattered.

We had but two more interviews—with the nuns at Ste-Catherine's and the police on the next two days. We would do both of them, if only to give the impression that we were finishing the investigation. If we learned nothing more, then I would have to conclude that Jean-Claude had fooled me like he had fooled everyone else.

I reread his "last will" very carefully with a French dictionary at hand so I could catch the nuances. Later on when I knew everything that was to be known, I reread it and told myself that I had been a complete eejit, as Nuala Anne would have said. Friar Jean-Claude had fooled me too.

The Paris papers the next morning reported another miraculous cure, this time at the head of the steps leading to the crypt. A young woman who had

not walked because of an accident ten years before
was able to walk down the steps to the crypt and climb
back up. She continued to walk across the parvis towards Notre-Dame to give thanks to God and the
Blessed Mother and the saintly Jean-Claude. *M. le Cardinal* had no comment.

The police had closed the crypt and cordoned off
the entrance, as if you can stop miracles by barring
access to holy places. The Cardinal of Paris was undoubtedly furious. So too were the rest of "them."

If Jean-Claude were still somewhere in Paris—as I
strongly expected he was—he must be puzzled about
what was happening.

The best thing he could do was to get out of town.
Immediately.

15

"*Père Renault wishes to see you,*" Frankie said on the phone.

"Ah?" I said, making no commitment at all.

"Laurent Renault. He is a Jesuit who is part of the *Figaro* circle. You know what *Le Figaro* is?"

"A daily paper which is kind of an equivalent of the London *Tablet* or the *Commonweal* in America."

"Close enough. Very influential among well-educated Catholics. Maybe a little right of center, but taken very seriously by all."

"Indeed."

"*Père* Renault was the Jesuit who defended Jean-Claude before the commission."

"When and where do we meet him?"

The man was certainly interesting. I needed another perspective badly after reading poor Jean-Claude's notes to himself.

"*Les Deux Magots* at one o'clock. You can see him before you visit the nuns at St. Catherine's."

"Excellent."

"You find out anything yet, Blackie?"

"Only that Friar Jean-Claude was a very complicated man despite his apparent simplicity."

"Yeah, I agree. Most people don't get it, however."

The next call was from the valiant, loyal, and virtuous, if bossy, *Demoiselle* Marie-Bernadette, seeking instructions for the day on a public phone up in

Belleville—where they had once torn bishops apart with their teeth.

"At three we visit the good sisters at Ste-Catherine's. However, I would appreciate it very much if you could arrive here at twelve."

"Bon . . . pourquoi?"

It was not a demand for an explanation, but a request for information as to how she should dress.

"To lead me once again to that excellent café *les Deux Magots*, lest I end up in the *Louvre*."

"Bon."

"We will have lunch with a good Jesuit, *Père* Laurent Renault."

"Oui."

"He was the one who spoke in favor of *Frère* Jean-Claude before the commission."

"Oui!"

"How is the excellent Jacques-Yves this morning?"

"He worries too much, Mr. Bishop."

"And you don't?"

"He wants to marry me, *bien sûr*. He worries that we will starve to death together. I say better that than starving separately."

"You are, of course, correct."

"That's what I tell him," she said with a bright laugh. "Eventually I will win the argument, of course."

"That is the way of it in our species."

At the third call, I had the sensation that I was back in the Cathedral Rectory and should grab for my ritual and stole and dash for a hospital.

It was, however, only my sole male sibling, the ineffable Packy Ryan.

"Some of our mutual friends," he began without preliminaries, "have raised some questions about your friends over there, which they need before they go ahead to push this matter through."

"Indeed."

"Do you have any indication that they want to come to America?"

A relatively clear question from Packy.

"Yes."

"And that indication is?"

"They are eager."

"You're sure of that?"

"Bank it."

"Any indications of criminal behavior in their past?"

"No."

"They married?"

I sighed. It was none of our mutual friends' business and certainly nothing that the exemplary Nuala Anne would ask.

"They will be."

"Yeah, well, that's about all. Our mutual friends will have to decide that they'll go ahead with the project and push it through."

That meant it was a done deal.

"Bon."

"Huh."

"French for good."

"Yeah."

The omens were good.

Later as we traversed the mysterious path from the hotel to the *rue* Bonaparte, I outlined for my translator the themes in Jean-Claude's notes.

"Le pauvre petit frère," she said softly. "Is he the only *prêtre* who has ever felt those things?"

She was wearing her worn but clean and freshly pressed gray suit, appropriate for meeting with a Jesuit and later cloistered Dominican nuns.

"Obviously not. However, he is a young and sensitive priest who, through no design on his part, finds himself a national celebrity. It is unfortunate that there was no one he could talk to."

"He could talk to you, could he not, Mr. Bishop, when we find him?"

"If he wants to, Marie-Bernadette, but only if he wants. . . . You look very tired this morning, *Demoiselle.*"

"My sleep often escaped me last night. I love my work. At night, however, I find myself still translating everything. *Le pauvre* Jacques-Yves sleeps in the same room with me. He worries about my restlessness." She dismissed him with the required wave of her hand. "He worries about everything concerning me."

"I am sorry that you cannot sleep."

"It will be only a few more days, *douloureusement* I will sleep the rest of my life."

"Arguably."

After a moment's hesitation, she added shyly, "We sleep in the same room, as do others, but we do not sleep together."

"Patently," I said, though it had not been patent, it should have been.

Through a miracle of grace or nature, she found the way to *les Deux Magots*. In my Chicago Bears windbreaker the good Laurent Renault would never recognize me. I glanced around the green awnings in front of the café. Sitting alone at a table was a slender, handsome man with neatly combed iron gray hair. He wore a gray suit and a thin, black tie and was absorbed in a book.

He might just as well have had the letters "S.J." emblazoned on his forehead.

"Ryan, Chicago," I introduced myself.

"Monseigneur." He smiled genially and rose to shake hands.

"Call me Blackie."

"Not Ishmael?"

Many points to *Père* Renault for that line.

"Sean Cronin is not a white whale."

He laughed cheerfully. *"Touché!"*

I introduced my translator. He smiled charmingly and shook her hand with just a hint of a bow. You really can't beat the Jesuits for turning on charm with women.

"I translate for Mr. Bishop Blackie," the little imp informed him. "However, I'm sure there'll be no need to translate in this conversation, *Père* Renault. Mr. Bishop Blackie likes to listen to the people we interview in French and I translate, even though he understands what they say, so that he can study them and prepare his next question. But that would never work with a Jesuit, would it?"

We all laughed together.

She caught my grin out of the corner of her eye and relaxed in the knowledge that she had not gone too far. In fact, she had said just the right thing. Soon she would be able to handle the investigation without my help.

We spoke about her first under *Père* Renault's lead. She was a musician, a violist who played Celtic music with her *fiancé* Jacques-Yves. They were from Celtic lands in France. Mr. Bishop Blackie had seen her begging across the street and been kind enough to hire her. She was so bold that he would probably soon regret it.

I noted what while *le pauvre* Jacques-Yves had been, as usual, dismissed with a wave of her hand, he had been promoted from boyfriend to fiancé. I wondered if that promotion had come after our conversation earlier.

Then we segued into the matter at hand.

"Might I say initially, uh, Blackie, that while it is an honor to meet you, we are a bit surprised at your role of a detective."

It was not clear in the conversation who "we" were. It was, however, more than an editorial "we." Perhaps a claque of very bright Jesuits who hung around *Le Figaro.*

"Auxiliary bishops do what they must."

"We know and admire your philosophical work, of course. There is some discussion of translating it into French . . ."

"An amazing honor."

He laughed without skipping a beat.

"We are delighted that you solve mysteries."

"Only locked-room mysteries."

The good Marie-Bernadette, having ordered the meal for us, filled our glasses with white wine.

"All the more a matter for delight . . . Now as to Friar Jean-Claude, we do not think that it will do to dismiss his work as that of a naïf, a simple *prêtre de campagne,* if you understand my meaning. Quite the contrary, we are inclined to believe that he has, perhaps more successfully than anyone in thirty years, adapted the theological insights of the Second Vatican Council to everyday preaching. He has combined new theological thought with traditional religious rhetoric with remarkable skill."

"Fascinating."

"Therefore, we are considering some writings of theological reflection on his underlying thought. It would appear that the Sisters at Ste-Catherine's have kept his files. Our Dominican colleagues are not opposed to sharing them with us. . . ."

"I have a file with his preparation for the homily which he did not, alas, give. I can testify that it indicates considerable reflection and sophistication. At the end of my investigation, I will turn it over to the Dominican Provincial."

"Excellent! . . . You agree with me that—"

"He was something more than a *pauvre prêtre de campagne?* Oh yes. He knew what he was doing. It surprises me that you were the only one on the commission investigating him that perceived that."

"Ah?" He smiled complacently. "You read the transcript of that dreadful interlude? It astonishes me that many of us read into a man's work what we want to find and do not hear what he is actually saying. Myself, I have noted a progression of his skill from the earlier broadcasts to the later ones. An analysis of this development should be most instructive, no?"

Poor Jean-Claude. Soon they would be writing doctoral dissertations about him. The French, of course, must analyze everything. It is not required, however, that they do anything about their analysis. We Americans do just the opposite. We do something and then analyze.

"I have watched several tapes and have noted this enrichment of his material."

"Perhaps eventually we will be able to trace the sources which have influenced him, perhaps even books that he has marked. Myself, I am convinced that his discussion of the Holy Spirit is influenced by the work of his late Dominican colleague *Père* Congar."

"Cardinal Congar," I corrected him.

"*Mais certainement!* The Vatican waited till the last minute, did they not?"

"Usually they wait till after a person is dead to honor him."

"*C'est vrai* . . . We believe that the drafts of his presentations, the theology books he used and, of course, the broadcasts he made, will provide fruitful material for reflection and perhaps, I do not use this word in the negative sense, imitation?"

"Arguably."

"*Enfin*, the matter is very delicate. We wonder if your work will clarify it for us."

Ah, that was the point of the luncheon. I nibbled on a mysterious-looking piece of fish. Quite good. I would not starve to death before the day was over.

"The matter is as you say, Laurent, very delicate. The miracles add to the delicacy, do they not?"

How about that for ducking the point!

He made a little face to indicate the embarrassment of the miracles.

"Indeed they complicate the matter, though perhaps not in a negative way. He was a very good man, Blackie. Holiness shone from his face and filled his speech, though my colleagues on the commission were blind and deaf to it. Miracles are a complicated matter. However, it would not surprise me if he were somehow or the other involved in them."

A sophisticated Jesuit theologian, a man of the *Figaro* group, thought that Jean-Claude might be a saint. Perhaps I had missed something.

"You read the text of our investigation?" he continued.

"Oh, yes."

"Was there not a touch of Jeanne d'Arc in his responses."

"And of the good Marie-Bernadette's patron."

"Oh, yes, indeed!" he said with beaming smile of appreciation. "That is very good, very good! A combination of innocence and intelligence, virtue and wisdom. I do not know whether this matter will ever go that far, still he had the material of a great man and of a saint."

"Arguably."

"If he had persisted in his work, I am sure that they would have silenced him."

They again. The *they* who had sent *Père* Congar off to Africa where his health was ruined for the rest of his life and made him a cardinal only on his deathbed.

"It's a little harder these days."

"*D'accord.* But if a priest belongs to a religious order, it takes a single command from the Congregation for Religious Orders to silence him. Perhaps Jean-Claude has escaped that."

"Perhaps," I said.

"Do you think he will return, Blackie? Naturally, we hope he does. Hence we suspend most of our work. However, we continue to analyze his homilies. Several articles on him should keep *them* at bay for a while."

"Indeed."

"Might one inquire gently and unofficially how your work is coming? One hears that you and the Cardinal leave in a few days."

"As I said, the matter is very delicate. We have many facts in hand and need only a few more for the picture to fit together. . . ."

Suddenly the picture did come together, more clearly than before. It was like a door to an elevator opened and I saw everyone who was in it in their proper places. Alas, the door slammed together before

I could identify where they were. It often happens that way at first.

"Mr. Bishop Blackie," Marie-Bernadette said with fierce pride, "always solves his puzzle, *tout le temps.*"

"So far," I said with as much modesty as I could under the circumstances. "This matter has special problems . . ."

"Doubtless," the good Jesuit agreed sadly.

"I will promise this," I said carefully. "Before Milord Cronin returns to Chicago, I shall inform you whether and to what extent your project should continue."

"*Très bien.* We could ask for no more."

The reader will perceive that this promise was outrageous. I was walking on very thin ice. However, the promise would put extra pressure on me to keep the elevator door open.

"Did you ever notice anything especially mysterious about the good Jean-Claude?"

"*Bien sûr* . . . He was charming, intelligent, and, I think, very holy. But yet . . ."

"Ah?"

"Many said that he was utterly transparent. I found him that way up to a point."

"And after that point?"

"Utterly opaque. There was something there, oh yes. Not unattractive but different from the rest of him. . . ."

"Contradictory?"

Laurent Renault screwed up his handsome face.

"No, not necessarily, but different . . . Fascinating in a way. A special kind of smile."

"False smile?"

"No, not false, but secret . . . As if he knew something wonderful that we did not know."

"I see."

In fact, I didn't see at all.

"Perhaps a smile"—*Père* Renault considered his words carefully—"that was more mystical than mysterious."

Not only was *Frère* Jean-Claude a theologian and perhaps a saint, he was also a mystic. I found this near canonization a little improbable. I had read his *cri du coeur* last night. Would a mystic and a saint agonize in such fashion?

Arguably. However, what did I know?

We bade farewell to Laurent Renault and walked back to the Luxembourg Gardens in full autumn radiance under an overcast sky which filtered soft, silver sunlight.

"I note with interest that *le pauvre* Jacques-Yves has been promoted."

"Comment?"

"He is still dismissed with a wave of the hand. Now, however, he is described not as a boyfriend but with a more serious term."

"You do not miss anything, do you, Mr. Bishop Blackie?" She looked away, flustered but delighted.

"Arguably . . . However, it will do no harm to our investigation if you wear the ring which you have secreted in your purse after you put aside the old ring."

She blushed and lowered her head.

"It is not an impressive ring, I fear."

The band she slipped on her finger was a novelty store ring, worth no more than two hundred francs.

"One measures the value of a ring by the quality of the love it represents, not by its cost."

Now she was crying happily.

"Since we were little children and did not know what marriage was, we knew that we would marry someday. It is now time, past time. Soon we will both become twenty-five and we can collect the twenty-five hundred francs a month from the government. I said to Jean-Claude that we should wait no longer. He agreed immediately. We will return home to Valence soon and become man and wife. Then we will come back here. Perhaps we can find somewhere a room for ourselves, maybe, if we are fortunate, an apartment."

A good deal more if we could help it.

"Congratulations and God's best blessings."

"Thank you, Mr. Bishop Blackie. You are the first to know."

A torrent of tears, now of great joy.

"Marriage," I said, quoting G. K. Chesteron and I hope not sounding too much like Polonius, "is both a sacrament of God's love for his people and an extension of that love."

She pecked at my cheek, leaned against my chest, and sobbed happily.

"Sometimes I thought it would never happen. . . . Mr. Bishop Blackie, what is the word you people from Chicago use when you want something from someone else . . ."

"A favor?"

"Yes! I need a favor!"

"Ask it and you got it," I replied using the appropriate Chicago rhetoric, knowing that I would have to lay in a new supply of melatonin.

"*Pardon?* . . . Oh, I understand! . . . It is terrible of me even to think of it . . . Jacques-Yves and I wish you would preside over the marriage Eucharist for us."

Preside over the Eucharist? They knew all the right words.

"I would have been offended if you hadn't asked!"

More tears, another peck on the check, and this time an embrace.

"Mr. Bishop Blackie, you make us so happy. . . . If you had not asked me to work with you, Jacques-Yves and I would not have had the courage to plan our marriage."

This I very much doubted. Passion and love would have worked out God's plan for the young lovers even if his bumbling servant had not come upon this young woman on the steps of *St-Germain-des-Prés*.

Marie-Bernadette devoted herself to drying her tears.

"Will the sisters know I was weeping?"

"Surely not. . . . And if they should, they will attribute it to happiness."

"What did you think of the plans of *Père* Laurent?" she said, changing the subject to less emotionally charged matters than wedding plans.

"I do not have a mind like that of a French Jesuit, Marie-Bernadette. I lack their ardor for precise analysis and detailed plans. However, I believe that he is on to something important about our friend Jean-Claude. I hope only that they do not analyze all the fire and the fervor out of his televised homilies."

"That would be very French, *n'est-ce pas?*"

"*C'est vrai.* . . . His perspective is also different from mine because I read his spiritual notes last night and understand the agonies that plagued Jean-Claude."

"He is *très compliqué, n'est-ce pas?*"

For Marie-Bernadette it was still a given that Jean-Claude was alive. I had thought that earlier. Now I wasn't so sure. Even if we found him, would he want to come back to the strain he had experienced before his disappearance? I didn't think so. The more I reflected on his suffering, the more I thought that he was edging close to a psychological breakdown when he had poured out those passionate words of protest against his fate.

Yet . . . Yet I was still surprised by the intensity of his pain. Most priests, if they have any sense and any imagination, wonder if they truly believe all the things they preach. Like Jean-Claude they both believe and not believe at the same time. Does not, however, the nature of human condition impose such doubts upon us all. We doubt the love of our beloved for us. We doubt that we truly love the beloved. We doubt that love is possible or that there is any such thing as love. Yet we act, perforce, like we are loved and love and eventually come to believe in it again. Only for the cycle to begin on some other day. Why was doubt so much more traumatic for Jean-Claude? Was there a human lover—of either gender—involved?

His notes were obscure on that question. He wrote of erotic fantasies, mild enough ones in truth. Did not Manley Hopkins write a poem about similar feelings? Yet Jean-Claude did not hint at a specific lover for whom he longed. Perhaps he was merely being prudent, lest someone someday find his notes.

And had he left the notes behind deliberately? At least subconsciously? Were they left as a last will and testament which would explain his disappearance? Could such a careful and cautious man have made such a mistake? Wherever he was now was he worried about someone—the police especially—finding his spiritual notes?

Could a man with the sophisticated and creative intelligence that Laurent Renault claimed for Friar Jean-Claude make such a mistake?

Sophisticated and creative people make mistakes, some of them terrible.

"You are thinking, *n'est-ce pas*, Mr. Bishop Blackie?"

"Ruminating, Marie-Bernadette, and not making much progress. Perhaps the good sisters can help us."

"Surely they adored *le pauvre petit frère.*"

"Nuns in general and contemplative nuns in particular are pretty hard to fool. Let's see if they noticed any strain in Jean-Claude."

16

When I asked Mother Marie-Dominique of the
Blessed Trinity and the Holy Angels (sic) that question, the Mother Prioress replied quietly that certainly
they noticed such a strain from the very beginning of
Jean-Claude's arrival at the Convent of Ste-Catherine.
Is it not natural in young priests, especially those who
have many different kinds of work and must run all
the time?

Nuns, and especially mother superiors, have a style
of discourse they use when dealing with priests which
is above all submissive and respectful while at the
same time telling the clergy nothing and suggesting
that they are at best foolish little boys. I notice this
style immediately, but I have yet to figure out how to
circumvent it.

The Convent of the Dominican Sisters of Perpetual
Adoration was on a small, narrow street just off Mt.
St-Étienne. It was very old, late middle ages perhaps.
Marie-Bernadette rang the doorbell and told the porter
person, an old, old woman not bound to cloister that
Mr. Bishop Jean-Blackie Ryan had an appointment
with Mother Prioress. We were conducted down a
series of narrow corridors, past wooden grills and into
an office with whitewashed stone walls, a high ceiling
and small stained-glass windows. Mother Marie-
Dominique of the Blessed Trinity and the Holy Angels sat on an old wooden chair behind an equally

ancient wooden desk, on which incongruously rested a Dell laptop computer.

She welcomed us with restraint, asked us to sit down in two chairs as old as her own, and offered us tea. She busied herself with an electric teapot and left us sitting in silence while she finished the task. She seemed to take no notice of my clerical shirt without a collar and Chicago Bears jacket. However, after a quick glance that took in everything, she nodded slightly at the appearance of my translator.

(I could not, of course, come to Europe without two jackets.)

Mother Marie-Dominique of the Blessed Trinity and the Holy Angels was a tall, slender woman in her late seventies. Her face was lined by time but still striking as were her piercing aquamarine eyes. In her white-and-black Dominican robes, she radiated serenity and intelligence. *Formidable*, as the locals would say. She had poured the tea into two very old cups and handed them to us.

I had begun with an innocuous comment that Friar Jean-Claude had been their chaplain for less than five years.

"Oh, yes, Mr. Bishop," she said in a linen-smooth voice. "I have been here at Ste-Catherine's since the war. He was the best chaplain by far we have ever had. All of us miss him very much."

You won't get much out of me, she implied.

I had sighed and asked my question about stress. She in effect had replied no reasonable person could expect anything else from one so young.

I said nothing. Mother Marie was too much a gentle woman not to fill the silence.

"We have had many chaplains here, old men who have worn themselves out by many decades of hard

work. Young men who were not interested in any
work at all. Troubled men who were afraid of women.
Tempted men who liked women too much. An occasional man sent here for a rest. Friar Jean-Claude is
like none of them. He is most *remarquable.*"

"Might I ask in what way?"

"In every way. He is a wise confessor, far beyond
his years, an excellent preacher as *tout le monde* knows
now, and he genuinely respects and admires our vocation. We could ask for no more."

"You wondered why the provincial sent such a sin-
gularly qualified man?"

Not a hint of a smile.

"When he visited us last I congratulated *Père* Duchamp on his choice. He seemed pleased."

"Indeed."

More silence.

"You doubtless understand, Mr. Bishop, that our
vocation is to pray. Everyone should pray of course.
Pour nous, however, it is our principal work. We support ourselves by making altar breads for use at the
Eucharist. Most people do not understand. They think
our work is medieval. Friar Jean-Claude did understand the vocation of the contemplative and admired
it. He did not patronize us, not once."

I thought I saw a way to thaw her just a bit.

"I wonder, *Mère,* if I could ask that you and the
sisters might pray for my colleague, *la petite* Marie-
Bernadette. This very morning she became the fiancée
of her childhood friend Jacques-Yves."

The forementioned *la petite* blushed happily as she
translated for me. The strategy worked beyond my
expectations. The old woman rose from her chair and
embraced Marie-Bernadette, wished her well, promised prayers, and said that she knew they would be

very happy. Both women were weeping. Then, still holding the hand with the magic ring, the nun turned to me and asked, mostly in mock seriousness, "*Bon.* You approve of this Jacques-Yves, Mr. Bishop?"

"He is a very fortunate young man, *Mère,* and is wise enough to know it."

Mother Marie-Dominique of the Blessed Trinity and the Holy Angels returned to her chair. My petite colleague (I never thought of her as little, by the way) dabbed at her eyes, pleased and flustered.

"I was engaged once," the nun said. "My fiancé died in the war. I came here then. I did not make a mistake. It was so long ago. Yet I pray to him every day. And weep for him too. One should never forget how to weep for a lost love no matter how long ago the loss, *n'est-ce pas,* Mr. Bishop?"

Now I was the one who felt like weeping. Human love is so fragile and yet so durable. And comes in such wondrous varieties.

"*Bien* ... You wish to know more about Friar Jean-Claude. Come, let me show you his room."

Her tone suggested that this was a last-minute decision. You're a clever man Blackie Ryan even if just now you feel like weeping for all the lost loves in the world.

She led us down several more twisted corridors to a large oak door. She opened it with a key from the chain at her belt—all mothers superior in my experience have such chains.

"I have a key to his rooms, Mr. Bishop, because once a week one of us would enter it while he was away and clean it. There was not much work to do. Friar Jean-Claude is a man of impeccable habits."

The quarters of the chaplain of the Convent of Ste-Catherine were Spartan indeed. In the tiny bedroom there was a single bed with an iron frame, a *prie-Dieu* with no pad on the kneeler, a plain crucifix above the bed, and a chair with a thin cushion. The walls were whitewashed stone like that in the nun's office. There were no windows and light such as it was came from two lamps, one by the bed and one by the chair. An alarm clock ticked on a small bed stand. The simple bathroom contained an old-fashioned tub and a single, clear glass window high up on the wall. The floors were stone, covered by several throw rugs.

His study accommodated massive bookshelves on three walls, a frayed easy chair, a battered old desk (with a laptop computer and a small printer), a large armoire, two lamps, and three neatly stacked piles of books next to the chair. A file drawer in the desk seemed to be locked. Light filtered in through two massive stained-glass windows. Like the bedroom and the bathroom, a couple of dubious space heaters provided the heat. A thin carpet covered the stone floor.

The newly constructed (though very ugly) priory of St-Jacques to which the provincial had transferred Jean-Claude would have seemed luxurious in comparison.

"Sister cleaned the room the morning he left us," Mother Marie-Dominique of the Blessed Trinity and the Holy Angels said. "There was never much to clean. *Le Frère* was fastidious. He told me that he felt embarrassed that a woman had to clean his room. I said to him that he was a better housekeeper than most men, but our peace of conscience demand that we do something for him."

"I notice the locked drawer in his desk."

"His private material. He alone had the key to it. When the fathers came to examine the room after he had left us, Father Provincial refused to let them open it."

I examined the books next to his chair: Chenu, Congar, Teilhard, Rahner, Küng, von Balthassar, Geffré, Josua—the great names of the council, most of them in French paperback covers. In another pile he had kept commentaries on the scriptures. All the books were dog-eared and heavily marked. Jean-Claude had done his work.

He had arranged the books on the shelves in alphabetical order. Never immune to the solicitations of vanity, I discreetly checked authors whose names began with "R." Sure enough, there was a copy of *The Achievement of David Tracy* by a certain John B. Ryan.

"It is your book, Mr. Bishop Blackie," Marie-Bernadette, who had been peering over my shoulder exclaimed excitedly. "*Le pauvre* friar read your book. . . . I did not know you wrote books!"

She deftly removed the book from the shelf and thumbed through its pages.

"He read it! See how often he has underlined what you wrote."

"It cannot be an important book, *chérie*." Mother Marie-Dominique of the Blessed Trinity and the Holy Angels laughed behind me. "It has not yet been translated into French." Well, we had won *Mère* Marie-Dominique over to our side.

"*C'est vrai,*" I said modestly.

My estimation of the intelligence of our missing friar soared enormously. He had underlined the proper sentences. Yet why was an allegedly simple, allegedly pious, allegedly transparent young French priest reading a minor commentary by an alas unknown American author on a brilliant, if admittedly difficult, American theologian?

"You see that he was a man of orderly habits, Mr. Bishop. He was never late for the Eucharist in the morning though we rise very early here. He never missed his scheduled times in the confessional. He was punctual and well prepared for our weekly conferences—and we were always behind the grille so he did not know whether anyone was listening. Meanwhile he was working long hours with the students and then preparing his broadcasts on television. *Formidable, n'est-ce pas?*"

"You watched him on TV, *Mère* Marie-Dominique?"

"*Naturellement,* we do not have television here. Friar John-Claude did not have one in his quarters either, even after he began to appear on television. However, at important times—the death of a Pope, the return of *le Général* from Colombey—the friars bring a small set over for us. Father Duchamp told us that we should watch Friar Jean-Claude."

"Were you surprised?"

"That he was on television? *Certainement!* But not by what he said. He was just like he was in his conferences for us—wise, devout, good, and very kind—and said the same things. He was *magnifique!* . . . *Bien sûr*, the strain soon became evident. When sisters discussed his broadcasts at our recreations we worried about him. He was working too hard, doing too much. *Enfin*, he had to appear like what he said was simple and spontaneous. That is not easy, Mr. Bishop, as I'm sure you know."

"*D'accord.*"

We walked out of the door of his suite into the darkened corridor.

"If the friar turned this way and walked a few steps down the corridor, he entered the chapel. In the other direction, a few more steps and there is that door which leads to the alley in the back and it is only a few steps to the metro station at Cardinal Lemoine."

The wooden door was massive enough to resist revolutionary cavalry men who wanted to break in and stable their horses.

We walked back to her office.

"Do you expect he will return, *Mère?*"

She was silent for a moment as she opened the door.

"We pray that he will return, Mr. Bishop. We pray with all our hearts for his return."

"That was not quite my question."

"*Je sais* . . . He has not come back yet. Does not that make it unlikely that he will ever return?"

That didn't quite answer my question.

"Do you think he is still alive?"

"Who would want to take his life? Do not the envious try to destroy the character, not the life?"

"That didn't answer my question either."

She shrugged as if to say that was too bad for you, little American priest. Then she thought better of it.

"What is the purpose of your investigation, Mr. Bishop?" she asked bluntly.

"To learn the truth about Friar Jean-Claude."

"And when you find the truth?"

"I work only for Cardinal Sean Cronin of Chicago, no one else. When I find the truth, I will be under no obligation to do anything which would hurt Jean-Claude or those who love him or ruin his reputation."

"You believe he is still alive, Mr. Bishop?"

"Yes."

"No one else has found him, have they?"

"Mr. Bishop always solves his puzzles," Marie-Bernadette insisted firmly.

"So I understand. . . . How close are you to a solution?"

"I know the solution, *Mère* Marie-Dominique. I have yet to recognize what I know. I will recognize it, however. Soon."

"So *la belle* Marie-Bernadette is correct that you always solve your puzzles?"

"So far. There always is the possibility of a time when I will not solve the puzzle. This will not be that time, however."

I sounded far more confident than I actually was. However, it was appropriate to talk tough with this tough and lovely woman.

"*M. le Cardinal* Cronin is fortunate to have you on his side."

"He has remarked on that occasionally."

She sighed, her mind made up. I was not altogether sure that I wanted to hear the truth she was about to tell me.

"I grew up in the years before the war, Mr. Bishop. We always believe that times were different when we were young. Some days we think life was easier then, some days we think it was different. I cannot say. Yet it is possible that life is more difficult for priests today than it was a half century ago, *n'est-ce pas?*

"Arguably."

"When I was young, it was still the Third Republic—we French had five republics while you poor Americans only have had one. The anticlericals were very strong. Discipline in the Church was very tight. Most priests were poor and surrounded by restrictions. The men in Bernanos's novels, if you are familiar with them."

"I am."

"His *curés de campagne* were marginally more literate

than the peasant priests of centuries ago. Some of them were good and holy and hardworking men, although the memories of the various excesses of the anticlericals forced them to live in fear. You know these things, of course."

"Never from the inside."

"Some drank, some played with little boys, some took lovers. Most lived narrow circumscribed lives in which it could hardly be said that there was much freedom."

"Patently."

"The war broke down many of the barriers in our society. The Church finally accepted the Republic, the Republic finally accepted the Church, both sides clearly with reservations. Then the Vatican Council finally transformed the Church, which was still fighting the revolution, *n'est-ce pas?*"

"Arguably."

Not quite completely, but nonetheless definitively.

"Many priests suddenly found more freedom than their predecessors ever had. There were fewer rules, fewer requirements for acceptable behavior. In the Middle Ages the rules were often broken. It was dangerous, however. One could be scourged or even burned at the stake. Now a priest can do whatever he wants and probably never be caught unless he goes too far."

"Oh yes."

"I do not know whether this is better or worse, but it is the situation."

"It is better, *Mère* Marie-Dominique. As your colleague from Aquino pointed out long ago, virtue is developed by the repetition of free acts."

I knew where the conversation was going and I didn't like it.

"There is not enough support for them, however."

"*D'accord.* . . . Religious communities are more likely to constrain than to support."

"I do not know whether there is less, how does one say, sexual activity now than there used to be."

"Those patterns do not change much over time, *Mère* Marie-Dominique, human nature being what it is."

"Yet it does not seem right in times like our own to forbid young priests sexual pleasure with a wife they love, does it?"

Not an argument I expected to hear from a mother prioress close to eighty.

"Arguably," I said, holding my cards very close to my Bears jacket.

"We know that *les prêtres de campagne* had wives for hundreds of years."

"One person alone could not survive."

"Can many of them survive alone in our time in which it is equally dangerous to be alone in its own way as the fourteenth century?"

Why, I wondered, this long and circuitous approach.

"*Le Frère* Jean-Claude was a friar, *Mère.* Even should the Pope decide tomorrow that secular priests might marry, those in solemn vows . . ."

"One could easily obtain dispensations and continue to serve as secular priests. With a wife."

She smiled and shrugged.

"I do not want to give offense . . ."

"Patently you are defending Jean-Claude."

"*Certainement!* One says to oneself that even if such a splendid and holy young priest needs to bring a woman into this convent at night then there may be something wrong with our rules. Should the Church lose such a good man because the juices in his blood are so strong . . . ?"

Marie-Bernadette's eyes were wide open in astonishment.

"There are answers to your argument, *Mère* Marie-Dominique, which I need not rehearse because you know them as well as I do. *Pour moi,* I wish there were a wider variety of ways of being a priest. I can also understand why a priest under enormous strain can feel the need of loving consolation."

"You yourself have felt such a need?"

I gave my standard answer.

"Only on Sunday afternoons in an empty rectory."

She laughed enthusiastically. Then she sobered immediately.

"Our *pauvre* Jean-Claude brought a woman into this convent on at least two nights, shortly before he disappeared."

"Ah."

Cherchez la femme? Was it all as simple as that? I doubted it. But maybe.

"She was certainly not there on one of the mornings, nor was there any trace of her. The other morning was not on the day we clean his room."

"The friar would surely have been discreet."

"One night, I had been working late in my office on our accounts. I looked out the window and saw a young woman walking down the alley. I was surprised because it is a dangerous place to be walking alone at night. I watched her walk down the alley and turn at the door to the chaplain's suite. She disappeared."

"It was dark."

"Not so dark that I could not recognize the gait and the shape of a woman's body."

"Even through the stained glass?"

"I said to myself that I had fallen asleep and imagined it all. I said that I could not have seen anyone at night through the stained glass. I dismissed it as impossible. Jean-Claude would never do something like that."

"Yet you continued to be suspicious?"

She spread her hands in self-defense.

"One is responsible for the reputation of this convent. One does not wish for a scandal."

"So?"

"I took the subprioress into my confidence. She is a sensible woman, much younger than I, though so is everyone else. We agreed that we would take turns keeping watch from a window on the second floor on subsequent nights for two weeks. If nothing happened, we would dismiss our suspicions as the dreams of a silly old woman who had fallen asleep when she should have been in bed as were all the other women in the convent."

"And nothing happened?"

"Not until the last night of the two weeks. Sister saw the woman go in through Father's door. She said that she was young and attractive."

"Even in the dark?"

"One saw certain outlines."

Marie-Bernadette looked like she had just heard of a death in her family.

"Yet you did not denounce the unfortunate priest?"

"No, Mr. Bishop, we did not."

I said nothing.

"*Premièrement,* we did not know that he had done anything sinful with the woman."

"*D'accord.*"

"Perhaps she could come only that hour for counseling. There was nowhere else where *le pauvre frère* could talk to her at that hour."

Frenchwomen used the word poor in a fashion, not unlike Irishwomen. In fact, it meant "poor dear."

"Arguably."

"We did not have enough proof to complain to Father Provincial."

"He would have demanded more than suspicions?"

"Certainement!"

"You did not search for grounds for further suspicion."

"We did not want to spy on him." She lowered her eyes as if admitting her guilt.

"*Enfin* you did not wish to lose the best chaplain this house ever had."

"Sister said to me, 'Madame, we are not God!' "

"She was quite correct."

"We told ourselves that, even if the young woman was his lover—and we did not know that—perhaps he would give her up, perhaps return to the strict practice of the Dominican rule. We owed it to him to give him a chance for that if one were needed."

"Patently."

"What do you think of our decision, Mr. Bishop?" Marie-Bernadette watched me closely.

"It was a wise and prudent choice, *Mère*. Very sensible, very Christian, *n'est-ce pas,* Marie-Bernadette?"

"*Mais oui,* Mr. Bishop, *très chrétien.*"

That settled that.

"You continued to worry, however."

"Especially that Friday after Easter when he did not return and the police came the next day."

"They did a thorough search, I presume?"

"No, Mr. Bishop, they merely asked us some stupid

questions and glanced at his room to make sure he wasn't hiding there."

Odd. The police weren't searching for him very hard. Someone didn't want him to be found.

"If you should find him, Mr. Bishop, would you please tell him that we wish he would come back."

Her request was as much an act of faith as a request.

"*D'accord.*"

"*Merci.*"

I stood up.

"Thank you, *Mère,* for your candor and courage. You can trust me to respect both. No one besides the two of us and Cardinal Cronin will ever know this part of the story."

"Mr. Bishop Blackie always keeps his word."

I had acquired in this young woman's eyes yet another virtue.

"And *le petit* Jacques-Yves?" *Mère* Marie-Dominique said with a grin.

"Has not he proven this very day his enormous prudence?"

On a note of happy laughter we took our leave. As we circled around the Pantheon on our way back to St-Germain, under a somber sky in which rain, perhaps even a downpour surely lurked, I reflected that Marie-Bernadette would never forget the events of the day of her engagement.

"So you have solved the puzzle, Mr. Bishop," she said duly.

"Oh?"

"*Frère* Jean-Claude ran away with a woman."

"Perhaps."

"*Madame la Prioress* thought so, despite the excuses she made."

"We have no evidence that the excuses were false."

"C'est vrai," she admitted.

"So, young woman, I suspect that a very important young man will be waiting for us on the *rue* Cassette. He expects to see his future wife smiling happily. We can leave the puzzle in God's hands till tomorrow, can we not?"

"Certainement!" she exclaimed cheerfully. "It is a happy day, the happiest yet in my life."

Nonetheless, Marie-Bernadette had grounds to be worried. Like the other Catholic students around the *Sorbonne,* she adored the young Dominican. Modern young people that they were, they were old-fashioned enough to expect that Friars, especially ones who were important to them, would keep their vows. There was no proof that he had not, but grounds for some suspicion.

Could a young priest intelligent enough to read *The Achievement of David Tracy* make such a foolish mistake as to make love in his quarters at the Convent of Ste-Catherine?

How had Cardinal Newman put it, quarry the granite slab with the edge of a razor, anchor a mighty liner with a silken thread and then you will be able to control with mere reason those two monsters, the pride and passion of man.

He would have said humankind today.

In front of the hotel, in his best jeans and sweatshirt I judged, Jacques-Yves was waiting for his future wife. As soon as he saw her he began to walk towards us, a huge, happy smile on his face. As his paced picked up, she walked rapidly ahead of me. The two of them covered the last ten feet which separated them in a single bound and charged into each other's arms.

Then after a moment of incoherent babbling, they separated and kissed one another with intense delicacy. Matters, as the locals would say, have arranged themselves well.

I waited discreetly till that enchanted kiss ended and offered my congratulations. Jacques-Yves hugged me and then his affianced did the same. She told him that I had agreed to preside over their nuptial Eucharist and I was hugged twice more.

"Cardinal Sean is in the hotel *avec madame sa soeur.* They did not like Versailles. They thought it vulgar."

Actually, Nora was the one who had thought it vulgar and Milord Cronin, as is his wont, agreed.

"Did you tell them our secret?" Marie-Bernadette bubbled.

"Without you? *Certainement non!*"

"Then we must go in and tell them and have a little celebration," I insisted.

Doubtless Nora had read the secret in Jacques-Yves's eyes.

We found them in the bar with their afternoon cup of tea. I whispered to the bartender, "A bottle of your best champagne . . . on *M. le Cardinal's* bill of course."

"We have a secret to tell you," Marie-Bernadette said, holding out her ring.

"We are engaged, we will be married soon," Jacques-Yves joined the litany.

"And Bishop Blackie will preside over the Eucharist."

"He'd better." Milord Cronin shook hands with Jacques-Yves with one hand and hugged his bride with the other. Nora kissed them both. The waiter poured our champagne and we toasted the bride and groom, wishing them long years of love together.

"And an eternity together after that," I imparted the final blessing.

"We'll have an engagement dinner tomorrow night,"

Milord decided. "You two be here at six-thirty and we'll celebrate at greater leisure."

The happy couple tried to disagree.

"Never argue with a cardinal," I warned them. "In most matters they are infallible."

So it was arranged.

"Are they really *that* poor, Blackwood?" Nora asked me after, arm in arm, the prospective bride and groom had left us.

In line with my late mother's exhortation to "waste not, want not, especially when it's expensive booze," I emptied the champagne bottle into my flute.

"Unbearably poor. When they turn twenty-five they will receive twenty-five hundred francs a month. A little better than four hundred dollars. They hope to find a room for themselves somewhere."

"She's a virgin, you know, Blackwood," Nora informed me.

"I yield to your expertise in the matter."

"He may be too, though it's harder to tell with a boy. She certainly is."

"In France?" The Cardinal seemed surprised.

"Innocence can exist anywhere," I contended, "although it is a special grace."

"It's time that they get married," Milord observed. "How is your scheme to get them to Chicago coming, Blackwood?"

"The matter arranges itself reasonably well," I said.

"Are you going to talk like a Frenchman for a long time when we get back to Chicago?"

"Arguably."

"Who's working on the deal?"

"My brother Packy . . ."

"Lots of clout there."

"And your good friend Nuala Anne McGrail."

He rolled his eyes as he usually did on the subject of "that one."

"The first team, huh?"

"Only the best."

"They should be able to pull it off. . . . Tell them they can use my name if they need to."

"I already have."

He didn't seem bothered at that.

"Well, they're good kids. Talented too. If we can help them, we should. They're from the neighborhood. We should always help people from the neighborhood when we can."

"From the neighborhood?" Nora asked. "I thought they were from the Rhône Valley."

"They're practically members of the Cathedral parish, which, in case anyone has forgotten it, is still my parish. . . . See to it, Blackwood!"

That settled that.

For Milord Cronin it was a simple matter. We had encountered this nice and talented pair of innocents. We could help them. Therefore we should. I was much more suspicious of the temptation to do good, especially when it changed dramatically the direction of people's lives. Truth to tell, however, when push came to shove, I normally decided that it was better to act than not to act and to leave the rest in the hands of God.

I was reminded that we were to have supper that night with Chuck and Rosemarie O'Malley at *Le Train Bleu* in the *gare de Lyon*.

I believe I made some tasteless remark about coming to Paris to eat in a diner. The Cardinal retaliated with a defamatory comment about the sophistication of the South Side Irish.

In my room, I realized that it would be vain to

attempt to rest my eyes. We had but two more full days in Paris. Tomorrow we would visit the police and learn whether we could bluff them into telling us more than they wanted to. I did not expect them to tell us why their search for Jean-Claude had been so perfunctory. That was a "State secret." However, they might slip and tell us something that we did not already know.

After that there were no other leads. I would spend the following day in a vain attempt to systematize my luggage, finally cramming it all in and sitting on top of the suitcase to zip it up. Then the next day we would fight our way through the mayhem at Charles de Gaulle Airport and leave for home. O'Hare was mayhem too, but it was our mayhem. I found myself yearning for the sight of Lake Michigan and then the towers of the Chicago skyline.

However, one must find Friar Jean-Claude before one permits oneself thoughts of home. What had I learned today. I began to type on my laptop.

At the end of this troubling day, we know two more facts about this troublesome priest.

1) He was much more theologically sophisticated than at first appeared. He had read all the books and then successfully translated them into the rhetoric of traditional piety, a most impressive accomplishment

2) He had so charmed the cloistered nuns that they were unwilling to denounce him to authority although he had brought a woman into his quarters at the convent.

The first fact proved merely that he was a very clever young man. The second was disturbing. Probably the nuns had not imagined the young woman. Probably he had engaged in sexual congress with her. However, I do not know the latter for certain. Yet when I combine the young woman in his quarters with the anguish of his journal, it becomes very likely that he was engaged in an affair of some sort. That being acknowledged, the balance of probabilities leaned in the direction that he had absconded with the woman and was living with her, hopefully nowhere near Paris.

If this is the case, there is little more that I can do. Friar Jean-Claude will appear again, if he ever does, when he is ready to reappear. Yet I feel uneasy with this scenario. It is probable. Indeed it seems likely. However, it is in fact little more than guesswork. I need not have spent the week confirming what many had already guessed. Moreover, I sense that there is something more at work, something more twisted and complicated.

That "something more" may appear the next time the elevator in my brain swings open and reveals to what I already know in my tacit knowledge. It cannot be forced open. It will simply happen.

So I must plod on tomorrow and perhaps the next day. I must gather facts and wait for the strobe light of insight.

Le Train Bleu, it developed, was an artful attempt to re-create the gilded age—purple velvet drapes, Second Empire antiques (confirmed by Nora Cronin), polished brass, bronze lighting fixtures, and waiters clothed to fit the scene. Phony, in my biased judgment. I withheld that judgment out of prudence (after all I was not paying) and respect for the food.

The Cronins and the O'Malleys recalled their experiences of growing up during the Depression and the War. Having been born in 1945, the axial year of the twentieth century, I had no recollection of those days. Places I had never seen lived for the second time this week in their memories—Motto's Pharmacy, Ryan's Magic Tap, Kallas's Pharmacy, Fred's Pool Hall, St. Ursula's school yard, the Ambassador Theater, Park 11, the Chez Paris nightclub. Unlike my generation, these men and women had lived through a momentous turnabout in the country, a line defined in the sand which marked two very different times in their lives.

The Cardinal and Rosemarie had never been poor. However, Chuck and Nora had seen difficult times. They laughed now, but in their eyes I saw difficult memories and residual fear that it might happen again.

The Cardinal told them about the young woman who was helping me on a "small matter" and her fiancé.

Nora shivered, "They're having their own Great Depression, aren't they?"

Chuck turned serious for a moment. "Can we help?"

"Blackwood has taken some measures," Milord Cronin said.

"I have seen to it."

"You snooping around Paris, Blackie?" Chuck asked, mischief in his eyes.

"Hunting for a disappearing priest." I sighed. "Incidentally, the youth unemployment rate here is no worse than that of young African-Americans till very recently."

The elevator rose again from the subbasement of my consciousness. Its door opened slowly. I peered in. The lights were out.

"The difference here, however," Chuck, sometime ambassador to the German Federal Republic, said, "is essentially a deeply flawed economic system. In America it's the residue of slavery and racism."

"Hope," I said, closing the discussion, "is in short supply for both groups, if anything shorter here."

The dinner went on amid much laughter and nostalgia, but the elevator remained stuck down there in the subbasement.

"We have plenty of time," I told myself. "Two whole days if I don't pack."

17

The police officials at the Sûreté reminded me of Robespierre's Committee of Public Safety about to order that someone be sent off to *Madame la Guillotine,* save that they lacked the required three cornered hats. They were lined up across from us behind a long and ornate table in a large and ornate office which was perhaps Second Empire, though I could never be quite sure about such matters. I promptly imagined them as the Three Stooges. Curly, the man in the middle might have been Robespierre. He was young, good-looking and possessed an enormous head of jet-black hair. On second thought, perhaps he worked for Bonaparte. His brown eyes, however, were dull and lifeless, as if there were no one there. He had risen to the role of deputy commissioner (which I think was his title) by hard work and an utter innocence of imagination and compassion. On his right, Larry, a little man with a high forehead and a perpetual sneer, glared at us as if he were about to call in Inspector Maigret and order our arrest. At the other end of the table, bored to tears, sat Moe, a large, bald man with an expensive suit which did not quite fit him anymore. He and Larry were, I gathered, some sort of assistant deputy commissioners.

Patently, their task was to intimidate us. They didn't know that I was beyond such pressures and that, as long as I was along, *Demoiselle* Marie-

Bernadette was also immune to them. She was perhaps wondering how I would deal with these three stooges. We'd let them go through their act and then decide how to scare them into telling us something we needed to know.

They doubtless had real names, but they had not introduced themselves. Larry, Curly, and Moe did as well as another—save arguably Wynken, Blynken, and Nod.

"So, Mr. Ryan," Larry sneered.

"Ah?"

"You realize that you are violating the laws of France? You are conducting a private criminal investigation without having a license from the State. You could be indicted and sent to prison for that crime."

"Indeed," I said, blinking my eyes rapidly behind my Coke-bottle glasses.

"Ours is a secular society that does not tolerate the interjection by the Church of itself into matters of State."

I remained silent.

"The police agencies of France have conducted a thorough investigation of the matter of this vanishing priest. They need no help from the Church or from America."

I smiled blandly.

"This is no small matter, Mr. Ryan," Larry sneered. "You have broken the laws of our Republic."

I continued to stare blankly at them.

"I have refreshed myself," Moe informed me in a basso profundo voice, "on all the measures that the police took to find this priest." He hefted an inch-thick stack of reports. "I can assure you that our investigators left, as you Americans would say, 'no stone unturned.' "

More silence.

Curly joined the game in a high, squeaky voice.

"We have agreed to talk with you at the request of the Cardinal. *En fait* there is nothing that we can tell you."

Three different characters—each playing their assigned role. *Commedia del Arte al'improviso*. A shame, in a way, to disrupt its perfection.

"My first question," I said briskly, "is who were the higher powers who told you to do a cursory investigation of the disappearance of Friar Jean-Claude? Who suggested that it would be much better for the State if you never found him?"

A moment of stony silence, then an eruption of babble. I motioned to Marie-Bernadette to ignore it.

"Virtually everyone I've talked to has told me that the police investigation was sloppy. I don't care about your records, Mr. Moe. Check if you wish, the report on the visit of your investigating officers to the Convent of Ste-Catherine. Does it tell you why they only glanced at the room to make sure he wasn't there but did not search among his belongings for clues?"

Moe thumbed frantically through his dossier.

Larry rose to the occasion, literally. He jumped out of his chair and gestured angrily at me.

"This is outrageous, Mr. Ryan! How dare you insult the honor of France, the honor of the Paris police, and our own personal honor!"

"I have the highest respect for the honor of all involved, particularly of the Paris police, Mr. Larry. The police of this city are respected all over the world for the diligence and the persistence with which they pursue their work. When I find that they are not exercising either diligence or persistence, I conclude the reason is that someone has told them not to. I do not imagine this order originated from you three. You merely passed it on."

"My name is not Mr. Larry."

"Indeed."

"The case still is open," Mr. Moe said, still flipping through his sheaf of reports. "We are still investigating."

"Don't be absurd, Mr. Moe. *Tout le monde* knows that while your statement is technically true there is not a single officer working full-time on it. As far as you are concerned the case is closed. You went through the motions, hoping you wouldn't find Friar Jean-Claude and, *bien sûr,* you didn't find him. Now you are acutely embarrassed because of the miracles at the entrance to the archaeological crypt. You and your masters are terrified that, as the miracles continue, someone will wonder why you have not found Jean-Claude or his body. In the hierarchy of the French State, that someone doubtless outranks those who told you not to find him unless you couldn't help it."

"You think you can find him?" Mr. Curly asked, his voice ascending even higher.

"Arguably."

"What is it you want from us?"

"Your personal conclusion as to what happened."

Curly looked at Moe. The latter shrugged indifferently. He glanced at Larry. The latter sneered, but nodded.

"Very well, Bishop Ryan," Curly squeaked on, "and without any references to your earlier comments, we agree to give you the unofficial judgment that was made here at *Sûreté* about the case of Friar Jean-Claude. Once we made this judgment we thought it inappropriate to pursue the matter further. There would be difficulties if the whole matter came to public attention, especially since there was no crime involved."

"Indeed."

He paused, pondering unemotionally the juggling balls he was trying to balance.

"We came to the conclusion that the unfortunate priest was engaged in an affair of the heart with a student at the *Sorbonne*. One had seen them together often. One had heard reports that there was ample proof of their intimacy. About this matter there was little doubt in the Latin Quarter. We interviewed the woman. She was of no assistance."

"Is she with him now?"

"We have no evidence of that. On the contrary, we believe he has left France. He may return eventually or she may join him. As far as the *Sûreté* is concerned that is a matter of no importance."

"And the young woman's name?"

He hesitated than shrugged.

"Chantal Mercier."

Later, Marie-Bernadette and I stood on the platform of the *Cité* metro station.

"It is not possible," she said sorrowfully. "No one thought there was an affair between Jean-Claude and Chantal. They were not each other's type. It could not have been a secret. Everyone would have known. They have made the story up."

Not for the first time in my life, my intellect had shut down for a rest.

"Arguably."

"We must talk to Chantal. She will tell us that it is absurd."

That seemed as good an idea as any.

"Where is she this time of day?"

"She had a dreadful course in early modern French drama. If she attends the class—and she often does not—after it is finished she walks over to a little café on the *Boulevard* St-Michel behind the *Musée de Cluny*, right near the metro station." She glanced at her watch. "She eats a croissant and a cup of coffee, smokes a cigarette, and perhaps drinks an aperitif. Maybe some of her friends join her. It is a kind of *salon*. She is very bright. Then she takes the metro up to her apartment in *Montmartre*."

"*Montmartre?*"

"She has a very nice apartment on the street across from the funicular which goes to the top of the *butte*, where there is the Church of the *Sacré Coeur*. There is money in her family."

"And a man in her life?"

"She flirts with many men, but as yet she does not find anyone who is her type."

"You never saw her with *Frère* Jean-Claude."

"I cannot say *jamais*. I cannot remember the many times I have talked to her with other people around. Perhaps Jean-Claude was there. It would be strange if he were not, because her table was a place of serious conversation."

"You saw no signs of intimacy between them?"

"When Chantal flirts, you know she is flirting. If she had flirted with Jean-Claude, everyone in the Quarter would know it. They were two of our celebrities. . . . What do you think, Mr. Bishop?"

"I don't know what to think, Marie-Bernadette, except that the police work was sloppy. Chantal Mercier, as one of the celebrities around the *Sorbonne*, might have been an easy target for them, if they wanted to put together an explanation."

"Still, after what we heard yesterday . . ."

"It is disconcerting."

"Chantal would never sneak into a convent in the dark of night for sex, Mr. Bishop Blackie. She didn't have to."

We climbed up the stairs of the *Cluny* metro station, turned a corner and in the bright sunlight, which had returned, saw Chantal sitting at a table and sipping an aperitif. She was wearing a black silk shirt and tight black slacks with a thin crimson sweater around her shoulders. Slimmed-down dragon lady, I thought.

She looked up as we drew near, dashed out of her chair, and hugged Marie-Bernadette fiercely.

They exchanged congratulations and affection in French too rapid for me, though I gathered that Marie-Bernadette had asked her to be the maid of honor at her wedding which, news to me, was now scheduled for two weeks.

"And Mr. Bishop Blackie will preside!" Chantal exclaimed enthusiastically. "*Comme merveilleux!* You are the *faiseur de prodiges.*"

A wonder worker, huh? We would see in a few minutes how wonderful.

She ordered another glass of the green stuff for Marie-Bernadette and the usual Bailey's for me. We toasted one another happily.

"No cigarettes, Chantal?" Marie-Bernadette asked.

"*Mais non, chérie.* I asked what I could do to pray for a wonderful marriage for you and your adorable man. I said I would give up the cigarettes for you."

"And for yourself too. . . . But you don't believe in such things!"

"There are some Catholic customs one cannot escape from."

Time for the wet blanket.

"We need a favor, Chantal," I said carefully.

"Ah, Mr. Bishop, a favor?" her face became a mask, her eyes turned cold and hard. "What would this favor be?"

Did she suspect what was coming?

A dark cloud descended on Marie-Bernadette.

"We would like you to take us to Friar Jean-Claude."

Her lips twisted into an angry rictus of fear. A classic "gotcha."

"You are quite insane," she snapped, much too late to cover up. "Why would I know where he is?"

"You know, Chantal, and we know you know. We wish no harm to either you or Jean-Claude."

She laughed bitterly. "No harm is it? Don't be absurd. You all mean harm."

"The police," my aide tried to intervene gently, "say that you were intimate with him!"

"The police are *merde*! Intimate with him? Ridiculous!"

"The nuns told us a woman who looked like you entered his rooms at Ste-Catherine in the middle of night," I added.

"You stupid priest! Do you think I have to sneak around at night to find sex?"

I struggled to understand her reactions. She was angry, she denied the specific charges. However, she did not deny that she knew where Jean-Claude was. It was probable that she did.

"We want to make trouble for no one. We wish merely to talk to him to clarify what has happened."

"NO! You want to keep your record perfect!" She leaped to her feet. "You are both evil. I thought you were my friends. You have betrayed me!"

She turned and walked rapidly towards the metro station and then disappeared into it.

Marie-Bernadette was crying softly.

"Chantal is very angry," she sniffed. "That means we are right."

"Not quite. It means only that we hit on a very sore spot in her soul. She knows something that frightens her, I think."

"What do we do now, Mr. Bishop?"

"We wait, Marie-Bernadette. Perhaps she will change her mind."

"I have never seen her so angry."

"I fear that I frightened her more than I intended."

"What else could you have done?"

Indeed.

Chantal had left without paying the bill. I picked it up. I also insisted that Marie-Bernadette and I finish our drinks.

We celebrated the newly engaged couple that night in the *Restaurant du Palais-Royal*, a terrace in the gardens of the palace. God cooperated by planting a full moon over the garden. Chuck and Rosemarie joined us, himself with his inevitable camera and photographer's babble. It was a wonderful evening for all.

When she pecked me on the cheek after dinner, the bride-to-be whispered, "It will be all right, Mr. Bishop Blackie. I know that it will."

"Your call," I informed the Deity, as I do in those all-too-numerous occasions when I run out of ideas.

18

"Did our friend Chantal say why she wanted to meet us?" I asked Marie-Bernadette as we bumped along in the *Porte de Chapelle* metro which we had boarded at the *Rennes* station down the street from the hotel. I was thankful that she was with me because I never would have been able to straighten out the mystery of why there were two metro stations within walking distance on totally different lines.

"No, Mr. Bishop, she did not. She does have an apartment up in *Montmartre*, however . . ."

"You did not speak with her?"

"She called one of our friends with a phone and he brought the message over to our commune. . . . Do you think she is the one the police and the *soeurs dominicaines* say was Friar Jean-Claude's lover? The police said the woman was named Chantal."

"She is certainly the woman they had in mind. It does not follow, however, that they were lovers."

I had awakened in the middle of the night, drugged still by the melatonin, convinced that I now understood everything. Content with myself, I fell back to sleep. Alas, when Marie-Bernadette's call from a public telephone jarred me out of my sleep, the insight was gone.

I had volunteered to meet her at the *Abbesses* metro station. She had laughed, quite disrespectfully I thought, and said, "I would be afraid to myself that we might lose you forever."

She was as bad as the porter persons at the Cathedral Rectory who were afraid to let me out of the house without a guide.

So she had met me in the lobby of *l'abbaye,* looking wan and disconsolate in jeans and North Wabash Avenue Irregulars sweatshirt, worried as I was no doubt about what we might find.

"The *Abbesses* metro station," Marie-Bernadette informed me, "is the deepest in Paris."

"Ah?"

I knew all of the tourist facts she was about to tell me since I had memorized the guidebook. However, it would have been churlish of me to spoil her fun.

"It is precisely 285 steps up to the surface. We, however, will ride the lift."

"Excellent."

Milord Cronin and Madame his sister were taking the train to *Chartres.* I had warned them that they would find it the most beautiful church in all the world.

"It was necessary to build the station on the bedrock because the *butte,* as we call the *Montmartre,* is honeycombed like Swiss cheese by the gypsum mines. Even though the mines closed 150 years ago, the government only recently has pumped compressed concrete into them to keep the *butte* from collapsing."

"Provident of them."

"It is called the Mount of the Martyr because St-Denis the Bishop of Paris was beheaded here."

"Being a bishop was never an easy job."

"It is said that he took his head under his arm and walked over to the mount we now call St-Denis. It is not required that we believe that."

"Sort of thing a bishop might do."

"That is where the Basilica of St-Denis is now."

"First Gothic church, it is said," I intervened. "Abbot Suger."

"*Précisément* . . . *Montmartre* is a very nice place, despite some of the *cafés* and the women who wander the streets at night. Quite safe. A *faubourg* we would call it. What is the English word?"

"Suburb, but I suspect that neighborhood would be more accurate."

"It is nicer than Belleville, where we live. . . . That was the last place that the National Guard held out in 1870. They hacked their prisoners to death, including the archbishop." She shivered. "It is not a nice place."

We left the train and entered the vast and crowded elevator.

"As I remember my history," I indulged in the game of matching facts, "the war began here in *Montmartre* when the National Guard executed the two delegates from the government in Versailles, an act which began all the terrible bloodshed."

"We French used to be a crazy people," she said sadly. "We used to think that revolutions would change the world."

A final judgment on hundreds of years of bloody violence dating back to the *Fronde*.

"We must keep our tickets," she informed me as we emerged into the gentle brightness of a perfect autumn day. "We will need them to ride the funicular to the top of the *butte* to see the Church of the Sacred Heart. It is free if we have our metro tickets. Our appointment with Chantal is in forty-five minutes."

I had not been consulted about that part of the trip. I had no desire to see a church which for ugliness was matched only by the shrine at Knock in Ireland.

"The church is not attractive, but the view of our city is."

"Ah."

"Are there views of Chicago that are striking, Mr. Bishop?"

There was a faint touch of longing in her voice, as though she would like to see Chicago someday, but knew it would be impossible.

"You will be the judge of that when you come to visit us."

Montmartre was, as she had suggested, very much a neighborhood—shops, women strolling with children, people talking to one another on the streets. Under the almost unbearably lovely autumn sky, I felt a longing for my own neighborhoods—the Cathedral parish and Beverly, the neighborhood of my youth.

"I would like that very much...."

She had no idea of the plots which the North Wabash Avenue Irregulars were hatching. Did we dare intervene in her young life as gods swinging down on the stage from their machine? Who did we think we were? By what rights did the Ryan Clan and the Irregulars take over people's lives?

Because they could of course.

"You could never leave France permanently," I said as we lined up for the funicular ride up to the top of the *butte*, a ride against which both my inner ear and my stomach prepared to protest, "could you?"

"Jacques-Yves and I speak about this often. Many of our friends say they could never leave France. We say that we would be sad to leave. Still we would leave. For us France promises only a life of poverty, of begging like I was when you first met me in front of St-Germain."

"I see," I said, partially freed from my worries of doing too much good.

"Except who wants two mediocre musicians?"

"Promising musicians," I corrected her.

"Without training."

"Or perhaps Celtic minstrels?"

"Oh yes, that would be much fun. . . . But who needs Celtic minstrels?"

Not wanting to get her hopes up, I didn't answer that question. There were many Celtic minstrels, but few who possessed the fire of these two gentle, young innocents.

I survived the funicular ride, the climb up to the church, and even its aggressive ugliness. Inside I prayed to the One in Charge that He protect my two young friends and that, if it be Her will, She would guide their paths to a better life than they could have dreamed possible.

I also prayed for Friar Jean-Claude and for wisdom in my search for him.

"Over there is St-Denis, where the bishop walked with his head in his arm," Marie-Bernadette said to me as we left the darkness of the church for the warmth and color of September in Paris.

"A bit of a walk . . . Some of us even have heads," I replied, "but do not know how to use them."

She giggled. "You will solve the mystery," she assured me, "perhaps today, *n'est-ce pas?*"

"Perhaps."

The view of Paris from the *butte* was impressive enough, though nothing like the view of Chicago from the John Hancock Center in my parish. But then I am arguably a biased Chicago chauvinist.

Chantal was waiting for us at the entrance to the metro station. She was wearing tight black jeans and a white blouse and skillfully administered makeup. Nonetheless, she seemed wan and vulnerable. Doubtless she had slept little the night before. We greeted one another cordially enough, as though the little scene in the *place de Cluny* had not happened. We began to walk in the opposite direction from the *butte*.

"We are going to the *Cimetière Montmartre*," Chantal informed us. "Our French cemeteries, Mr. Bishop," she said, "are as much museums as burial grounds. "While our little *Montmartre* cemetery is not as elaborate as that of *Père Lachaise*, it still has its famous people. Emile Zola, whom I suspect you wouldn't like, was buried here for a time, but now he rests in the Pantheon."

"I would quite agree with him," I responded, "that clericalism is the enemy."

She smiled briefly.

"Mr. Bishop Blackie is a radical," Marie-Bernadette assured her. "He doesn't like *Sacré Coeur*."

"Perhaps he merely has good taste."

Inside the *cimetière* Chantal showed us the tombs of Stendhal, Dumas, Offenbach, and Degas and the tomb of Hector Berlioz, safely tucked in between his two wives. I made polite sounds of approval. In truth I did not especially like cemeteries. Did not the Boss say, "let the dead bury their dead?"

I wondered about Chantal as we strolled along the quiet walks of the cemetery. I assumed that she would show us a tomb which she would claim was that of Jean-Claude Chrétien. She seemed to be the only one of the young people I had met who did not have a hyphenated name. Given the custom, if she were really named after the saint, should she not be Jeanne-Chantal or even Jeanne-Françoise-Chantal. However, they did not seem to pile up three names, only two.

We turned a corner in the path and came upon a small section of new tombs with modest headstones. Yes, indeed: we were to be shown a tomb in which Jean-Claude Chrétien would be alleged to be buried.

Then the illumination which had teased me and slipped away so often, exploded from the dim sub-basements of my brain into full consciousness. The elevator door opened and remained open. Blackie Ryan, I informed myself you are a complete and absolute idiot and you have been for many days now.

Could it be?

Of course it was! It fit everything we knew!

Remarkable! *Remarquable!*

Even fascinating!

My heart pounded vigorously. With difficulty I restrained a smile.

Then I felt infinitely sad. Such a terrible tragedy. I wished that Marie-Bernadette was not with us. No, I was glad she was here. There was much healing to be done and little time to do it.

"You see, Mr. Bishop," Chantal said, "the tomb of Friar Jean-Claude?"

She gestured at a headstone which said simply, "J. Chrétien 1969–2000."

"I see it," I agreed.

"When the furor about his death dies down, we shall add his full name. It is not time now."

"Will it ever be?"

"In the world of the mass media, men are forgotten very quickly."

"Saints, even saints who work miracles?"

"He was a very good man, but not a saint."

"Many of the people of France think that he is."

"They will forget him. . . . I helped him escape, you understand?"

"Oh, yes," I agreed. I understood a lot more too. The elevator door remained wide-open for the first time. I saw the whole astonishing picture. *Etonnement!*

"He had a fatal disease. We need not trouble ourselves as to what it was. Not a sexually transmitted disease. You will understand that he wanted to die privately, away from the noise of publicity. I helped him slip away and then took him to a place where they would care for him lovingly. A priest was with him at the end. A mass was said privately. Now he is with God, if there is a God."

"Indeed."

"You must believe, Mr. Bishop Blackie, that Jean-Claude is buried under that stone. You could demand that he be exhumed . . ."

"That will hardly be necessary," I said. "I believe that you are telling me the truth, Jeanne-Chantal. Your brother Jean-Claude is indeed buried underneath this ground and is surely with God."

Marie-Bernadette's pretty face locked in a deep frown. She was not quite sure what was happening, but didn't like it very much. I could not blame her.

"I have told you the truth," Jeanne-Chantal said, her lips quivering in fear. "Is that not enough?"

"You have not lied," I admitted. "You have not, however, told the whole truth. You did help your brother, your twin brother indeed, disappear, you did see to his burial, he is indeed buried here. What you omitted was the fact that he died five years ago in Rome."

"You cannot prove that!" she spit out furiously. "You can't prove a thing."

"Jeanne-Chantal," I said gently because now the healing must begin, "I do not need to prove anything. I do not represent the police or a *juge d'instruction*, nor the Archdiocese of Paris, nor the Dominican Order. I represent only Cardinal Cronin. Your secret will not go beyond the three of us, save for the Cardinal and of course Jacques-Yves."

The young woman burst into tears. Marie-Bernadette threw her arms around Jeanne-Chantal and led her to a bench. Hands jammed into the pockets of my Bulls jacket, I waited for the sobbing to stop. When Jeanne-Chantal finally gained control of herself and wiped her eyes with a tissue that the good Marie-Bernadette provided, I began my story.

"It was easy to escape from the archaeological site. You left your companions behind, darted into one of the more elaborate ruins, pulled off your wig, your jeans, and your turtleneck and jammed them into your briefcase. Now you were a young woman again with a womanly figure under a tee shirt perhaps and a tourist's shorts. Your hair was straight and short. You were carrying a briefcase just as Jean-Claude always did, perhaps bulging a little, but not suspiciously. You had accomplished this change many times before and, skilled actress that you are, could do it quickly. Maybe you wore sunglasses. You strolled by the admissions desk, smiled at the clerks, bid them good day in your woman's voice and walked out into the sunlight. You turned towards the Cathedral, slipped into the tunnel, and out in the Ste-Chapelle. Then you disappeared into the Paris crowds. Even the most skilled cop would not have recognized you. Doubtless you disposed of the remains of Jean-Claude in a place where they would not be found. Friar Jean-Claude was dead, this time permanently. He could not have survived after he had moved into the new priory of St-Jacques."

"My brother said that when they made me leave the convent of the nuns it would be a sign from God,"

Jeanne-Chantal said, dabbing at her eyes for a final time. Then she removed makeup from her purse and repaired the damage caused by her tears.

"Chantal is *Frère* Jean-Claude?" Marie-Bernadette demanded. "How can this be? Did she not watch him with us on television? Did she not make fun of him?"

Jeanne-Chantal hugged her young friend. "*Chérie*, the programs were all taped, *n'est-ce pas*? I did think that Jean-Claude was funny even if I were playing him. I laughed at him often when he was still alive. We were twins, just as Mr. Bishop Blackie, has guessed. We loved each other very much. *Bien sûr*, we laughed at each other."

Marie-Bernadette looked at me for confirmation. I nodded.

"You must realize how close we were when we were growing up. We played a game of saying what the other was going to say before it was said. We loved each other so very much. We played very little with other children because we enjoyed each other more. There was nothing that we would not do for one another. Nothing. So when he knew he could not be a priest and wanted me to replace him if for only a time, I could not refuse, *n'est-ce pas*?

"It was an Irish Dominican who suggested this"—I hesitated for the right word and settled for—"impersonation?"

"Oh, no! Two of them helped us. It would have been impossible without them. However, it was Jean-Claude's idea. He wanted to be a priest so passionately. He knew he would not live long enough. He became obsessed with the plan that I should take his place. I know it seems insane now, but, because of my love for him, it seemed quite sane then. He was, you see, the one with the deep religious faith like *Madame ma Mère.* I was the skeptic like *M. mon Père.* I believed in nothing. We were of different gender and different religions but otherwise we were almost the same person."

"So you saw nothing sacrilegious about acting as a priest for a few weeks to keep him happy during his last days?"

"Not at all. I thought it was amusing, a challenge to my skills as an actor. I am an alto, he was a tenor," she said, easily changing her voice to that of the priest on television. "I could drop my voice an octave when a conversation began so I sounded like him. Then people didn't notice."

The young woman was relaxing, confident now that I was not an avenging angel.

"You were shielded by your friends at San Clemente?"

"It was easy there. A Dominican habit"—she gestured at her slight figure—"can cover many things. At Ste-Catherine's, of course, I had all the privacy I needed. I left my woman things in a locker in a metro station. It would not have been helpful for the nun who cleaned my room to have discovered any traces of menstrual blood or its anticipation. At first my . . . my little drama frightened me. So many things could have gone wrong. Then I became a polished professional on a great adventure. Then perhaps I became careless."

"You did not think of yourself as a priest?"

"*Pas du tout.* I was an actress playing a challenging and difficult role. It was easy with the nuns. I could slip out of my private suite at night and be a woman again. I had to do that to protect my sanity . . . I did not violate my vow of chastity, however. I could not do that. . . . I tried and could not. Perhaps by then I had become a priest most of the time."

"But you had made no vow of chastity," I said.

I thought I knew the psychological condition Jeanne-Chantal had created for herself, yet I wanted to hear about it from her.

"Jean-Claude had," she said sadly, glancing at her brother's gravestone. "I felt I had to keep it for him. I still keep it. Once I stopped being a priest it was not *très difficile*. Soon perhaps I will begin to search for a man with whom I can share the rest of my life, perhaps even all my secrets."

"The nuns thought you had a woman visitor at night," I said softly. "They admired you so much that they decided not to report you."

"The old dears!" she exclaimed with a broad grin. "I loved them all . . . I usually became Jean-Claude in a woman's washroom. Towards the end I fear I became careless."

"That," I said, "was the crucial clue which I missed for far too long. The nuns, who were nothing if not good observers, saw a woman come into the suite but never saw one coming out. It should have been obvious that she came out the next morning as Jean-Claude."

"Those nights saved my sanity, Bishop Blackie. I could be a woman again, act like a woman, talk like a woman, smoke like a woman, laugh like a woman, even flirt like a woman. Then the demands of the priesthood—it is so demanding, is it not, would call me back. I would be exhausted when they were over. So I would wear my woman things back to the suite at the convent. Then the next morning I would put them in my briefcase and return them to their hiding place in the metro station."

"The police thought that Jean-Claude was involved with a woman named Chantal."

She threw back her head and laughed. "That is very funny! Oh, yes, he was very much involved with a woman named Chantal! It is amusing, is it not, Mr. Bishop?"

"When did you first begin to think of yourself as a priest?"

"*Je ne sais pas*... When everyone treats you like a priest and you put yourself inside of the role of a priest, you begin to think and act like one. I did not worry about it because I knew I would play the role only a short time, till my brother died."

"And you brought his body back to France," I said gently, "buried him up here, and bought your apartment on the *butte,* presumably from your still very ample inheritance, so that sometimes you could be close to him?"

"You know too much, Mr. Bishop. You understand me too well. Or am I," she laughed again, "as transparent as they thought Friar Jean-Claude was on television?"

"He was very transparent, as are you," I murmured.

"You wonder," she said, rising from the bench, "why I continued to act like a priest? Come let us have a cup of tea and an apéritif. I know a wonderful little café where we can talk quietly."

"You read Mr. Bishop Blackie's book," Marie-Bernadette chirped excitedly as we climbed up the *butte*.

"Really! . . . You wrote the book about *Pere* Tracy?"

"I must say that I thought you had underlined it wisely."

The two women laughed at my discomfiture.

"It was such a sweet book, I never thought a bishop could have written it."

My brilliant doctoral dissertation sweet? *Hélas!* as the locals would say. The next step would be for Jeanne-Chantal to decide, as my assistant had some time ago, that I was cute, *très malin, n'est-ce pas?*" It has been my lifelong fate to make the journey from a dangerously brilliant detective to "sweet" and "cute" in a humiliatingly short period of time.

This wonderful little café, near the *Abbesses* metro station, also had delightful French pastries, in honor of which I did not pollute my palate with a Bailey's. We sat in a dark quiet corner where no one could overhear perhaps the strangest conversation in the history of the *Montmartre*.

Jeanne-Chantal poured the tea for us and raised a very French eyebrow when I told her that I drank it black. American savage.

"*Bon.* It was easy to be a priest. Jean-Claude," she resumed her story which now she was eager to tell, "and I had similar education. I knew all the religious words and phrases and doctrines as well as he did, though I never believed them. I knew how he said the words. I could easily imitate the fervor of his faith. The good nuns loved it, even the more sophisticated ones. When I stumbled in my first attempts at presiding over the Eucharist, they thought it was because I was a newly ordained priest still not familiar with the ceremony. At first I felt a little guilty preaching to them when I had no belief and giving them the Eucharist in which I did not believe either and which I was not even capable of making present. . . . Or was I, Mr. Bishop Blackie?"

She looked at me quizzically, a touch of hope in her eyes.

"The Pope would not think so," I replied. "I'm sure God was pleased with the love between you and the sisters."

"They did love me. I have never really been loved since our parents died, except for Jean-Claude, of course. Or was it Jean-Claude they loved? I can no longer separate the two of us."

"You liked being a priest so much," Marie-Bernadette interjected, touching Jeanne-Chantal's hand, "that even when you had fulfilled your promise to Jean-Claude, you continued to be one?"

"At first," she said sadly, "I liked the game I was playing, I enjoyed deceiving everyone, I would laugh myself to sleep at night. Then the laughter died. I hated myself for my treachery. Then . . ."

"Then," Marie-Bernadette continued, "you found that you liked being a priest. As Mr. Bishop said to me 'it's not difficult being a priest when you like the work the priest does.' "

And we all know that Mr. Bishop is always right, *n'est-ce pas?*

"I don't know when it happened," Jeanne-Chantal said sadly. "I suppose that it was gradual. Not only did I like being a priest. I began to think of myself as a priest. I would tell Jean-Claude when I said my prayers at night that he had made me a priest and I was now perhaps a better priest than he would have been. . . . It was the way we used to talk to one another. Then towards the end I *was* a priest."

She was not the first actor who overidentified with her role. Bela Lugosi, the famous Dracula, demanded that he be buried in his Dracula garb.

"So," my good translator continued her interrogation, "you even began to pray?"

"*Mais oui!* Are not priests supposed to pray, *chérie?*

I prayed before I believed. I recited my lines and then as time went on I believed them. Jean-Claude had made me a priest so that he could make me a Catholic!" She laughed wryly. "It was the sort of thing that *mon chèr frère* would do. And then we would both laugh at it."

"You could have left the nuns after you buried your twin's body over in the *cimetière,*" I said as I polished off my third pastry. "You could not, however, leave the students. The nuns did not need you. The students did."

"C'est vrai. You do know everything, Mr. Bishop, don't you? . . . The young people, like *la petite* Marie-Bernadette"—she touched the girl's hand—"did need a priest who understood them, especially the young women. I was not Jean-Claude the student chaplain. I knew it could not last. I knew it might end badly. Yet they had become my . . . dare I say . . . my vocation?"

"You began to read books about theology and scripture?"

"Certainement! So I could preach better. I was glad I did when *they* had their silly little inquisition. . . . Did you read it, Mr. Bishop Blackie? Wasn't it funny?"

I sighed. "You enjoyed every minute of it. I had the key to the puzzle even then. I said you sounded like Ste-Jeanne or Ste-Bernadette. I should have realized that only a woman could tie men in such knots."

"And the television?" Marie-Bernadette asked with a worried frown.

"At first I thought it was all foolish. I complained to my brother that he had put me in a very dangerous situation. I was certain that people would see through my disguise on the TV screen."

"You even tried to tell us," my translator remem-

bered, "that you thought Jean-Claude looked femi-
nine. We all laughed at you."

"Yet the disguise was wearing thin after all the
years, was it not?" I asked.

"Very thin, Mr. Bishop. My friend Friar Marcel
told me I looked exhausted. The nuns prayed for my
health. I could not sleep at night. I worked very hard
for my broadcasts. I wrote them and then memorized
them and practiced them. Everyone said how natural
I was. They did not understand that I was now an
actor playing two roles. I believed in what I was saying. I was terrified of the scandal should I be found
out. More and more I wondered what *le bon Dieu*
thought of me. I knew that eventually I would crack."

"So you decided to disappear before that happened?"

"I prayed over it, Mr. Bishop. I begged God to tell
me what to do. I knew that many people liked my
silly homilies and that I was helping them in their
lives. I also knew how shocked they would be when
I was revealed as a fraud."

"And God told you to quit while you were ahead?"
She laughed again.

"Something like that. . . . It was very easy to arrange. Indeed, I did it on the spur of the moment
when I saw the opportunity. I had hoped that day to
come up here to calm my nerves. So I wore my Chantal shorts and tee shirt under my Jean-Claude clothes
and my woman's lingerie. Jean-Claude walked into the
crypt with his two colleagues, slipped ahead of them,
hid in one of the Roman homes, and became Jeanne-
Chantal with her shorts and very tight tee shirt and
her taunting breasts and sunglasses and a dab of lip-
stick. I shoved Jean-Claude into my briefcase. After
they had all dashed out to search for me, I sauntered

out of the crypt and up the stairs. I stood right behind them and listened to them talk. I felt guilty because I had made them worry, but they would have suffered far more if the truth should become known. I stood right in front of them to see if they would recognize me. They did not. . . . Nor did you, *chérie*. You did not once realize that I was also Jean-Claude."

"Even now," Marie-Bernadette admitted, "I know you are Jean-Claude but it is impossible. You are still Chantal."

"It was a risky strategy," I observed, "but then the whole five years was risky. Early on, as you have said, you enjoyed the risk."

"Even to the end, I enjoyed it, though I feared I might be going mad. Yet I had to flee from that pleasure. . . . As you said, I escaped through the tunnel. You did not guess that I boarded the metro at *Cité*, changed to the purple line at *Châtelet* and rode up here to *Montmartre. Tres ingénu, n'est-ce pas?*"

"Your breasts are very pretty, Jeanne-Chantal," my translator insisted. "It was unfortunate that you had to hide them all those years."

Jeanne-Chantal blushed to the tips of her hair.

"*Bon.* It was wonderful to be a woman again," she said. "I drank half a bottle of champagne in my apartment that night to celebrate. I was astonished by the reaction the next morning. I had no idea how important Jean-Claude was. However, Jean-Claude was dead, was he not? Then there were the flowers and the reports of miracles. I worked no miracles, Mr. Bishop, believe me!"

"As Jean-Claude said in his talks, who are we to put limits on what God can do?"

"*C'est vrai.* Still I don't think there are any miracles."

"Your twin did, however, perform one wonder,

even if it does not measure in as a miracle."

"What was that!"

"He made you a good Catholic," Marie-Bernadette insisted. "Mr. Bishop is right."

Jeanne-Chantal shrugged.

"Sometimes I thought he was whispering in my ear. Or inside my head. And of course laughing at me. Or acting through my body and my soul. You know, Mr. Bishop, how close twins are. Even death . . . does not seem to stop that." Bemused, she shook her head, trying to understand what had happened. "Sometimes I *was* Jean-Claude."

"Merveilleux!" Marie-Bernadette exclaimed.

"I don't know, *ma petite*. He was a much better person than I. I always knew that. Somehow he has made me more like himself. He always wanted to do that too."

Grace was at work everywhere in this strange story.

"I thought the baron and baroness were silly foolish people. I never wanted to have anything to do with rich and dumb Royalists. Bah! I said they should all have gone to the guillotine. Yet, I had to be nice to them when they befriended me. I did not want their money and in truth they never offered it to me after I had declined for the first time. They are not intelligent but they have a certain dignity that I came to respect. Their silly notion that I would remake the people of France and then the *Duc* could become king was, after all, harmless. Then, despite all my wishes to the contrary, I came to like them. I helped them a little in their marriage, I think. They are happier now. I confess that I miss them."

Marie-Bernadette remained silent. Too much grace—strange grace, the work of a God who by Her own admission is strange.

"And Sarah and Pierre?"

"You make me feel guilty, Mr. Bishop. I loved them too. Such good, kind people under their veneer of tough journalists. Only after I worked my little magic trick, did I realize how much they would worry about me. I did not want them to suffer, but then it was too late. It would have been worse for them if *tout le monde* found out what I really was. I did not think . . ." She paused. "When I started my . . . my impersonation how many people I would hurt."

"And perhaps help too."

She shook her head dubiously.

"I don't know that, Mr. Bishop."

"Everyone was better for knowing you," Marie-Bernadette maintained. "That is why you miss them."

"Not as much," this haunted young women went on, "as I miss the students. I was a very arrogant young woman. I thought that most young students, even those a few years younger than me, were boring. Jean-Claude forced me to change my mind. I had to be open and humble with all of you, *ma petite chérie*. I had to love you and let you love me. You made me very happy. . . . I miss you."

She struggled with her tears again.

"You see us often down in the Latin Quarter," Marie-Bernadette argued.

"But as Chantal—or Jeanne-Chantal perhaps now. Don't you see, Marie-Bernadette. I do not see you as Jean-Claude. That changes everything."

"A great miracle!" Marie-Bernadette whispered softly. "God and Jean-Claude changed you and changed us."

"It was very clever of both Jean-Claude and God. However, I will have nothing to do with miracles. I have worked no miracles. I will not accept that."

"Perhaps your brother is responsible for the miracles."

She was startled and then added with a wry grin. "That would be just like him."

"The police came to see you?" I asked, steering away from the intense emotions, for the moment anyway.

"Not up here. They interviewed me down in the Latin Quarter. They asked many stupid questions. They claimed that I was the lover of Friar Jean-Claude. Many people had seen us together. Was that not hilarious? No one could ever have seen us together, *n'est-ce pas?*

"Perhaps your opinions on him gave some people the idea that you loved him."

"The police were not trying very hard to find Jean-Claude. All they knew was that I was Chantal Mercier. The identity papers that I had purchased told them so. Jeanne-Chantal had died in Italy. Jean-Claude had disappeared in Paris. They did not recognize me. Soon they lost interest in me. I then became confident that no one would ever find out. I did not like it, Mr. Bishop, when you came around asking questions. I thought you were far more dangerous than the cops. I was right, *n'est-ce pas?*"

"Mr. Bishop always solves his puzzles," Marie-Bernadette said proudly.

"What was the hint?" Jeanne-Chantal asked meekly. "Why did you look at me and see my brother?"

"Rather I think I looked at your brother and saw you. I had been told you were twins. As I explained to *la petite* Marie-Bernadette, I do not reason to my solutions like M. Poirot or Mr. Holmes. I see them like that other detective Father Brown in a moment of illumination. It is very difficult to sort out the steps in the process. Your name is Chantal. I thought idly that, if you had the kind of hyphenated name that seems so popular in France, your name might well be Jeanne-Chantal like the saint who is patently your patron. Then I realized that I had heard that Jean-Claude's dead twin sister was called Jeanne. Twins—Jean-Claude and Jeanne-Chantal. The names parents might give twins with matching initials. All speculation until finally I glanced at you and realized that you looked exactly like the friar on television with short hair and an ingeniously concealed figure. From that perspective all the other aspects of Jean-Claude's story fit perfectly. The woman who came into the convent but did not come out. The womanly wit with which you fended off the theological commission. Then finally, I remembered that several of the people we interviewed said that on rare occasions you smiled magically at them. It was not so much magic as a woman's smile of affection—ordinary in a woman, magical in a man."

The three of us sighed together.

"So it is all over," Jeanne-Chantal said. "What will happen now?"

"Not much," I said. "I will tell Cardinal Cronin. He will enjoy the story. . . . It is, after all, a remarkable story. He will tell the *archevêque de Paris* the absolute truth, Jean-Claude Chrétien is buried in *Cimetière Montmartre*. He died of a particularly virulent form of tuberculosis. He wanted to die privately, away from all the publicity. He had the sacraments at the end and a Mass was said."

"And what will the Cardinal do?"

"Virtually nothing, except to hope that the flowers at the crypt and the miracles stop. To reveal where Jean-Claude's body is would complicate life for the

Catholic Church in Paris. The secret will remain reasonably safe, though there will be certain obscure rumors. The real secret will remain a secret for a long time."

"Forever!" Jeanne-Chantal pleaded.

"At least till the Catholic Church changes its mind on the ordination of women."

"That will never happen!" Jeanne-Chantal insisted.

"As a sometime president of the United States once remarked, never say never because never is a long time."

Jeanne-Chantal was silent for a couple of moments. Then she nodded. "I will worry about what that would mean for me when and if it happens."

"Précisément."

"Will you have to tell anyone else?"

"I will personally pass on my conclusion to Father François—the same message that Cardinal Cronin gives his Parisian counterpart: Friar Jean-Claude died a holy death in the presence of a priest, received a Christian burial and is buried in a grave that is tended by those who loved him."

"That is all true," Jeanne-Chantal shrugged. "Anyone else?

"I will keep my promise to our mutual friend *Père* Laurent Renault that there is no reason why he and his team should not continue their analysis of your work!"

"What!" Her eyes opened wide.

"Père Renault and his colleagues believe that your homilies integrated the insights of the Second Vatican Council and the rhetoric of traditional piety better than anyone has done in the last thirty-five years. He thinks your work is sophisticated and intelligent and its style needs to be imitated."

"Impossible!"

"Arguably. However, he expects to find marked passages in your theology books which correspond to your broadcasts. Thus he thinks your remarks on the Holy Spirit show the influence of your great Dominican colleague Cardinal Congar."

"Mais certainement," she said shaken, but pleased, by this appraisal. "When I would pray to Jean-Claude sometimes at night I would tell him that I knew more theology than he did. . . . I will read *Père* Renault with great interest."

"Doubtless."

"What happened to the folder I left on my desk at the station? I was so nervous about what I intended I forgot to lock it up. Did the police find it?"

"Sarah hid it for you."

She nodded in relief.

"I hoped she would."

More silence. I motioned for the *compte*. Jeanne-Chantal snatched it from my hand.

"I have one more question, Mr. Bishop Blackie, if I may ask it?"

I knew what it was.

"Of course."

"What about all the Eucharists, all the sacraments of reconciliation? Were they valid?"

She was using the liturgically correct term. Kids born after 1965 almost never heard "Mass" or "Confession."

"What do you think?"

"The Pope would say that they were not, *n'est-ce pas?*"

"D'accord."

"And what would God say?"

"What do you think, Jeanne-Chantal?"

"Maybe He would laugh and say that was a silly

question and I should let Him worry about it."

"Her," I said automatically.

Both my devout French Catholic women gasped in surprise and then grinned together.

"God is not angry at me?" Jeanne-Chantal asked hesitantly.

"You have forgotten your own sermons."

"You suggest that God is proud of my deception?"

"Minimally, God is proud of you Her beloved child and of all the good work you've done in His name. Is that not enough?"

"If I believe what Friar Jean-Claude said on television, it is certainly enough."

"*C'est vrai,*" Marie-Bernadette said.

Jeanne-Chantal began to weep again. Then she embraced me.

"*Merci,* Mr. Bishop, you have saved me from madness."

That I very much doubted. God and Jean-Claude had used me as their willing tool.

"I almost said to you both yesterday, '*Je suis Jean-Claude.*' I was too frightened. Last night I could not sleep. I resolved that I would carry out the deception. Yet so much I wanted to talk about it. Thank *le bon Dieu* that you solved the puzzle and I could talk."

"A huge burden has lifted?"

"I have confessed all my sins. Could you please give me absolution."

I did.

"It will be all right now," Marie-Bernadette said confidently. "Only Bishop Blackie and Cardinal Sean and Jacques-Yves and I will know that the maid of honor at my wedding will be a priest!"

Epilogue

"I'll be damned!" Sean Cronin exclaimed. "Not very likely," I said in dissent.

"Are you sure that it's all true?"

"Oh yes."

He pondered the story for a moment.

"She became her brother?"

"At some point she was perhaps more Jean-Claude than Jeanne-Chantal. . . . She had the good sense to desert the drama while she was still sane."

"Tough young woman."

"Patently."

"She was a damn good priest, wasn't she, Blackwood?"

"Indeed."

"It just goes to show you," he said with a faintly ironic laugh.

Always the discreet auxiliary bishop, I did not inquire what it went to show me.

"Our mutual friend in Rome wouldn't like it."

"What the poor man doesn't know won't hurt him."

"She sure fooled them all, didn't she?" he said, rubbing his hands in satisfaction. "As your friend Nuala Anne would say, good on her."

"Arguably."

Two days later we flew home to Chicago. Lake Michigan never looked so good. But two weeks after that return we had to fly to France for the marriage of Jacques-Yves and Marie-Bernadette in Valence. Mr. Cardinal presided and I said the Mass, oops, presided over the Eucharist, and preached. The celebration was in a small country church outside of the city surrounded by vineyards under a warm late-autumn sun with the Rhône glittering in the distance.

Cardinal Sean (usually pronounced "Jean") and *la belle* Nuala Anne were the center of attention, though so graceful is their charm that they directed that attention to the glowing bride and the dreamy groom. As for *le petit evéque,* arguably *le pauvre petit evéque,* no one noticed him save for the children. Even they abandoned him when during the party the aforementioned Nuala Anne led the urchins, including her own Nellie and Micky in various ditties, the first of which was appropriately "Sur le Pont d'Avignon."

There was unaccountably applause for him after the exchange of vows when both the bride and the maid of honor (Jeanne-Chantal naturally) embraced him enthusiastically. He soon slipped back into his deserved (some say practiced) obscurity.

I had told my notorious Celtic story of why God made strawberries—*Pourquoi le bon Dieu a-t-il fait les fraises*—much to the delight of all the self-proclaimed Celts in the congregation, although, as I explained, in fact the story came from a Cherokee princess named Gail Ross. The bride had to translate the story, with much giggling. All arranged itself well.

Once upon a time, long, long ago, there was Earth Maker and First Man and First Woman. They lived in a whitewashed stone cottage on the edge of a green field with a silver lake and a road leaving over the hills and out beyond. First Man and First Woman were very much in love and very happy together. Earth Maker was pleased with himself because it appeared that his experiment of creating male and female had been a huge success. Oh, they argued a few times a week, but never anything serious.

Then one day they had a terrible fight. They forgot what they were fighting about and fought about who had started it and then about what the fight was about.

Finally First Woman was fed up. You're nothing but a loudmouth braggart! she said, and stormed out of the cottage and across the green field and by the silver lake and over the hill and out beyond.

First Man sat back in his rocking chair, lit his pipe, and sighed happily. Well, at last we'll have some peace and quiet around here. The woman has a terrible mouth on her.

But as the sun set and turned the silver lake rose gold, he realized he was hungry. Woman, he shouted, I want my tea. But there was no woman to make the tea. Poor First Man could not even boil water. So he had to be content with half of a cold pratie (which is what the Irish call a potato). Then as a chill came over the cottage and First Man felt lonely altogether, he sighed again, let his pipe go out, and felt he needed a good night's sleep. He didn't light the fire because, truth to tell, he wasn't very good at such things. First Woman did all the fire lighting in their house because she could start fires in a second.

The poor fella shivered something awful when he pulled the covers over himself. Well, he told himself, she did keep the bed warm at night. He didn't sleep very well and when he woke there was a terrible hunger on him. Woman, he shouted, I want me tea! Then he realized that there was no woman and no tea. So he had to be satisfied with the other half of the cold pratie.

Well, he was sitting in front of the cold fireplace, puffing on a cold pipe, wrapped in a thin blanket, when Earth Maker appeared.

Let me see now said Earth Maker. This is earth and I made ye male and female. And you're the male. Where's herself?

She's gone, your reverence.

Gone?

Gone!

Why's she gone?

We had a fight!

You never did!

We did!

And she left you?

She did, your reverence.

You're a pair of eejits!

Yes, your reverence.

Do you still love her?

Oh yes, your reverence, something terrible!

Well then, man, off your rocking chair and after her!

She's long gone, your reverence. I'll never catch up with her.

No problem. I can move as fast as thought. I'll go ahead of you and slow her down! Now get a move on!

Poor First Man, his heart breaking, trundled out of his chair and down the path across the green field and by the silver lake and out beyond.

Meanwhile Earth Maker caught up with First Woman. She was still furious at First Man. She walked down the road at top speed, muttering to herself as she went.

The woman has a temper, Earth Maker reflected. But that fella would make anyone lose their temper.

So to slow her down, said ZAP and created a forest. Didn't she cut through it like a warm knife cutting through butter.

Then Earth Maker ZAP created a big hill. Didn't she charge over the hill like a mountain goat?

So ZAP Earth Maker created a big lake. That'll stop her, he said to himself.

It didn't stop her at all, at all. She charged into the lake and swam across it, Australian Crawl.

I don't know where she learned the stroke because Australia didn't exist way back then. But she knew it.

Och, said Earth Maker, there are problems in creating women athletes, aren't there now? Well, the poor thing is hungry, so she'll slow down to eat. ZAP. There appeared along the road all kinds of fruit trees—peach trees, plum trees, grapefruit trees, apricot trees (no apple trees because that's another story).

What did First Woman do? Well she just picked the fruit as she was walking and didn't slow down a bit.

Sure, said Earth Maker, won't I have to fall back on me ultimate weapon. I'll have to create *les fraises*!

ZAP

First Woman stopped cold. Ah, would you look at them pretty bushes with the white flowers.

As she watched didn't the flowers turn into rich red fruit.

Ah now isn't that gorgeous fruit and itself shaped just like the human heart.

She felt the first strawberry. Sure, doesn't it feel just like the human heart, soft and yet strong and firm. I wonder what it tastes like. Sure, doesn't it have the sweetest taste in all the world, save for the taste of human love.

Well, she sighed loudly, speaking of that subject, I suppose the eejit is chasing after me, poor dear man. I'd better wait for him.

So didn't she pick a whole apron full of *fraises* and sit by the strawberry bush and wait for First Man.

And finally, he came down the road, huffing and puffing and all worn-out.

This is called the strawberry bush, she said, pointing at the bush. And doesn't the fruit taste wonderful. So she gave a piece of fruit to First Man, like the priest gives the Eucharist.

Oh, says First Man, isn't it the sweetest taste in all the world, save for the taste of human love. So they picked more strawberries and, arm in arm, walked home to their whitewashed cottage by the green field and the silver lake and the hill and out beyond. 'Tis said that they lived happily ever after, which meant only three or so fights a week.

Now I want all of you here, especially Jacques-Yves and Marie-Bernadette, to remember every time from now on when you taste *les fraises*, that the only thing sweeter is the taste of human love. And remember too that love is about catching up and waiting and true lovers know how to catch up and wait.

After she had translated my final sentences, Marie-Bernadette burst into tears and grabbed her almost husband's hand. He was weeping too. *Le bon Dieu* would certainly bless and protect them.

At the party after the Eucharist someone (doubtless Milord Cronin who had heard the homily, as he remarked, to the point of nausea) provided huge bowls of strawberries with vast dishes of heavy cream. Various and assorted leprechauns stole mine before I could finish my plate.

Nuala Anne, who had come over with her stalwart Dermot Michael as well as the two urchins, sang a French wedding hymn at the Eucharist and, together with the bride and groom, entertained the party well into the night with Celtic music, the kind of music one might have heard millennia ago when the first tribe of Keltoi arrived at the Rhône.

The young couple were to leave shortly for Chicago, where they had a three-month contract at the Abbey Pub, an agreement for recording their disk of Celtic music, a contract for the Nuala Anne Christmas show, and a scholarship at the American Conservatory. The North Wabash Avenue Irregulars and the Ryan family had done themselves proud. The parents of the newly-weds were sad to see them go but happy for their opportunity, especially when the ineffable Nuala Anne showed them a picture of the apartment waiting in Chicago, just down Southport Avenue from where she and Dermot Coyne lived.

Jeanne-Chantal was accompanied by a slender, handsome young man with a touch of silver at his temples. He was attentive and respectful—so respectful that he insisted on calling me *"Monseigneur."*

"You realize of course, Mr. Bishop Blackie," she said, toasting me when the young man had discreetly drifted away, "that I concelebrated that Eucharist with you and Cardinal Sean."

"I would have assumed as much."

"What do you think about that?"

"I would hope that you don't expect a third of the stipend."

"A third of nothing is still nothing."

"Arguably," I admitted.

"You saw the Cardinal talking to me?"

"Oh yes. Charming man, isn't he?"

She grinned wickedly.

"*Très charmant* . . . He told me that if Rome should decide that I am a real priest, he would want me as his auxiliary bishop. He said I would be a distinct improvement."

"Doubtless."

Then I added, "The young man seems very attentive?"

"Jean-Laurence? Oh, yes. He is an *avocat*, a lawyer I suppose you would say. He is not without some interesting qualities. A widower, poor man. He needs someone to take care of him."

"You told him that you were a priest?"

"Certainement!"

"And?"

"He is a Breton and very devout. At first he was shocked, then amused. . . . Everything I do amuses him, except my smoking. So, I no longer smoke."

"Matters then arrange themselves nicely?"

She looked off into the distant vineyards, warm in the soft late autumn sun.

"Bishop Blackie, we are so blind and deaf. The world is transparent. God is everywhere whispering to us, talking to us, shouting at us. Usually we do not hear. Sometimes we do. Then we know that everything is grace."

So, I thought, *Frère* Jean-Claude lives.

Author's Note

I have great admiration for the Irish Dominicans especially those in the priory at San Clemente in Rome. I am sure that none of them would have any part of something like the conspiracy I spin in this story. To protect Cardinal Cronin from investigation by the Vatican, I must note that what he had in mind when he said to Bishop Ryan "it just goes to show you" was that women would make better priests than men, not that they *should* be made priests!

Look for Andrew M. Greeley's
latest Blackie Ryan novel

THE BISHOP
IN THE
WEST WING

Available in hardcover
from Forge Books July 2002

1

Your good friend was on the phone earlier this evening."

Cardinal Sean Cronin leaned casually against my doorframe as though he was posing for a fashion magazine shoot, in light blue pajamas and royal blue robe. He had never appeared at my doorway in such array. I noted with some pleasure that he did not wear his cardinalatial ruby to bed at night and that his slippers were also royal blue, not crimson.

"Ah," I said as I turned away from the purgatorial task of catching up on my e-mail. Naturally I had no idea who the friend was—a beautiful but troubled woman, a penitent Mafioso, a haunted priest, someone from Rome, a mystic with revelations that must be passed on instantly to the Pope. The rhetoric of Chicago discourse, however, required that he begin with such an indirect approach, as though all the rooms of the Cathedral Rectory were wired by hostile law enforcement agencies.

"The Megan thought I should talk to him since you were not around."

It was therefore a serious matter. None of the four porter person Megans who presided over the entrances to the Cathedral Rectory from after school to 9:30 would dream of disturbing the Cardinal Archbishop (whom they adored as "extreme cute") unless some important game was afoot.

(One must understand that for the younger generation "extreme" has become an adverb.)

"Indeed!"

"We have you on the 6:00 flight. Your friend Mr. Woods will pick you up at 4:30."

"P.M.?" I said, knowing full well that it was not.

Milord Cronin permitted a frown to furrow his handsome brow.

"The monks get up a lot earlier, Blackwood."

"Such as they are these days. However, patently I am not a monk."

"He was going to send Air Force One to pick you up, but I said it wouldn't look good for a lowly auxiliary bishop to fly around in that. Create a lot of comment, which he doesn't need right now."

"Arguably," I conceded.

So that's who "my good friend" was—John Patrick McGurn, POTUS, aka to the media "Machine Gun Jack."

Without asking my permission—he never does—Milord Cronin opened the secret cabinet on the wall of my study (hidden behind a portrait of our currently gloriously reigning Pontiff), removed a bottle of my precious Jameson's Twelve Year Special Reserve, and poured himself a good-size splash into one of the attendant Waterford goblets.

"You're proposing to assign me to the White House," I protested. "That won't look too good."

"You always say that you're the little man who isn't there. They won't notice you." He leaned against the door and sipped complacently from his goblet, looking all the more like a cover for *GQ*.

"The Nuncio won't like it."

"I'll worry about him."

If he did worry about the reaction of the ambassador of the Holy See's reaction to my translation to the White House, it would be the first such worry in his career.

"Why is it necessary that I abandon all my serious responsibilities here in your Cathedral parish?"

A weak argument, I acknowledge. Yet the game had to be played out.

The Ryan family has a gene that inclines them to resist travel. In my own case the power of the gene is primordial. The upper limit of my tolerance is the drive from Chicago to South Bend, Indiana, home of the fighting Black Baptists. However, the apparent need of the first South Side Irish Catholic from Chicago to become president of the United States overrode my reluctance, though not without a loud west-of-Ireland sigh which might suggest an attack of asthma.

John Patrick McGurn indeed needed help, though he would have been the first to deny it.

The media, especially the *Wall Street Journal,* the *New York Times* and the *Washington Post,* hated President McGurn. They persisted in calling him "Machine Gun Jack" because the name broadly hinted of the Capone era and Chicago Irish political corruption. So deep in the subbasement of Chicago memory is the name of that alleged perpetuator of the St. Valentine's Day massacre that Jack McGurn had never been identified with a machine gun during his brief career in Chicago politics.

"He has some serious problems," the Cardinal continued with a sigh as loud as mine.

"Surely not the sexual harassment charges!" I protested.

Milord waved his hand in a graceful, dismissive gesture.

"Those go with the territory if you're a Democratic president. Jack will survive them."

"Arguably," I said without much conviction. The top national media hated Irish Catholics, especially from Chicago. They were determined, even though they would piously deny it, to drive Jack McGurn from office. Such assaults sold newspapers, increased TV ratings, satisfied needs to experience pious self-righteousness. Typically Jack did not shy from the Chicago identity, though he and his family had been at best minor figures in the various Daley administrations.

"Though I deserve little credit for it"—Jack would smile and his blue-green eyes would glitter with mischief—"I am proud to be identified with the most effective municipal administration in America."

"Why then," I persisted, "this late-night emergency call for the lowly sweeper to the Cardinal Prince of Chicago?"

This was a none-too-oblique reference to my conviction that an auxiliary bishop's main *raison d'être* is to sweep up his Ordinary's messes, as the worthy Harvey Keitel had done for the Outfit in the film *Pulp Fiction.*

"Ghosts," Sean Cronin said in his most gloomy apocalyptic voice.

"Ghosts!"

I warned myself mentally that I must not seem too enthusiastic.

"Ghosts. Or psychic phenomena or whatever."

"Legend has it that Mr. Lincoln's ghost haunts the building."

"It's more than that."

"Ah?"

Sean Cardinal Cronin hesitated, something he almost never does.

"There are psychic phenomena happening all over the White House—in the West Wing, including the Oval Office, in the bedrooms, in the family quarters on the third floor, in the various museum rooms on the first and second floors, in the basement offices under the West Wing, in the guest bedrooms like the Lincoln Bedroom and the Queens' Bedroom, even out in the Rose Garden and the South Lawn . . ."

"Appalling!" I murmured with little conviction. "Of what sort are the phenomena?"

"The usual junk—doors slamming, chains rattling, paintings falling off the wall, vases flying across the room, windows springing open during snowstorms, thermostats going crazy, televisions switching on and off . . ."

"Nothing ever breaks, I presume?"

"No."

"Poltergeists," I said with some disappointment.

"Presumably . . . There's a twist to it . . ."

"Ah?"

The Cardinal hesitated again.

"The rumors around the White House, which still includes some service personnel who worked for the last president, are that Ellen has come back to harass Jack over the sexual harassment."

"Absurd!" I said hotly. "Ellen was not and is not that kind of woman! She might burn the White House down if she were sufficiently angry, but poltergeist phenomena are beneath her."

"Steady, Blackwood! You and I know that and so do most people in this city. However, the media have stirred up so much hatred for Jack and his family that the public is capable of believing anything about them.

Irish Catholics from Chicago are capable of bringing every kind of evil to the White House, even ghosts. Many people will think that the ghosts are proof that he did mess around with those campaign bimbos."

The harsh truth about political campaigns that you will never read in the papers is that they are airborne orgies, traveling brothels in which boredom with the political rhetoric provides an excuse for the hangers-on, including the self-righteous journalists, to indulge in day and night promiscuity. John Patrick McGurn's campaign was, heaven knows, not boring. Nonetheless, the habits of promiscuity continued. Sex on campaigns is far more important than the issues that allegedly divide the candidates. If the candidate's wife is not with him, then speculation erupts about whom he is sleeping with. In the bawdyhouse atmosphere of a campaign it is taken for granted that everyone is committing adultery, especially a candidate who has recently lost his wife. It is alleged indeed that some young women, one might call them groupies, join a campaign so that they can sleep with world-famous journalists and even perhaps spend a night with a man who may be the next president of the United States. Two such young women, who might not be utterly innocent of Milord Cronin's accusation that they were bimbos, filed sexual harassment suits against him three days before his inauguration, alleging that they had not received promised White House jobs because they resisted the candidate's sexual advances.

Those who did not know John McGurn as we did could easily have believed the charges. Most Americans did not know him very well. Indeed they were surprised that he was sitting in the Oval Office and had begun to wonder if they had made a serious mistake.

"Poltergeist phenomena," I observed, "are usually associated with an early adolescent, especially of the female variety. Does not the President have two such in his family?"

"It may surprise you, Blackwood," the Cardinal said with a touch of superiority permissible in an encrimsoned prince, "to learn that I know that about the playful spirits. However, Deirdre is back at Notre Dame and Granne is living with her aunt in Chicago until she graduates in June from St. Praxides Grammar School, your alma mater, if I'm not mistaken."

His Eminence had begun to talk like Sherlock Holmes, which was my role not his.

"Then our mutual friend needs an exorcist. If I am not mistaken, you have one such on your staff, against my advice I might add."

"You've been working too hard lately, Blackwood," he said with mock disappointment. "What would the *Washington Post* do or the Calvinist Vatican on Forty-second Street should they find out that the Catholic Church had sent an exorcist into the White House?"

Milord was always amused to describe the *New York Times* as a Calvinist newspaper.

"Especially one as eager to appear on television as your staff exorcist."

He ignored my sally, which was all he could do under the circumstances.

"Besides, we know from past experience that all you have to do is to walk into a haunted house—or aircraft carrier as far as that goes—and the playful spirits go out of business."

That lamentably was the truth. The adolescent who was, not altogether consciously stirring up trouble, knew better than to mess with Father Blackie.

"You yourself have observed that I have been working too hard," I said, knowing that the battle was lost. These battles were always lost, but it was nonetheless necessary to play out the scenario.

"The *Post* and the *Times*," Sean Cronin continued implacably, "know about the phenomena from their spies inside the administration. They are hesitant to use it because of their ideology that there is no such thing as the supernatural."

Having conducted a token search for a coaster, he placed his empty goblet on top of a stack of computer output.

"So they will wait till the supermarket tabloids run it and then they'll play it as a media story," I observed.

"And the sharks will swim in from all sides for a feeding frenzy."

We were both silent for a moment. American journalism had come a long way from its assumption that major public figures were entitled to their private lives. Even the most responsible media outlets would salivate at the prospect of poking into a president's parapsychological life.

"Blackwood," the Cardinal intoned, "John Patrick McGurn is a good and worthy layman of this great Archdiocese. I baptized him, I officiated at his marriage, and I baptized his kids. I said his wife's funeral Mass. Now that he is also president of the United States of America it is unfitting, offensive, and intolerable that he be haunted by ungodly spirits, especially when a revolution is sweeping China."

"Ah," I murmured.

"Moreover the bimbos that are suing him are also ungodly spirits. I expect that you will be able to deal with them too."

Swept by the power of his prose, Milord had just doubled my assignment.

"I won't have it," he said solemnly. "I simply won't have it."

"Indeed."

"See to it, Blackwood!" he ordered as he turned towards the dark corridor whence he had come to disrupt my late-night tranquility.

He departed from my study with the swoosh of a passing but lordly hailstorm.

"Tomorrow!"